Deadly Alchemy

by Julie Morgan

This book is a work of fiction. All characters in this novel are fictitious. Any resemblance to actual events or locales or persons, living or dead, is entirely coincidental.

This book is intended for mature audiences. It contains scenes of violence, sex, shifter's, vampires with serious adjustments to reality, descriptions of torture, and adult situations.

ISBN-13: 978-0-9913482-6-8

Photo Image by Studio Smexy

Cover Image and Back Page design by Stella Price

Editing by: Editing by Rebecca
https://www.facebook.com/EditingByRebecca

Editing by Tiffany Tillman

Books by Julie Morgan

Chronicles of the Fallen

Fallen

Redemption

Atonement

Culmination

Southern Roots series

Southern Roots

City Lights

Fueled Desire *(coming soon!)*

Driven Hunger *(coming soon!)*

Paramour *(coming soon!)*

Stand Alone

Deadly Alchemy

Acknowledgements

To my readers, thank you for hanging by my side, believing in me and never forget, you are AMAZING!!! May there always be fantasy in our world of reality.

To my beta readers, you ROCK! Thank you for helping make this story come together.

To Rebecca and Tiffany, thank you for making it BETTER!

To Leah, thank you for jumping into this adventure with me when I first told you about this story. Our conversations kept me going, between the laughs and the pissed off moments, we had a wild ride! Don't lose your faith and keep pushing through.

To Jenn for capturing what is now the characters for Deadly Alchemy! They are amazing!

To Stella and your MAD graphic skills! Damn!

And finally, to my husband John, my muse for wolf character. I love you!

Deadly Alchemy

To Leanna,

May your imagination never stop amazing you.

Deadly Alchemy

Julie Morgan

Table of Contents

Deadly Alchemy

Chapter 1

"I did it! I can't believe I actually did it!" I find myself bouncing lightly on my stool while conducting the final experiment on X280. Carefully setting the tube in the slender holder, I press a cork gently on top. I grin and press the tips of my fingertips together. "This will win me every prize known to man! Besides, it's about time a woman won an award or two," I huff to myself.

Grasping my pencil, I quickly jot down a few important details in my notebook.

The experiment of batch X280 was successful. After the death bite had taken place, the facility received the cadaver patient. As his body began the transformation from human to vampire, we administered X280 and it instantaneously stopped the transformation from taking place. The cadaver then began to breathe oxygen again and his heartbeat started up on its own. Recovering from his death state, rigor mortis failed to set in, and the victim soon became a survivor.

Smiling to myself, I close my file folder and tuck it securely into my carry bag, pencil tucked behind my ear. As I clean up the remnants of today's adventure in the lab, I take a few steps back and almost scream when I bump into someone.

"Eva! Oh my gosh! I didn't hear you come in!" Sighing as I catch my breath, my supervising leader steps out of the shadows and farther into the room. I am not sure how I did not hear her coming as her heel strikes the tile floor with each step she takes.

The woman is absolutely stunning. Her dark hair, pulled back into a bun, frames her face nicely with a few whispies hanging down. Her bold, chocolate brown eyes, lined with the darkest of eyeliner, seem to accentuate her beauty, and her makeup looks refreshed on her tanned skin. Her slender frame fills her corset in places that would make a man drool.

"Amelia, love, were you successful in the experiments today?" Eva looks around my lab and takes in the area with a raised brow. Her fingers gesture as if suggesting what I do may be beneath her—in a way, I suppose it is.

Eva has not *always* been an Alchemist. She came by her talent through training. Where, with me, it came naturally. Family stories have it my bloodline descends from those who created the original serum for the first original vampire, Henry VIII. Then again, that is just speculation.

My superior looks back toward me again and I realize I have been staring at her for a moment. "Oh, umm yes, ma'am. I successfully created a positive cure of vampirism! Oh, Eva, I'm so..."

She suddenly cuts me off. "Shh!" She brings a single digit to her lips and stops me from speaking anything else. "Ears are everywhere, Amelia!" She lowers her voice and steps forward. "You have everything documented? Everything is in its place? You were able to duplicate the efforts?"

Looking to my left and right, maybe expecting someone to be eavesdropping, I nod a few times. "Yes, ma'am. The cadaver brought in today," lowering my voice to a whisper, "I was able to bring him back successfully." My lips stretch into a wide grin. "He's recovering nicely at the hospital next door and..."

"That's enough for now. You've done well." She smiles and pats my arm casually. "Make a duplicate of your notes and leave them on my desk first thing. I will need to review this with our investors. We need a reason to continue our research, you know." Eva smiles, but it does not reach her eyes. She turns away from me and walks back out the door. "Oh, and Amelia," she looks back at me slightly over her shoulder.

"Yes, Eva?"

"No word of this to anyone, understood?"

"Yes, ma'am."

"Very good." She smiles and continues down the hallway as her heels click away, echoing in the silence.

"How did I not hear her before?" I ask myself. Shaking my head and pulling my carry bag underneath my arm, I pin my small hat to the top of my head. As I cross the room to the coat hanger, I pull on the matching dark blue jacket of my dress. The bustle catches in the shadows, and for a moment, I am reminded of the shadow rooms I have frequented in the museums.

After safely locking X280 in the lab cooler, I lock the main door behind me then venture out into the night air. With summer coming soon, the air at night is still cool in Savannah—tonight is no exception.

Making my way toward my driver, I look around, finding myself alone. I mumble to myself,

"Too bad the moon does not offer more of a guide at night."

The sound of a struggle erupts from the side of my coach. My heartbeat speeds up, and standing frozen in place, my eyes roam the area in hopes of seeing what is happening... before it sees me. Vampires are plentiful in our world; however, as an Alchemist, it is my duty to protect the humans from attacks. If I am attacked... "Well, I can't think about that right now."

Taking in a deep breath, and pushing the thoughts of a vampire attacking me by the lab out of my mind, I take a few steps toward my coach. "Henry?" I call for my driver, "Are you alright?"

Tentatively, I reach inside my bag. My fingers search for a vial of liquid sun. Years ago, when becoming a master at my craft, the best decision I made was creating this solution. As the Undead burn from the inside out, their bodies explode as if the sun was actually shining from within.

Clutching it tightly in my grasp, I think for a moment I might break the glass within my grip. Slowly pulling it out of my bag, I take another tentative step forward. "Henry? Please talk to me!"

Suddenly, a growl pierces the night air, followed by a figure moving so quickly, I am afraid I might have imagined it. A scream pierces the night from somewhere nearby and I drop the liquid sun on the ground where it explodes at my feet. I cover my mouth with my hand to keep from screaming along with whoever is being tortured. Panic and fear build quickly and I am afraid I may pass out from the adrenaline rush I am experiencing. I take a few steps back when a man peers from around the side of the carriage.

"Madam, has harm come to you tonight?"

His voice has an accent—French maybe? Shaking my head a few times, I am scared to move from the shock of what has just happened. "Where's Henry?" I ask the stranger. Not that he even knows who Henry is, but considering the circumstances, this is the best I can come up with.

"I'm sorry, madam; I'm not sure who your Henry is." He steps farther around and I suddenly gasp. Blood settles on his chin and some has spilled on his shirt.

"No! You need to keep your distance! Henry is my driver and I simply wish to return home!" I reach into my bag again and realize the glass I dropped was the only one I had. *Dammit*, I think to myself.

"Madam, I do not wish to attack you. I simply wish to..."

"Please, don't come any closer! I *will* scream and someone will come!"

Suddenly he is directly in front of me and I suck in a sharp breath, taking a step back. "Who, exactly, would come? You *do* understand I could quickly snap your neck before you even *think* of screaming."

Swallowing thickly, my eyes widen as I take in his features—dark, almost black hair, down to his ears, his dark blue eyes seem to glow in the darkness. His lips pull back in a smirk and his teeth peek through his thin lips. Fangs are on display, most likely for my benefit. I can only nod a few times.

"Why are you nodding?" He leans in toward me, the blood already drying on his lips and chin. "Did I ask you a yes or no question?"

"N-No." I look from his eyes to his thick, broad chest, back to his eyes again.

"Like I said," he pulls away from me and straightens the gloves on his hands, "I will not be attacking you tonight." He turns his back to me as he continues talking. "I believe it is your Henry who was not so fortunate."

Finding my voice, I whisper, "Wait, what?" Keeping the distance between us, I follow him toward my carriage. "What happened?"

He turns back toward me and glares. A look of rage fills his features and my heart quickly climbs into my throat. "A man was just attacked on the other side of your ride here, madam. Most likely, *you* would have been next." He looks down my body then slowly brings his eyes back up, meeting my gaze. A slight shiver runs through me. "Blood calls to blood. I came to investigate, to see what had occurred while in the area. I found one of my kind attacking one of yours." He bows and brings an arm across his body. "You're welcome, madam, for saving your outstanding, most important life tonight." He stands back up and the look of rage shifts to chagrin.

My lips part as his insult sinks in. My own rage begins to fuel my body and heat my face. Feeling my cheeks and ears redden from my circulating blood, I step forward, finding a boldness I usually do not carry in front of strangers, especially if said stranger is a vampire. "I'll have you know..."

"Just stop, madam." He crosses his arms over his chest and raises a brow. "No apology necessary."

Gasping, my mouth opens in astonishment. "Sir, I will have you know I had *no* intention of apologizing, for you have offended me!"

He laughs and his voice echoes into the air. "*I* offended *you*? Madam, I saved your fucking *life*! You know, it does not matter now. The least I can do is offer you a ride home since your driver is obviously now indisposed. That is, of course, unless you are too offended by me to take said ride."

Biting my tongue, I can feel the blood pool in my mouth. *Exactly what you need to do, Amelia. Attract him to your mouth where your blood is oozing.* "I'll find my own way home, thank you very much." Turning my back to the stranger, I begin walking toward the cab station.

Just as fast as before, he is in front of me. He runs his hands down his jacket as if dusting debris from it, lifting his eyes to meet mine. "Allow me this favor, madam. I can guarantee the vampire would have attacked you. I took it upon myself to save you from such fate. Please, allow me the honor of getting you home safely." His tone has changed from sarcastic to serious.

My brows lift in surprise and I blink a few times. "Fine," I offer and my gaze drops to the ground. A throbbing begins in my shin, and when I raise my leg, blood is oozing from a cut. I gasp and remember the glass vial of the liquid sun I dropped earlier. I immediately look up to the vampire in front of me. He has just had dinner and now I am presenting myself as dessert.

He reaches into his breast pocket and withdraws a handkerchief. Taking a tentative step forward, he lifts his palms up as if offering surrender. "I simply wish to apply pressure to stop the bleeding. Nothing more."

The vampire bends down in front of me and slowly glides his hand around my calf. The touch is cool and his skin soft. Slowly, he moves his hand up my leg as he pulls it toward him. The other hand presses the handkerchief to my shin.

"Umm, thank you, sir..."

"Michel. Michel Gauthier," he offers, and then looks up, catching my gaze.

I offer a hint of a smile then nod. "Thank you, Mr. Gauthier."

He looks back down at my leg and continues holding the material against my wound.

"Please, I insist you call me Michel. I believe the vial you intended to use on me…"

"No!" I clear my throat as he quickly looks up, "My attacker, not you."

He slowly forms a smile. I am the first to look away when he removes the handkerchief. "Look, all is well." Michel stands and I realize he is almost a half-foot taller than I am now that we are standing so close to one another.

Swallowing hard, I nod and look away. I blush and now I am grateful for the night sky. "I would appreciate that ride home, Michel." Glancing at him again, I offer my hand. "I'm Amelia Rimos."

"Miss Rimos," he takes my hand, lifts it to his lips, and kisses it, never breaking eye contact. I have completely forgotten about the blood on his clothing and chin. "My night has become saved by your beauty and by merely being in your presence."

I find myself biting my bottom lip and lower my gaze. "Please, Amelia, and thank you, Michel."

He pulls my hand into the crook of his elbow and walks us toward his carriage, opening the passenger door for me. After sliding in, he shuts the door. Watching him as he walks around to the other side of his ride, I smooth down my dress. He climbs inside, starts up the engine and it roars to life. Vehicles like Michel's have not been in existence for too long and only the fortunate and wealthy own one. I am not sure at this moment if I am lucky to have met Michel tonight... or unfortunate. Time shall tell.

After offering directions to my home, Michel opens my door and escorts me to the front step of my building.

"Miss Amelia, it was my pleasure to make your acquaintance tonight. I do hope to call on you again, if I may?"

My brows rise at this, having no idea how to respond. It is not common for vampires and humans... especially Alchemists...to fall into courtship. However, I have not disclosed I am an Alchemist, either. "I frequent the library if you ever find yourself in the area. I adore historical artifacts." I smile and look toward my door.

Michel nods and takes my hand again, lifting it to his lips and kissing it while watching me. "Until then, Miss Amelia." He releases my hand, takes the steps down to the walkway, and turns to head back to his carriage.

I grin and unlock my door, excited to fill my sister, Rachel, in on tonight's events, adventure, and Michel.

23

Chapter 2

Shortly after returning home from what had been one of the most intense nights of my life, I knew my sister would want to know about my meeting Michel. The words of my superior briefly came back to me.

Do not tell anyone of this.

Deciding now is obviously not the time to fill her in on X280, I begin with my news of how Henry was attacked and how the vampire Michel came to my rescue. She is taken aback with the news of my meeting a vampire, until I fill her in on the details. "I need you to understand, Rachel, this could have been a tragic attack," I begin explaining to her, "Rachel, he was," I pause for a moment as images of Michel flood my mind, "somewhat charming. Moreover, do not forget, he saved my life. You mustn't worry yourself over anything."

"I mustn't worry? Well, this is certainly something," she begins. "Please remind me, if I ever meet this vampire, to thank him. You need to be more careful, though, Amelia." Her voice was thick with worry, and then she went on with a soft sigh, "Alright, so, Friday night. You and I will have dinner and then some dancing. I know of quite an interesting place; I think you'll enjoy it." I could tell she was forcing a smile over the phone.

My interest piqued, I go along with the change of subject. I make sure to remain quiet about the discovery of the cure, despite wanting to tell her. "Alright, we'll also celebrate."

"Celebrate?" she asks.

"I'll explain later. I'll see you Friday night… with bells on," I laugh softly. "Now, I am exhausted and need sleep. I will talk to you soon, sister. I love you."

"I love you, too. Rest well."

I hang up the phone then stare across the room for a moment, gathering my thoughts from tonight's adventure.

First, I finally completed the right chemical compounds to create X280. Then, Henry is attacked in the parking lot. How will this news go over? It is a good thing the man has no more family to consider. I have no idea how I would explain his premature death. Animal attack?

Shaking my head, I stand to prepare for bedtime. After making a call to the local law enforcement office to disclose the discovery of Henry's body, telling them that an animal had indeed attacked the man made me feel like a complete fool. I do not make it a habit to lie about anything, or to anyone. Having to keep a secret from Rachel is completely eating me up on the inside.

Letting out a long sigh, I double-check all the doors and windows before stepping into my bedroom. Loosening my corset enough, I unclasp the busk enclosures then slip it off. The momentary reprieve at removing the garment from my skin is next to amazing.

After folding my clothes over my armchair, I slip my cream-colored nightgown over my slim figure and run a brush through my golden locks. Looking at myself in the mirror, dark circles, from lack of sleep, have plagued my eyes. My fingers gently pull at my skin as the laugh lines disappear.

"Whoever called them laugh lines has apparently never experienced them," I tell myself.

Making my way across the room, I pull the covers back on my bed then relax comfortably against the cool sensation of the fabric. Feeling restless, I close my eyes in an attempt to force myself to sleep, replaying the night's events in my memory.

The night is dark, one of the darkest I could recently recall. I find myself alone in the streets of Savannah. With the shops closed for business, the only light I have to guide me is that of the flickering street lamps. One by one, they start to darken as if a wind has picked up, dimming the streets into a greater darkness.

Realizing the darkness is making its way toward me, panic sets in and I flee from it.

Looking back over my shoulder, there is a figure in the shadows, not too far behind me. The person begins moving too fast for a human. He is moving at what can only be explained as supernatural speed.

As each light dims, he is that much closer. Whatever it is, whoever he is, it is absolutely not human. Feeling as if we are playing a game of cat and mouse, I quickly dash into a nearby alley to hide in the forgiving shadows.

Hoping to find something to use as a weapon, I am afraid my pursuer will discover me from the loud beating of my heart. Suddenly, he is gone. The pursuit is over and the panic begins to subside, until I feel a presence behind me. My eyes close with unimaginable fear. Holding my breath in an effort to keep in the scream begging to escape, I dare not face whatever is behind me.

Then he speaks, "Once again, Miss Amelia, you save the night by your beauty. I did not mean to frighten you." Recognition sets in immediately. Strong hands lightly grasp my shoulders as Michel turns me to face him. He offers a grin and the tip of his fang glistens in the darkness of the alley.

Swallowing hard, I try to calm my nerves. "You scared the life out of me, Michel!" I offer him a somewhat nervous smile.

"Oh, come now," he steps forward. Placing his hand on my cheek, his thumb brushes my skin. I cannot help but lean into his touch. I am lost in his blue eyes, almost as if I am hypnotized.

"I..." Before I can even finish, he hushes me.

"Shhh," leaning toward me, he places soft, gentle kisses along my cheekbone. As I gasp at his touch, he kisses my cheek once again, and then begins a trail toward my lips.

His lips are gentle, yet longing for passion. He gently cups my face as he tilts his head, deepening our kiss. His tongue parts my lips, asking for entrance. He gently massages my tongue with his. Chilled lips leave mine too quickly as they began to wander to my neck.

I begin to lose myself in him. Closing my eyes, my body gives into the way his lips feel against the warmth of my skin. Michel slides a hand to the back of my head and cradles it, while the other supports my lower back. He leans into me and the passion he unleashes upon my neck unnerves my senses. My hands clinch his biceps as they flex and relax against my touch.

His tongue traces the vein of my neck as he nips at my skin. I whimper softly with pleasure. Before I realize what is about to happen, he bites into my flesh. I begin to struggle, to move, but his hold only becomes stronger.

Tears stream down my face. "P-please, I beg of you, Michel, don't do this!"

Michel finally releases me. Leaning against the wall for support, my hand grasps my neck. Blood pools into my palm, and as I pull it down, I gasp. Looking at him, the look of triumph covers his features and realization has struck me. He plans to turn me into one of the Undead.

I hold my bleeding neck, backing away from him. Tripping on something behind me, I fall to the ground and hear the sound of my dress ripping. I sob into the night, "H-how could you do this?"

He flashes me that devastatingly handsome grin of his, my blood dripping from his lips and fangs, before the alley echoes with his laughter. I can feel the venom coursing through my veins, and I quickly stand as he suddenly disappears into the shadows. Not wanting to spend any more time in the darkness of this alley, I try to take off in a run, trip on the rags of my dress, and fall. Screaming from the pain in my neck and my anger at allowing this... monster... to feed on me, I push away the dizziness threatening to claim my mind.

There are only two things I can think of right now: my lab and the cure.

Running, I realize at some point that I have removed my shoes, as I am now barefoot. Finally reaching the lab, my hand remains pressed down on the wound on my neck. The blood seeps through my fingers, dripping down my neck to the collar of my dress. My vision starts to blur as I hold on to the walls, leaving bloody handprints. Grasping onto what humanity I have left, I need to reach X280; I have to intervene the change before it is too late.

I finally approach the gentleman at the lift. He is paler than usual and does not give any notice to the bleeding wound on my neck. He merely nods, pulling the lever, which closes the door. I can feel the floor move beneath me, and I will the lift to move faster. I am running out of time.

We finally reach my floor and I quickly take my leave, running down the hall. The hall seems longer than usual. The harder I run, the farther my office lab seems.

Sobbing as I finally enter the room, leaving a bloody handprint on the door handle, I reach my desk where the slender tubes of X280 are stored. Opening the cooler, I gasp with horror and panic when I realize each tube is empty. My fingers fumble around each, tipping them over. I drop one and it breaks into shards on the floor. "No, this cannot be! Please, it cannot be!"

"Amelia? What are you doing here?" I had not realized at this point that Eva is behind me. She lifts her perfectly shaped brow and looks around the lab as if I have been trespassing.

"Eva, I... do you know what happened to the X280? I, I need it," I sob, trying to get a hold of myself. "I've been attacked!"

Eva furrows her brows in confusion, "X280? What on earth are you talking about, Amelia?"

A low growl sounds throughout the room. As I continue to stare at the woman in front of me, I realize the sound has escaped from my throat. It is not a sound I have heard coming from myself before this. "The cure for vampirism! I have been working on this for months! How is it you haven't a clue what I am talking about?" I am losing control of my anger; I am losing all sense of who I am, becoming something else, as the venom spreads.

"Amelia, what has gotten into you? Have you taken something? Are you hallucinating? You will not speak to me in such a manner! Have you lost your mind?" Concern washes over her features before she laughs nervously.

"Did you not hear me? I was attacked!" Suddenly, pain erupts in my mouth and something sharp stabs the inside of my cheek. I hiss, "I'll speak to you any damn way I please! You are nothing to me, you mean nothing," I tell her with a low growl, showing a hint of fang, before lunging for her at a supernatural speed. She screams as I *bite into her neck. Warm, crimson liquid flows into my mouth and it is the most amazing, most intoxicating feeling I have ever experienced.*

Feeling something, or someone, watching me, I raise my eyes, meeting Michel's as he stands in the doorway with a smirk, watching me.

"NO!" Suddenly, I awake with a scream and sit up in my bed. My pillow is damp from a cold sweat. Quickly, my fingers swipe under my eyes to brush away my tears. I whisper to myself, "It was just a dream. It was just a dream." My heart racing, my chest heaves deep breaths as I struggle to calm myself.

Rising from my bed, my bare feet touch the cold, hardwood floor of my loft. It makes sense I would dream of Michel, even of my experiment. However, to dream of Michel turning me into a vampire? "You need to venture out more, Amelia," I tell myself. Last night was quite the scare and Michel was the handsome devil. Almost literally.

I quickly bathe and dress. The life of an Alchemist is demanding on occasions, such as the current predicament I find myself in. Pushing the thoughts of the dream behind me, I become a bit giddy thinking of the plans I have made with Rachel. Celebrating my success this coming

Friday is exactly what I need, despite her nervousness over my meeting Michel.

Now, without a driver for the time being, I hail a carriage and head to the lab. I find myself looking at the doorknobs and walls for evidence of my bloody handprints. Still visibly shaken from my dream, I take the lift to the second floor, my usual morning routine. I smile at the gentleman who works the lift and notice he is not as pale as I dreamed.

We reach the floor and he tells me, "Have a pleasant day, madam."

Giving him a nod, I smile in return, "Thank you, sir." My heels strike against the tile as chills from last night's dream continue to haunt me. With a sigh, I push the door to my lab open and step inside.

The first thing I do is check the X280. I find myself smiling and letting out a breath I realize only now that I have been holding. The slim vials are all in place. Taking a seat at my desk, I pull out the notes and paperwork for my project.

I note down everything I have learned, making sure Eva has duplicates of everything for her own records. The way she appeared to me in my dream, it almost makes me hesitant to record anything for her. Then again, I know I am being silly considering any such thing. Friday night is upon me, and soon, my night with Rachel will begin.

Chapter 3

Pulling my stockings up my legs, I then slide my boots on, my bustle lying in wait on my bed. The sheen of the black fabric reflects a hint of the light in my room. My fingers work the buttons on the side where it molds to my hips and waist. The corset planned for tonight's outing stares at me like a necessary evil. Holding the material to my body, my fingers tug on the strings and my waist slims a little tighter, my breasts spilling slightly over the top of it.

I turn and look in the full-length mirror in my bedroom. The red corset is a bright contrast to my blonde hair. The black skirt over my bustle is short in the front, while the back is long, almost touching the ground. Reaching for my red lipstick, I apply it then press my lips together. Taking in my full appearance, I shake my head slightly. "I look like a harlot." I cannot help but smile.

A part of me is hopeful I might run into my savior, Michel. The other part is almost reluctant to see him ever again. I have been using his kind as test subjects for many years. The thought of Michel ever lying on my lab table... dying... well, it is a lot to consider. Working on a subject you have no attachment to is different from actually knowing the subject personally.

My grandfather clock rings in the new hour and, coming back to the present, I quickly grab my handbag and hurry out the door. Locking it securely, I head out of the apartment and onto the sidewalk. The night air skims over my exposed cleavage and the hairs on my body stand at attention.

The streets are busy tonight with automatic carriages coming and going, along with a few horse driven ones. Since Henry's demise, I find myself without a driver. I had not considered this prospect until now, and I bite my lip. Stepping toward the curb of the roadway, I am hopeful to wave down a carriage, or maybe a driver looking to escort someone around town. I wave my hand to someone who is passing by, but he continues on his way. A woman sitting relaxed in his carriage glances toward me then waves as if to tell me, *my ride, find your own.*

"Excuse me, maybe I could be of assistance?" That voice, his voice.

Turning quickly, I find a carriage has parked just next to the curb where I am standing. Considering it was dark the other night, and I was completely out of sorts, I am not sure I would have recognized Michel's carriage even in the daylight. "Michel? Well, it is fancy to see you about again." I cannot help the smile on my lips. I do my best to hold it in place as the dream comes to the forefront of my mind.

"I was hoping to maybe come pay you a visit." My brows shoot up in surprise as he holds up a single hand. "Oh, let me explain, please. I simply wished to see you to make sure you were well. Nothing more." He smiles tenderly then continues. "Well, that is unless we decide to go on a date together."

"Oh," my cheeks blush as I break eye contact with him. "Tonight, I'm actually headed downtown to the pub."

"On a date, I presume?" I can sense a little jealousy in his voice. It is almost cute.

"Hardly. I'm meeting my sister, Rachel."

"Your sister? That is delightful news." He steps out of his carriage, and within a few strides, he is beside me. "May I have the honor of escorting you to your destination?"

"Michel, that is very thoughtful of you, but not necessary." Waving again, an older gentleman with a horse drawn carriage pulls to a stop.

"Need a ride, my lady?" he calls out.

"Yes, sir. Please provide me with one moment while I tell my friend here good evening." I glance back at Michel, who looks disappointed. "I told you, you can always find me at the library." Offering him a smile, I lower my gaze and begin to step out onto the roadway.

Michel takes my elbow and pulls me back. As I am about to protest, he leans in and kisses my cheek gently, then whispers softly, "I'll see you soon, then." He releases my arm and makes his way back to his carriage. After disappearing inside, the engine roars and he drives down the road. My cheek tingles slightly from the kiss he left.

A short while later, the carriage driver pulls to a stop in front of the pub where I had am meeting Rachel. I offer him his wage and he gladly accepts. Helping me down from the carriage, I smile up to the older gentleman. "If you're making rounds tonight, sir, I may need a way home this evening."

"I'll see to it that I am around, madam. Have a good evening." He tips his hat then climbs back into his carriage and gives the command to the horse to walk.

The pub is busy tonight with people walking in and out of the establishment. Gentlemen with their freshly cleaned suits and top hats and women with hairpins, hats, and new boots stand about, talking amongst themselves. A few wear monocles and are smoking cigars. Across the room, someone has a mechanical type eye socket that extends out from his temple. Assumptions race through my mind to how he lost his eye. Another man has gears attached to his arm.

"Amelia!" Rachel calls over the crowd near the door as she makes her way toward me. Her long, dark hair, such a contrast to my blonde, has been pulled to the nape of her neck. A bright green hairpin with a peacock feather in it stands in her hair. Her emerald green corset and skirt bring out the green of her eyes in a way that makes them glow. Her lips shine with fresh rouge and she smiles as she pulls me in for a hug.

"Sister, you look beautiful," I tell her.

"As do you!" She takes my hands in hers and gives me the once over.

As the older sister, she never lets an opportunity pass to pretend to be interested in what I am actually doing with my life. *Who is the latest beau? What do you do with your time at night? Why do you frequent the library so often? No man in his right state of mind will marry a woman who is a scientist and a bookworm!*

She smiles at me with mischief in her eyes. "So, tell me of this Michel."

"Well, you did not waste time jumping to the subject matter, did you?" I smile and let out a soft laugh. "There's nothing to tell. He's a very good looking man…"

"Vampire," she cuts in.

"Semantics," I continue. "Did I mention he came by my place again tonight? He just happened to be on the street and wanted to visit."

"Wow, sounds romantic." The sarcasm thick in her voice, she continues, "Amelia, he's a vampire. You are an Alchemist. Eventually, he will find out."

She is right—of course, he will find out. Although, *how* he will find out is the question. Whether I tell him or he discovers it himself, I am not prepared to handle that conversation. I wave the air as if waving off Rachel's warning as indiscretion. "I have some news to share with you!" I cannot help the excitement I am feeling right now and am hopeful my sister will share in my joy.

Having embraced my talent as an Alchemist, my sister has tried everything in her power to forget it. She refuses to work with what she has been blessed with and keeps up the appearance of a designer. She loves fabric and clothes. She enjoys making different garments and has been known to dress a few of the politicians before banquets.

I slip my hand into the crook of her elbow and lead her toward the entry of the pub. Two gentlemen on the other side, who appear to be the bouncers, escort us through and offer directions toward a few open tables. Offering a nod and a smile, I turn back to Rachel and continue.

"I found it! I did it, Rachel!"

"What did you do, exactly? Discover the cure for boredom?" She laughs at her own joke.

Pulling her to a stop, I do not find anything funny in her words. "I take my work very seriously."

"Yes," she offers with a smile. "I can see that. I meant no harm. Please tell me, what did you find?"

My frown changes into a grin so wide it hurts my cheeks. "I found the cure, Rachel!"

Her eyes widen, and in this moment, I cannot tell if it is from excitement in my news or possibly fear. "Shh!" She grabs hold of my arm and pulls me toward an empty table. She looks to her left and right, then settles her gaze on me. "Do not talk about things like this in public, Amelia! You know better!"

"Coming from the one who fights as hard as she can to deny her birthright? Humor me, please." My arms cross over my chest as I glare at my sister. The very fact she can say anything like this to me burns me on the inside. It would be like me coming to her with orange. You cannot dress the patriarch in black; it must be orange. She would slap me across my cheek if I allowed her.

Rachel takes my hand and pulls me into a seat at our table. She leans in and rests her elbows on her thighs. Her voice low, "There are ears everywhere, Amelia. Someone, somewhere, is always listening."

I nod slowly at first, raising a single brow. "You *do* realize half the people here are drunk, the other half are most likely ignorant. There is no way anyone here would care what we are discussing, unless it is our lingerie or if we were being scandalous."

"I realize that," she begins, "just please, not here."

"Alright, fine. Not here." Relaxing back in my chair, the sounds of the pub begin to heighten as if someone important has just walked in. We both turn to find a fight has broken out over some poker game. I roll my eyes and turn back to my sister, offering her an *I told you so* look.

She shakes her head then waves her hand at the waitress. The woman, who is dressed like a bar dancer, makes her way over. A few of the men offer a whistle of appreciation at her and she visibly ignores them. She looks between us with a forced smile. "What can I get you two ladies?"

"I'll have a scotch on the rocks," I tell her. Rachel orders the same and the woman turns to leave.

Someone from the corner of the pub catches my attention, or maybe it was something shiny in his pocket. I am not positive, but when I look across the room, Michel is on the other side... watching me.

Lowering my gaze, I slowly turn back to my sister. My lips part as I am about to tell her Michel is here.

"Amelia? What is it?"

I meet her gaze then casually look back over my shoulder again. I blink when someone else is standing in his place. "What?" I whisper to myself. Turning in my chair to face where I just saw Michel standing, my eyes roam the room, but he is nowhere to be seen.

"Amelia? Are you alright?" Rachel asks me.

I nod then let out a sigh as I turn back to her. "I thought I saw someone I know, that's all."

"Someone you know or someone you hope is here? The smile on your lips and the blush on your cheeks indicates the latter."

"What?" My fingers causally touch my cheeks and she is right—they feel warm. "Well, truth be told, I thought I saw Michel."

The waitress comes back to the table and sets our drinks out for us. The ice cubes gently clink against the sides of the glass as she points to the bar. "Compliments of the gentleman."

Rachel and I both look over and a young, good-looking man offers a wave.

Rachel gasps. "I met him the other night! I had no idea he would be here!"

I take a better look at him and nod a few times. "He is easy on the eyes, sister." Glancing back at her now, *she* is the one who is blushing. I laugh and take her hand in mine. "How long have you been seeing him?"

"Oh, we're not seeing each other, not exactly," she starts. "We met at a convention a few weeks ago. We talked for a few hours, and when the event ended, we decided to spend the afternoon together. He walked with me around town after the sun had set. He eventually walked me home." She blushes again, this time lowering her gaze.

"Well, he sounds like a real gentleman. Would you like to go talk to him?"

"Oh no, I'm here with you tonight, not him. Besides," she picks up her scotch and takes a long drink. "We need to dance soon." She winks and takes another drink.

"Oh, Rachel, I'll need a few more of these in me before I decide to venture onto any dance floor."

We eventually consume another two drinks, and my body is feeling loose. I know I am ready to take on the dance floor. We stand and make our way over to the open wooden floor. A few couples dance together, and as we take in the others watching, Rachel giggles, then pulls me into her arms.

"I'll lead, you follow," she tells me

"Oh, like this is any different than when we're sober?"

She laughs and pulls me out onto the floor. She leads me across the floor as we twirl and laugh with one another. Looking at us from afar, one could not tell we were kin. If one were lucky enough to get a closer look, our faces look almost identical, except for my blue eyes and her green.

A light tap touches my shoulder, and when I look back, the gentleman who bought our drinks tonight asks to step in. His dark brown hair is short and his dark hazel eyes stare into Rachel's. She is right; he is very easy on the eyes. He is almost a foot taller than Rachel is and his body is strong. I wonder briefly if he works on a farm. No office worker would have a body like this man. Smiling, I hand over my sister then take my leave from the floor. I lean on my elbow at the bar as I watch my sister and her friend dance together.

On the other side of the dance floor, someone laughing catches my attention. Whatever they are discussing seems to be quite humorous. I look back at Rachel as she smiles while dancing, and then glance back at the man who continues to talk and laugh. Something about him seems familiar, and in that moment, he turns to face me.

"Michel?" I whisper to myself.

As if hearing me, his gaze meets my own. His lips pull into a smirk as he lifts a glass toward me, offering a cheer.

"I knew I saw you earlier," I whisper to myself.

"Did you, now?" he replies in a whisper.

My eyes widen in astonishment. How can he whisper to me from across the room? I blink, and when I look at him again, he is in conversation with a woman. I wonder if I am imagining things or if this actually just happened.

The female next to him shifts her weight on her feet. Her profile comes into view, and this woman is absolutely the most beautiful woman I have ever seen. Her lips are full and her skin is tan... almost exotic. Her jet-black hair is pulled to the top of her head with beautiful pins holding it in place. Her dark eyes are lined with black liner, and when she looks my way, I momentarily lose my breath.

Breaking eye contact with her, I turn toward the bar and request another scotch. Bringing the glass to my lips, I take a sip, and then set it down. My fingers skim the top of it as I consider Michel being here with a beautiful woman. *Maybe she is just a friend. Maybe she is his sister.*

I glance back over again and find him watching me. He smiles and lifts a finger and motions for me to come join them. Michel glances to the exotic woman and she smiles, and then leaves his side. He glances back at me again, and then makes his way toward a darkened corner of the pub.

Scotch in tow, I begin walking to where Michel is standing. A part of me wishes to pull away, grab Rachel, and leave. The other wants to continue the path of least resistance. I need to see Michel. I need to talk to him. More than anything else, I have a need for him to kiss me.

Before I realize it, I am standing almost directly in front of him. He takes the drink from my hand and sets it on a table next to us. His fingers gently glide over my cheek as his blue eyes bore into my own. The sounds of the pub, the music and the talking, die down around us. All I can hear is my own breathing and my heart beating in my ears.

Michel reaches for me and slips his hand around my waist. He pulls me, bringing me closer to him. "I've been waiting for you," he tells me. He leads me toward the dark corner and presses my back against the wall. Michel leans into me and his body presses against mine. My breath catches in my throat as his fingers touch my cheek then glide down over my breasts. "I have been waiting a while for this, Amelia."

My breath comes out in a ragged exhale and I close my eyes. "How... how could you have been waiting for this for?" I swallow hard and begin losing my thoughts. His palm presses against my cleavage and he moves it toward my neck. Fingers gently grip my jaw as he lifts my face up just as his lips claim my own. Exhaling into his mouth, it is almost as if he is my oxygen and I need him desperately to breathe.

He presses harder against my body and warmth reaches my sex. I need him closer; I need to feel his naked body against my own.

As if reading my mind, his knee presses against my thighs, opening my legs. He lifts my body and my legs wrap around his waist. His hardened cock rubs against me in a way that almost forces me to moan in pleasure. He grinds hard against my body and I whimper, wanting more. His hands move down to my corset, and grabbing the busk of it; he rips it open, freeing my breasts.

Gasping aloud, his fingers pinch my nipples and knead my breasts.

"Michel," I whisper his name.

"Amelia?" My arm shakes, and looking to my side, Rachel is staring at me vividly. "Amelia, are you okay? Wow, you are seriously blushing! Oh, what were you just thinking about?" She grins, and I think she may have bounced in excitement.

I take a moment to gather my bearings when I realize I had been daydreaming. Michel, the kissing, him ripping open my corset... nothing had happened. I glance across the room to where I saw Michel and, like earlier, he is gone.

"I think I'm losing my mind," I whisper.

"I wonder if you've had too much to drink, sister!" Rachel tells me in playful banter.

***

After calling it a night, my friendly carriage driver, as promised, is waiting for me outside. Offering him a generous tip for being my escort home, I make my way into my loft. Double-checking my locks, my heart flutters slightly at the thought of having Michel in my home.

"Oh, the things I would let him do," I tell myself.

The blush touches my cheeks, and I smile to myself and remove my clothing. Cleaning up for bed, the scotch has almost worked its way through my system. Tomorrow is a new day and I have a feeling the library may be where I need to be.

Chapter 4

The sunlight peeks through the cracks of the curtains the next morning, providing enough light to wake me. Immediately, memories of last night with my sister bring a smile to my lips. We had fun, laughter, and nice drinks. I can feel my face flush again when I think of Michel—his body pressing against my own as his coveted mine.

With a sigh, pushing the covers back, I stand. My feet touch the cool, wooden floor of my bedroom. Lifting my arms over my head, I stretch for a moment then relax. I turn around and begin to tuck the seams of the blankets into the bed. My mind begins to wander for a moment as I stare at my bed, wondering what it would be like to roll around on it with Michel.

All I can think about is him, and how I wish our intimate encounter had been real. It all seemed so genuine: his staring across the pub, his sensual whisper, and the coolness of his fingers against my skin in the dark corner. Just thinking of his lips claiming mine and the heat I'd felt as he stood between my legs as they wrapped around his waist... it was enough to heat my body down below. Just the sheer thought alone did things to my body, but it was not my reality, just wishful thinking.

I blink slowly, mumbling to myself, "For heaven's sake, Amelia, snap out of it. Time for a cold bath." I laugh softly once I finish tucking in the corners of the blankets. Making my way into the bathroom to prepare for the day, I stare at myself in the mirror then shake my head. "Even if he knew the truth about who I was, there is no way he would be okay with any of this."

After running the bath water, I bathe myself then wrap my towel around my body. Droplets of water touch the floor as I begin drying myself. Anxiety touches my mind for a moment as I consider going to the library again. "What if he shows up? Would he show up? I hope he shows up." I glance into the mirror again then wipe my hand across the steam-filled mirror. A part of me hopes to find Michel behind me, waiting for me. What I do find is just emptiness—partly my home, partly my heart.

Hanging up my towel, I sit at my vanity and put on my make-up then brush my hair. Placing it at the nape of my neck, I set a few hairpins in to secure it in place. One of these pins is a silver peacock I received from Rachel a few years ago.

I open the closet door, searching for my teal corset dress. Smiling to myself, the silkiness of it feels amazing against my body. Unfastening the busk clasps in the front, I wrap the corset around my body then tug the strings, closing it tight. My dress, being strapless, flows beautifully as I continue preparing for the day.

I grab my handbag on the way out and step into the warmth of the day. Locking my door securely before descending the stairs of my loft, excitement fills me for the possibilities of what lies ahead. Walking into the familiar streets with horse and buggies, as well as the newly invented automobiles driven around by the wealthy, I make a mental note to ask around about drivers. The demise of Henry has been horrid. My mind briefly considers hiring someone who would be a vampire hunter for my own protection. Considering how ridiculous that would sound, I dismiss it immediately and hope I will come into some luck with a replacement today... maybe I will even see Michel.

***

Arriving at the market place, I had expected the place to be quite busy. The market was the thing to do on such a beautiful Saturday afternoon. I make my way through the busy crowd. My mind is elsewhere; all I can think of is *him.*

I spot a stand, selling exactly the fruit and vegetables I am looking for: strawberries, apples, broccoli, cucumbers, and other fresh greens. I smile as I approach the gentleman behind the stand.

"Good afternoon, madam," he smiles.

"Afternoon," I tell him with a nod. Sorting through the selection, I begin pulling out what I need. I notice the red tomatoes and pick one up, holding it in my grasp.

Michel invades my mind again and the memories of last night... or what I thought was last night...come to the forefront. His lips over mine, his erection teasing me so.

"Madam! You must pay for that tomato!" He stares at me intently before my eyes lower to the squashed mess that covers my hand.

"Oh my, I do apologize!" He lifts a brow, handing me a rag to wipe my hand without a word. I take hold of it, wiping the crimson juices from my palm. For a split moment, the nightmare I had where Michel attacked me crosses my mind. I swallow with an uneasy feeling. Remembering my blood stained hands, the bite on my neck, I quickly dig through my purse, shaking away the unpleasant thoughts. It was, after all, just a nightmare. After paying for everything, including the damaged tomato that went to waste, I step away from his stand.

Covering my face with my cleansed hand, I hope to block anyone from staring at the embarrassment I have brought upon myself. I quickly walk away from the market and stand on the outskirts facing the street. Looking down at my lot, I wonder briefly if the library would have a fit if I took these inside with me. My home is not far from here, but the effort of walking home, just to walk back again, is not appealing.

"I really need a driver," I muse.

After dropping the fresh fruits and vegetables off at home, I feel anxious for what the evening would bring, I huff as I walk the distance back to the library.

I eye the man in charge of the carriage. "Excuse me, sir? Do you know of anyone who is in need of a job? I have recently," I pause for a moment, choosing my words carefully, "I am recently in need of a new driver, due to some personal circumstances he needed to attend to. I will pay quite the reasonable price." What would it hurt to tell a little white lie? I highly doubt I would get anyone interested in the job if I explain it as an *animal attack.*

The gentleman clears his throat, "I am quite sorry, madam, I do not."

I sigh, forcing an understanding smile. "That's quite alright, thank you."

Making my way upon the crest of the library, my hand absentmindedly presses against my carrier bag, feeling the vials of liquid sun inside. Doing a mental sigh, I walk the short distance up the steps of the library.

My fingers wrap around the door handle as I give it a tug. The stagnant air from inside fills my nose immediately and I suddenly feel at home. The aroma of books, the new and old pages alike with book glue, and the newspapers laid about smell like home to me.

As the doors close behind me, I find myself looking around in hopes of finding Michel. Partial disappointment fills me, and I inwardly become fearful I will not see him. An older woman at the front desk greets me. "Good evening to you, miss." She nods and I offer a polite smile to her.

"Good evening to you as well, ma'am."

I make my way through the large building in the familiar pattern toward the Alchemy books. A brief thought touches my mind. *If Michel does come in tonight, he cannot find me here doing my actual research.*

Letting out a sigh, I change my direction and head toward the romance novel area. A part of me wants to look into the history of who I am— old stories of other Alchemists before myself. The other part knows I cannot risk being caught with such literature. That would be a dead giveaway to who and what I am. I cannot risk it… at least not yet.

Just as I turn the corner and head down the romance aisle, I see him. Our eyes meet and my breath catches for a moment.

Michel offers that devilishly handsome grin of his before he steps toward me. His strides forward to close the distance between us, and his movement is graceful; it is almost as if he is floating.

"Miss Amelia," he bows, leaning forward, taking my hand. Like the gentleman he always is, he lifts it to his lips and kisses it softly, never breaking eye contact. I relish in the coolness of his lips against the warmth of my skin.

I press my lips into a small smile. "Good evening, Michel." I remain calm and hide the excitement I feel at the sight of him. I have not noticed the stares we receive from onlookers.

"We meet again. You are a vision of beauty, my lady."

I try not to blush but fail miserably. I lower my eyes in a sheepish, flattered manner. He never lets go of my hand and holds it in his grasp. "Indeed, we do. I was just on my way toward the romance literature. Care to join me?" My smile turns into a small, nervous grin as I raise my eyes again to meet his.

Ignoring the nervous butterflies fluttering around in my stomach, his grin widens. "Perhaps I can offer some assistance." He pulls my hand into the crook of his arm, leading the way.

I sneak a glance up at his handsome features. "Hmm, perhaps." I lower my gaze for a moment, books being the furthest thing from my mind.

His eyes search for the perfect novel, plucking a choice from the books before him. I remove my hand from the crook of his arm, taking the book he hands me. "*Marquis De Sade*?" My slightly widened eyes rise to his. "*120 Days of*

Sodom?" The title itself gives me a clue just how intense and graphic the contents will be. Once again, I am blushing. "I feel as if I'm going to turn to salt, just by that title alone," I whisper with a nervous laugh, referring to the old Bible tale I have heard preachers tell on Sundays.

He leans in with a whisper, "Mmm, I assure you, Miss Amelia, you will enjoy it."

Flashes of the night before at the pub wash over my memory. It was almost as if he knew what I was thinking. *Such a thing has to be impossible,* I think through furrowed brows. I feel as if I am holding my breath. He leans in, merely inches from my lips. "I..." Suddenly, a gentleman beside us clears his throat. I glance over to him and see a disapproving glare. Releasing the breath I have been holding, I take a step back now that the moment has passed.

I change the subject immediately. "Well, I do look forward to reading this."

He once again places my hand into the crook of his arm as we begin to walk around the different aisles of the building, my free hand grasping the book. "You may have to tell me your favorite parts of the story." He takes a sideways glance at me then smirks. "Thank you for the recommendation."

He chuckles as we make our way toward the front of the building. The older woman that had greeted me when I first walked inside now refuses to make eye contact with us. She glances at me first then lifts her eyes toward Michel. She gives him a distasteful look. This is turning into quite an awkward evening.

"Is there a problem, ma'am?" I ask the older woman, as I do not take kindly to rudeness in any form.

"I tend to keep an eye on his kind, miss. I should hope you will do the same, for your safety." Her expression disapproving, she presses her lips together. Michel and I have managed to anger two people tonight.

In turn, Michel gives the woman a smug grin. I can tell he could not care less about her words, though his eyes are piercing right through her.

I quickly respond. "Well then, it is a good thing I do not care for other's opinions. We are turning into a modern society. It is a shame you are such a bitter old woman and insist on being quite rude to your patrons. He has a right to be here just as much as I do. You have a good evening." My expression and my tone were clearly equally disapproving of her.

She stamps the return date on the book with a huff before disappearing into the back room. I calmly walk with Michel toward the exit, cradling the book against me with my free hand. I was not about to make any more of a scene than that which had already happened. Michel pushes the main door open and holds it for me, and I nod with appreciation. My lips form a smile, despite the rude encounter.

"Why, thank you, Michel."

He steps beside me, the door closing behind us. "You are quite welcome, my lady. And it is you, who I should thank."

"It was nothing. You did not deserve the treatment from the likes of her." We descend the steps of the library together, the street busy with carriages and people walking. Michel's eyes are upon me, watching as if to see what I might do next. I turn to him, meeting his eyes, getting lost in those piercing blues for a moment. "Is something wrong? Did I make a funny face of some sort that you should be staring a hole right into me?" A small, nervous smile manages to cover my defensive behavior. I have never had anyone look at me the way Michel does. It is as if he sees directly into my soul.

His lips form upward into the grin I have grown to adore. "Not in the least, Miss Amelia. I was merely staring at your beauty. My, how awfully feisty you are." His grin widens as he leans close to whisper in my ear. "I like that. You are different from any of the other women I have met."

I bite my bottom lip for a moment, glancing up at his handsome features. His face remains inches from my own. "Right, well. Thank you. I'll take that as quite the compliment."

Michel tilts his head to the side for a moment, "I would love for you to join me for dinner tonight."

I swear my heart feels as though it has skipped a beat as he makes such an offer. I let on as if I am debating it, a thoughtful expression crossing my features. "Hmmm, well?" The butterflies are back with a vengeance. "Alright. I suppose tonight would be acceptable. I have yet to eat dinner." I offer a polite smile.

He steps back slightly and his grin turns into one of the most charming smiles I have ever seen. "I shall pick you up tonight then." We begin to walk again as he continues, "Do me the honor of allowing me to accompany you home?"

It is then I realize we are standing in front of his carriage. "Really I do not mind walking in the least. I do not wish to trouble you."

He leans in again, almost as if he wants to drive me insane. "I insist, my beautiful lady." He offers a wink as he opens the door to the carriage, and taking my hand, helps me enter. I place the book down before lifting my dress slightly to prevent the fabric from tearing. Smoothing it out, I take my seat. He closes the door before going around to his side.

Soon we arrive at my loft. Michel reaches across and unlocks the inside of the door. He is so close, and if he turns slightly to his right, we could kiss. His eyes look at me for a moment then he retreats to his side again.

My heart slams against my chest and I hope he does not hear how my pulse has quickened. He is out of the carriage and to my side in a quick moment. He opens my door and takes my hand, escorting me to the door.

His fingers gently glide across my cheekbone as he gazes into my eyes. I feel myself drifting, almost as if he is hypnotizing me. That is a silly notion since I do not believe in hypnosis. There is a cause and effect for everything. This is what I believe. However, being here with Michel, this almost challenges any beliefs I have ever had.

"I had a wonderful time at the library," he tells me. "Especially when you blushed. Your cheeks lit up as if a flame was burning from within."

"Oh," my gaze locks with his and I hesitate for a moment then lose my nerve. I look away and a smile pulls my lips. Maybe I am being coy; maybe I am a little shy. Whatever it is, Michel brings it out in me.

His chilled fingers gently touch underneath my chin as he lifts my face. Our eyes meet again and he leans in to me. "Until this dinner, my Amelia." Michel softly kisses the corner of my lips and my breath suddenly catches. His scent, his body... everything about him pulls me in. I want... no, I *need* him.

When he pulls away, it is almost too much. My breath leaves my lips in a rush and I think he notices. Well, if the smile on his lips is any indication, he most certainly did. Michel turns away and descends the steps toward his carriage. I smile as I close the door behind me.

Chapter 5

As I make my way up to my loft, I notice my door is unlocked and slightly ajar. My fingers barely touch the wooden door as I gingerly push it open. Peeking inside, I am not sure what to expect as not many know my residence. Well, aside from my sister and now Michel.

Turning the handle, I push the door closed to avoid the sound of the lock clicking into place. I reach for my purse and fumble with it for a moment until I manage to hold it firmly. Opening the top, I pull out my pistol. A mirror sits atop the table beside me in the front entry. Glancing into it, I try to see down the hall, but nothing is there, save for the empty wall space.

After setting my purse down, and using both hands, I pull the trigger back on the pistol and hold it at arm's length.

"Whoever is here, I warn you now. I am armed!"

Rachel steps out of my bedroom and I suddenly scream. "Rachel!"

"Amelia? Dammit, put that pistol away before you hurt me or yourself!" She ducks back into my bedroom quickly.

"What are you doing here?" My heartbeat finally slowing down a few paces, I gently release the hammer on the pistol then slide it back into my purse. "Honestly, you should have warned me you were coming."

"Well, I needed to borrow a dress you own for my date tonight." She peeks out at me from the bedroom door. She smiles then playfully rolls her eyes.

Stepping into the bedroom with her, I gasp to see she has pulled most of what I own out onto my bed. "Rachel! You *will* clean up this mess before you leave!"

She waves me off, paying me no mind. "Fine, fine. Where is that red number you own? I need to borrow it, please."

Sighing, I make my way toward the bags of recently laundered clothes. "I'm surprised you have not rummaged through these as well."

"They were next."

I glare at her over my shoulder and she shrugs. "Here." When I hand over my favorite red corset, bustle, and matching jacket, she squeals in delight.

"Oh, this will be perfect! Thank you!" She bounces slightly where she stands, then skips across the room to kiss my cheek. "So, now that we're alone, tell me more about this... cure? Is that what you called it?"

I grin and gasp in excitement, as it is my turn to bounce in my step. "Oh Rachel! I cannot believe it myself! I finally did it! Compound X280 is the miracle cure for the Undead! Vampirism will no longer be an issue in our community or our world!" I go into detail about how some of the chemicals I used were combined and how some were a dead end. Then I go over the details of the cadaver I brought back to life.

"It was the most exciting, most innovative thing I've ever done in my entire life!" I yell out the last part as I lay across the heap of clothes on my bed. "I could absolutely die happy. Right now!"

"Oh, no... no you can't. You must turn in your findings first! Then once the recognition is paid to your efforts, dying *could* be an option." She laughs and grasps my hand, giving it a squeeze. "I knew you could do it. You have been working on this for so long. Congratulations, sister. You deserve nothing but the best."

"Rachel, thank you so much." Sitting up, I sigh for a moment as my smile begins to fade, as well as my excitement. "There's just one problem now."

"Hmm? What's that?"

I watch my sister for a moment as she places the red corset around her body, modeling it in front of the mirror. She is probably thinking what it would look like on her, how she will do her hair. "How do I tell Michel?"

"Don't." She turns to look at me and folds the corset, lays it down, then sits beside me on the bed. "Who said you have to say anything?"

My brows rise at this. "Because it would be the right thing to do?"

"Says who?"

"Says me. Honestly, Rachel, I *must* tell him. I feel as if I have been lying to Michel this entire time by not telling him I am an Alchemist. On top of that, I discovered the cure for Vampirism.

"I mean, what if he does not wish to be human again? What if he enjoys the life he has? Who am I to take that away from him?"

Rachel watches me for a moment then shakes her head. "It is quite the dilemma." She stands and gathers up the clothing for her date. "I suggest two different paths here, Amelia. One, you tell him and get it out in the open. If he does not like you after that, he does not deserve you. Two, break it off with him before it becomes too deep.

Then you will not have to worry about saying anything. Besides, you have barely just met him. It shouldn't be too hard to break things off."

That is where she is wrong. I feel as if I have known Michel for a while, at least in how he is with me, how I react to him… how he reacts to me. "You're right," I tell her just to save face, but in all honesty, I need a backup plan.

***

After putting away my fruits and vegetables from this afternoon, I bite into an apple and rummage through the clothes Rachel left strewn across my bed.

"Honestly, she should be here cleaning up rather than going on her date!" Shaking my head, I take another bite then pull out my lavender dress. My head tilts as I look it over. The corset is heart-shaped and would really accentuate my breasts. The skirt is long and flows effortlessly. I am not so sure this is the look I am going for, but the garment is beautiful. "At least I can pull a shawl over my shoulders."

Stripping my clothes from this afternoon, I pull on the skirt then tighten the corset on my body. Turning toward my bedroom mirror to inspect myself, my eyes widen as my breasts definitely spill over the top of this dress. "Oh my."

My cheeks visibly blush in the mirror. "Well, if I'm going on a date, I might as well go all out."

Setting my hair in drop curls, I push in a few hairpins then add a small hat. I apply a layer of rouge to my lips and powder to my face. A knock sounds at my door and I suddenly jump. Checking the time, I realize Michel is a few minutes early.

My heartbeat picks up quickly as I clear my throat. Grasping my perfume, I spray the air then quickly walk through the fragrance.

"Coming," I tell him as I approach the door. "Oh!" Quickly, I turn back and pull my favorite black shawl from my bed. Thankfully, Rachel throwing my clothes about saved me a few minutes of time, not that I will ever tell her as much.

Pulling the shawl over my shoulders, I look out my peephole and find Michel standing there. He holds a bouquet of blood red roses. They look as fresh as if they were painted on a canvas. The color is absolutely brilliant. My eyes travel over his body which is covered in a dark gray three-piece suit and a tie as red as the roses. The heavens knew what they were doing when they created this man.

I audibly sigh as I swoon on my side of the door.

"Amelia? I can see you looking at me through the door." His smile grows as it reaches his eyes.

Gasping, I step back for a moment and gather my wits. I slowly open the door and my eyes are downcast. As Michel comes into view, my eyes roam up his body, the body of this beautiful man, underneath those clothes. Our eyes meet and it is all I can do to contain myself.

"May I come in?" He casually steps closer as his eyes lock on mine.

"Y-yes," I tell him then step aside.

Michel steps through, but just enough to stand beside me. He looks into my eyes and we are so close, his breath fans across my lips. "I bought these roses for you. They reminded me of your beauty." His eyes travel down the length of my neck to my breasts.

I imagine, for a moment, his face buried between my breasts, suckling my nipples as his fingers move inside my sex. I bite my bottom lip as I watch his lips smile. I wonder if he is thinking the same as I am.

I clear my throat, "Thank you, Michel. Allow me to get a vase for these." Finally breaking the intense eye contact between us, I take the roses and walk toward my kitchen. Putting a little distance between us is most definitely needed. I am not sure how long I had been holding my breath, but it was not until I got into the kitchen that I realized I had been holding it.

"Beautiful home you have here," he tells me. He leans against the wall and watches me, arms folded over his chest. I can just make out the outline of his strong biceps through the material of his suit jacket. "Amelia?"

"Yes?" Water begins running onto my hands, and when I look down, the vase had overflowed. "Oh!" Quickly turning off the water, I pour some of it out. I look up at him and smile, feeling like a damn fool. He returns the smile while I fumble for a knife to cut the ribbon off the flowers.

"Ow!" Seething, I look down at the cut I have given myself. Without hesitation, I look up at the concern on his face then watch it as it shifts to what looks like hunger.

"Here," he is by my side in a second and takes my hand. "I promise I won't hurt you." He stares at my finger the entire time he speaks.

"What are you going to do?" My voice squeaks slightly at the end and my heart is now racing. If he did decide to hurt me, no one would know. I would not be able to scream in time, I would not be able to outrun him; I would… "What are you doing?"

Michel pulls my finger inside of his mouth, completely catching me off guard. His eyes close for a moment as he sucks lightly then pulls it out. He examines it closely then licks his bottom lip. His eyes meet mine as he releases my hand. "Good as new," he grins, "and if I may be honest, tasty."

"Umm, thank you." I pull my hand to my chest and look at where I had cut myself. No blood is present, just a healing wound. "How?" Lifting my gaze to his, "How did you heal me?"

"It is what we do as vampires. We have the ability to withdraw blood, and at the same time, we are able to cease the blood from flowing out of the wound. If we did not, well, let's just say a victim would most likely bleed out."

My eyes widen in surprise at his honesty. "I have no idea what to say to that."

"Then say nothing." He smiles then picks up the roses and puts them into the vase. After setting them on the counter, he turns back to me and offers his arm. "I told you, I will not harm you. Now, shall we?"

I look into his eyes and consider, just for the briefest second, saying no. His eyes and lips both smile as he watches me. Michel does not appear to be a threat to me, so why should I hold him to the standard of a predator?

Nodding a few times, "Yes, we shall." I smile then slip my hand into the crook of his arm.

Leading us to the front door, he pulls it closed behind me and watches as I lock it. He leans in behind me and whispers in my ear, "You look and smell radiant tonight." My breath catches in my throat as his skims across my neckline. He has tasted my blood tonight, so if I smell radiant to him, it must make my scent overwhelming to him. "I love the perfume you wear. It is perfect for you."

I casually look at him over my shoulder with a smile of relief. "My perfume?" He smiles and I laugh softly. "Of course."

***

We are seated at a beautiful, elite restaurant in town. It takes months to get reservations at a place like this. My thoughts begin to run for a moment.

"Michel, may I ask you something?"

He reaches across the table and takes my hand. "Of course."

I gaze across the restaurant and take in all the patrons. Everyone here is well off from money earned, money inherited, or money in politics. As I get ready to ask him how he got us in, I notice a woman in the back. She looks familiar to me, but I cannot quite place her.

Her gaze meets mine and she smiles, turns, and walks into the kitchen.

"Amelia?" My attention comes back to Michel. He turns to follow my gaze then looks back at me. "Is everything okay?"

"Oh yes, I just thought I recognized someone, but it is nothing." I smile and wave it off. "I did wish to ask you something, though."

"Okay, let's have it." He squeezes my hand slightly.

"You're a vampire," I tell him in a whisper. He nods. "You do not eat food." He nods again and blinks slowly. "We have not known each other that long."

"The first two are correct. You lost me at the third." He chuckles and I continue.

"Right. Well, I was hoping to ask how you managed to get us in here without reservations. Believe me, I'm flattered, but you almost have to know someone, or make reservations a few months in advance."

"Hmm, I see your point." Using his free hand, he taps his chin in a playful manner. This brings a smile to my lips. "Let's just say I know who runs this place. Anytime I would like to come in, I have a standing table in my name."

"Really?" My lips pull into a bigger smile.

"Really. I saved his life one night, much as I saved yours. He feels he owes me a great debt, so this is how he repays me." He shrugs as if this were an everyday occurrence for him.

"Oh," I had not considered this before. Does he feel like I owe him a debt now for saving my life? "That is not something I had considered." My eyes shift downward as I stare at my empty plate.

Just then, the server returns with our food and places my steak with vegetables in front of me. Michel's plate remains empty as he watches me. The server refills my glass of red wine and offers some to Michel.

"I'll actually have a glass of brandy," he tells the server.

"Right away, sir." The young man bows and takes his leave.

"Amelia, I would never require you to pay a debt to me for saving your life. This is what the restaurant manager insisted. Who am I to deny this luxury?" He smiles again then leans in closer to me. His hand reaches around my face as he cups my cheek. "My sweet Amelia, I would never ask you to do such a thing." He leans in and leaves a soft kiss on the corner of my lips.

My eyes close for a moment as I inhale his scent. He is intoxicating to me. All I would need to do is move my head slightly to the right and our lips would meet. As I am about to do just that, he begins to pull away.

I watch him for a moment; his piercing blue eyes watch me. My lips part as a hushed breath escapes my lips.

"Your brandy, sir." The waiter returns this time with a full glass in hand.

Michel sits back in his seat and nods. The waiter sets the glass down, bows, and takes his leave.

Immediately, I pick up my glass of red wine and take a few sips from it. I need a break from this man. I feel I could drop my panties here and now for him. I would feel no shame in begging him to taste me under the table.

I can feel my body temperature rising and I turn away from him to avoid the embarrassment. Setting my glass down, I clear my throat and pick up my fork and steak knife. I cut my first piece and place it on my tongue. The flavor explodes and provides me a moment of reprieve from my vulgar thoughts.

We dance, we laugh, and we drink. The live band picks up their rhythm as the evening draws later. Michel surprises me with his dancing. He is definitely skilled in an area not many men are.

At one point, he pulls me close as the music slows for a song. His arm snakes around my body at my lower back, his fingers grazing the top of my backside. Placing my arm around his neck, he holds my other hand as he leads me across the dance floor.

We do not break eye contact as we dance, our bodies in fluid movements across the floor. He leans in over me and my back arches into a dip. I close my eyes and my head falls back, and I shudder softly as his breath cools across my breast line. His lips barely skim down between my breasts to my neck. My breath catches again in my throat as he slowly pulls me back up, his lips running the length of my neck until he stops at my ear.

Slowly, Michel brings his face around to meet my own. He stares at my lips for a long moment, then into my eyes. "I want to kiss you." His voice comes out in a growl.

My body shudders again, and more than anything, I want that kiss as well. The heat rises between my thighs and I feel my panties become wet. "I want you to," is all I can say before his lips are on mine.

At first, he is soft, tentative, like he is careful not to hurt me. My fingers move to his neck then into his hair. I pull him closer and Michel tilts his head the other way, deepening the kiss. His arms pull me closer and our kissing intensifies. My heart slams into my chest and a soft whimper escapes between us.

Someone nearby whistles and I suddenly pull away. Forcing myself to catch my breath, as well as my heart, I glance up into Michel's eyes. The hunger, the need in his eyes, does not go unnoticed. I gasp softly then, touching my swollen lips, I turn and leave the dance floor. I gather my purse at our table then pull my shawl over my shoulders.

"Amelia?" I jump slightly at his touch as he stands at my side, touching my shoulder. "Did I do something wrong?"

"No. I just... I can't, I'm sorry." Without looking into his eyes, I turn and start toward the restaurant door. I make it just a few steps before he grabs my arm, pulling me back.

"No, tell me what this is about. Why are you trying to leave? Did I upset you by kissing you?"

"Yes, but not in the way you may think." Glancing up, I can see hurt, and possibly anger or resentment in his eyes. He is probably not used to women turning him down. How long did he say he has been the Undead? I hand a bill over to the maître d'. "I need a ride home, please." He nods and accepts it, then picks up the phone.

"Amelia, allow me to escort you home," Michel insists.

I shake my head no. "I'm sorry, I can't." I start toward the door. Taking a deep breath, I am fearful to see the hurt, the rejection in his eyes. Slowly letting my breath release, I turn to look back over my shoulder. His eyes are sad and he looks completely defeated. "I am engaged tomorrow," I tell him in a softened tone, "but I'll be at the library in the evening." Lowering my gaze, I step out into the cool night air.

Wrapping my shawl tighter around my body, the carriage pulls to a stop and the driver opens the door for me. Light from the lamppost shines on his arm and I notice the driver has a few gears up his elbow. He turns to look at me and has a pair of goggles on his top hat with a few monocles attached.

My head tilts slightly as I take this in. "My sir, forgive me for asking, but the gears and the goggles?"

"Ahh yes, my lady," he begins as he assists me into the carriage. "I fell into a fight with an animal and I almost lost my arm. The glasses here," he taps the goggles on his top hat, "are for when it rains. Or when I require looking upon a beauty such as yourself." He winks and closes the door. After this evening, a little bit of humor is what I need. A single tear streaks down my cheek and I quickly swipe it away as the carriage takes off into the night toward my home.

Chapter 6

Morning has finally arrived. I push the events of the evening behind me and ready myself for the day. It will be my time to shine. I will be able to deliver my test results to our board staff of investors and the Noble Prize will be hand delivered in a matter of weeks.

Feeling confident, I decide I will take the train into work today. The ride is not too long and I figure it will allow me time to gather my thoughts on my presentation.

First, I will need to run it by Eva. I am sure she will want a part in this as well. As often as she is on the sidelines, a moment in the spotlight is something she will never pass up. *Workers do the work; she claims the glory.* I recall a former colleague informing me of that upon my hire at the laboratory.

Handing over my ticket for the train ride, I take my seat next to a window; the compartment is otherwise empty. Crossing one leg over the other, I pull out one of the folders from my bag and open it across my lap. The black fabric of my dress bounces slightly as the train picks up speed.

Test subject John Doe showed remarkable progress after receiving the X280 serum. It is amazing how his heart began beating on its own again and his blood began to flow. His toxicity level of venom showed a significant decrease while his white and red blood cell count increased.

The compartment door slides open and I look up, closing my folder with my notes.

"Good morning," calls a gentleman who takes the seat opposite of mine. He is older with gray hair and spectacles. His black suit appears old and worn, and his white button up shirt has a stain, which looks to be coffee. He catches me looking him over and offers a friendly smile.

"Good morning, sir," I return with a smile. Opening my bag, I slide my folder of notes back in it, and then close it tight.

"Studying for a big test?" he asks.

"Something like that, yes."

The train begins to slow, and looking out the window, my stop is just ahead. "Well, it was nice to share this with you for a moment or two; however, the compartment is now all yours."

Grasping my bag, I stand and take hold of the railing.

The older gentleman also stands and opens the door for me. "Enjoy your day, lovely lady."

"Thank you, sir," I offer as I cross the threshold. The door firmly closes behind me. I glance back inside to watch the man for a moment as he adjusts himself in his seat. He pulls something out from his breast coat pocket and writes a few notes on it then shoves it back inside, mumbling to himself.

"Odd behavior," I say to myself.

"A man scribbles on paper and that is odd to you?" a female voice asks of me.

Turning in her direction, I raise a brow. "Not necessarily, no. However, when one joins one's coach and scribbles, followed by mumbling, yes, I find it odd."

She looks down at my bag and back up at me. She shrugs, paying me no mind, and continues on her way. I glance back in on the man again and find him watching me. My brows rise in a question of *yes*? He then smiles and turns back around.

The train comes to a stop and the coachman offers his hand to assist me down. I glance up at the window where my coach was, thinking I would see the man but he has now gone. *Hmm, where did he go?*

Not necessarily caring, I set out on my way to work. Only a few blocks from where my building, I stop at a local coffee parlor and order a beverage. Considering today is a big day, I decide pastries and maybe a few other sweets are in order.

The sun is shining bright, and a light trace of perspiration forms on my forehead. As I approach my building, I hurry my steps to catch the door. "Hold the door, please!"

A tall gentleman, who seems close to six foot four, maybe six foot five, turns in my direction. He has to be the tallest man I have ever seen in my life. His dark brown hair is combed back just so and his dark, almost black eyes peer into my own. His skin is tan and his lips are slightly full.

He stands to the side and pulls the door open wide for me. "Thank you. Very kind of you, sir."

"It is no problem, miss." His voice is heavy, thick with a southern accent. He smiles and his face lights up.

"I'm not sure I have seen you around here before, sir. Do you work here in the building?" My heels strike against the tile as we walk inside the building together.

"No, miss, I do not work here, but I do keep a residence nearby. I'm an entrepreneur and work for myself."

"Oh, well good for you!" This man seems kind and very good looking. Where Michel is dark and seductive, this man is like a ray of sunshine on a cold, damp day. I almost feel warmer standing in his presence. Finding myself staring at him, I quickly look away with a soft laugh. "Where are my manners? My name is Amelia Rimos." I offer my hand to the gentleman.

He takes it and gives it a firm shake. "Nice to meet you, Ms. Rimos. Now if you'll excuse me, I have a meeting to attend." He smiles then releases my hand, walking in the opposite direction.

I must admit he is quite the man to watch as he walks away. I shake my head for a bit then smile as I turn toward the lift. "Oh, I didn't get his name. It is just as well since I'll probably never see him again, anyway."

The elevator opens and the operator offers a nod with a tip of his hat. "Morning, Ms. Rimos."

"Good morning."

A few moments later, I am unlocking my door and as soon as I walk inside, Eva is on my trail.

"Amelia, good, you're here. We need to talk." She bustles in behind me quickly then shuts the door.

"Eva, well good morning to you, too. I brought in fresh pastries and..."

She quickly cuts me off. "No time for that! We are in a bit of a bind right now." She sighs and looks me over from head to toe. "You look well this morning. What have you been up to?" As I am about to answer, she waves me off. "Never mind, it doesn't matter. What *does* matter is we have been cut off. They have halted our research. I need you to write up all your notes on everything and have it ready by the end of the week." She stares at me for a moment then raises her brows. "Did you hear me, Amelia?"

"Yes, Eva, I did; however, I'm unsure of what to say. Did they give a reason as to why they have stopped us? I have only just scratched the surface here! How can they…"

"Oh they can," she starts, "and they have. Now, I need you to do the right thing and gather up all your evidence. I need to be able to present this to the board as to why they must continue our funding. Do you understand?" She raises her brows and crosses her arms over her chest.

I nod a few times then glance over at my bag. My research, my notes… the last few years of my life are in this bag. Now? Now it is all over. "I still don't understand," I whisper.

"What's to understand? We make progress; they call it complete. We want to do more, they say no. It's their call, Amelia, not ours." Eva sighs and steps closer, placing her hands on my shoulders. "No matter what happens, you've done well. Remember that."

I nod a few times and lower my gaze. Eva turns and leaves my lab, her heel strikes softening in the distance as she makes her way down the long corridor.

"This was not the Monday I was expecting to walk into today." Letting out a sigh, I open the trash bin and drop all the fresh pastries inside. I take my time in moving throughout my lab, gathering all of my research—my evidence—everything I need to build my case for why we need funding. Opening the cooler case where I last stored the X280, I remove the test vial and place it securely within in my bag.

After double-checking each file and cabinet, I am satisfied and ready to go. I am not positive yet if they have permanently removed me or if we will continue our work here. Either way, my next step is to find work, whether it is Alchemy or otherwise.

***

The warmth of the sun takes on a different appeal than it did an hour ago. Walking in, I felt on top of the world. Coming back out, I now feel as if the world is on my shoulders. How did this happen? How do I convince those I do not even know that my research is worthwhile? How...

Does not matter now. I cannot be here. I cannot be here as the reminders of what I was working toward torment me further.

A carriage pulls up next to me, interrupting my thoughts. I look up at the driver and notice something familiar about him. Tilting my head, the sun glances off the goggles around his hat then I see his arm. Gasping, I realize it is the driver from the other night. I smile and begin to approach him.

He looks down at me from the carriage and raises a single brow. He then looks over my head and I have a feeling someone is behind me. I turn and find the tall, good-looking man I talked with earlier hovering over me.

"Good morning again, Miss Amelia." He grins then quickly shoves a handkerchief over my mouth. I try to scream but the sound is muffled.

The carriage door is thrown open and I am quickly shoved inside. Fear and adrenaline spike inside my body and I kick against my assailants. What will they do to me? What do they want with me? Everything I have been working toward could possibly be lost and now I am being taken captive? No, this is not happening!

Kicking at the door and at the captives who are holding me, the tall one from this morning holds my arms to my sides as I lay across his lap. Another tall, thick man holds on to my legs. I briefly wonder what they are feeding these men that makes so enormous.

"Just breathe deeply and all will be settled once you wake," the familiar man tells me.

I scream against the handkerchief again and my vision begins to blur. Realization begins to sink in as I recognize chloroform. My mind clouds as well as my sight. My body becomes still and I hear mumbling from one man to the other, "She's almost out. We need to move quickly to make this work!"

Chapter 7

My pulse beats softly in my ears. My fingers twitch lightly at my sides and voices are but a mumble in the distance. The room is dark, or at least I think it is. I cannot tell yet if my eyes are even open. A grogginess has set in, as well as nausea. I try to force myself to turn on my side, but I cannot move.

Hands quickly grab at my arms and the grip is tight. I want to scream but nothing comes out. My breathing picks up rapidly and the pungent smell of body odor fills my nose. Heavy breathing fans across my face and I try to turn away from it, to no avail.

"Leave her be!" a voice growls and whoever is holding me lets go. "She's barely awake!"

"Yes, but the time is now! We must know," he starts. The voice nearest me yelps and a wind passes my face. I hear his body hit the ground and I wonder if he has been struck.

I try speaking again, but cannot. My mouth is dry and something is shoved into it. A gag of some sort? I know now that I am blindfolded. My fear climbs higher and tears slip down my cheeks.

I have no idea what will happen to me and I have no way to reach Rachel to tell her I love her.

Hands touch the back of my head and I try to scream. Short breaths escape around my gag and my head shakes side to side in an effort to keep the assailant away from me.

"Amelia," he starts and his voice is familiar, "you need to calm the fuck down! I'm not going to hurt you, for fuck's sake!"

I do not care what he says. I try to scream again. Then the blindfold is removed from my eyes.

It takes a moment for my eyes to adjust to the room. The light is bright and the sun shines directly on my face. There is a man kneeling down in front of my knees, but I cannot make him out yet. I test my legs and find they are also tied to my chair.

As the difference from blackness to extreme light begins to adjust, so do the settings of the room. The walls are white and there is a pair of windows allowing in the sun. My chair is beside one of them. The house appears to be almost run down, possibly condemned. There is no way in hell Rachel would ever find me here.

Taking in the features of the man in front of me, my eyes widen in recognition. I met the man this morning in my building. I try to scream against my gag again, but this time, more out of anger. His face settles on chagrin while his counterpart, another male behind him, plays with a smirk.

My eyes watch the other man for a moment. His red hair is cut short and freckles adorn his features. His eyes are an emerald green, and any other day I would find him attractive. However, right now, all I wish to do is stab him with the heel of my boot.

"She's feisty, John. I like it," calls the redheaded man.

His accent is one I have not heard too often. He sounds almost Australian. Moreover, the tall man's name is John? *Well, John, I am about to be your worst nightmare,* I think to myself.

John leans forward and rests his elbows on his thighs. "Shut the fuck up, Adam." He glares back at the man then shifts his glare back to me. He raises a single eyebrow and his head tilts slightly to the left. His brows furrow in anger as he continues to glare.

The man he called Adam leans against the wall behind him. "She won't tell shit."

I look between the two men and continue to pant into my gag. Shaking my head, I growl into it, trying to tell them to remove it. I know they cannot understand me but I need to ask what they want of me. How I wish for my pistol right now. I have my doubts this lot are vampires considering we are set up next to sunlit windows.

As if reading my mind, John leans forward tentatively and reaches for the gag. "I'm going to remove this for a while," he tells me. "How long all depends on you and if you scream. If you sound like a damn banshee, it goes back up. Understood?"

His voice is deep and has a certain tone to it, almost like a commanding sound. I nod a few times. His fingers maneuver themselves between my cheeks and the gag then he tugs it down.

Inhaling deeply, the oxygen floods my lungs in a much-needed gasp of air. My head tilts forward slightly as I pant, and then my dry tongue licks my lips. "Water," I manage to get out. "Please."

John shifts in his chair and I hear the one called Adam groan and leave the room. John shifts closer to me and waits. I am not sure what he is waiting on as I have no idea why I am here and all tied up.

I lift my gaze to his and patience adorns his features. "We have all day, Amelia. As soon as he returns with some water, we'll get started."

"What?" I croak out. Adam returns to the room and hands over the glass of water to John. He stands and leans over me, lifting the cup of water to my lips. I am grateful for the cool water as it touches my lips and immediately, I need more. Gulping down the fresh liquid as fast as I can, it is gone before I am anywhere near done.

I lick my lips again. "More."

"Not until you talk," John instructs me.

I shake my head, confused. "Talk about what? You took me. I have nothing you want or need." My legs, as if on their own reflex, close tighter together.

Adam snorts against the wall. "Right, because we take women only to molest them." He rolls his eyes and looks at John. "She has no idea why she's here?"

John shakes his head. "She is either playing stupid or oblivious. I hope, for her sake, it is the latter."

"I will play along here with your," I start, then building confidence in my words, "what-does-Amelia-know-game. I am oblivious here. I have no idea why you took me. Now please, release me!" I hold my head up in hopes the falsity of my confidence does not show through.

John leans back in his chair and allows his long legs to extend out in front of him. "Well, let's start from the beginning. You're an Alchemist." My eyes slightly widen at this statement, but others in this town know that about me. "Your lineage stems from the original Alchemist himself, Zosimos."

"How do you know this?" I yell out to him. "How is it you know about my family? Who are you?" I cough as the dryness of my throat sets in.

"You also managed to create what you're calling," and he quotes himself, "*a cure* for vampirism. Let me know if I am getting closer."

My mouth opens but nothing comes out. No one knew of this. Well, no one but Eva and Rachel. Whom would Rachel tell, and why would she? It had to be Eva! Her investors? "What do you want?" I ask in a quick breath.

"So you acknowledge these facts then, correct? You are THE Amelia Rimos?" John smirks as he stands and hands the glass back to Adam. "Get her some more water."

Adam nods and leaves the room. John makes his way back over to me and takes another seat. "Amelia, look, we're not here to hurt you."

"Really?" I tug against my restraints and let out a huff. "Could have fooled me! Let me out of these, right now!"

"No." John's eyes flash so quickly with his statement; I think I may have missed it.

"Excuse me?"

"I said, no. We need to know you'll comply with our demands before releasing you." He crosses his arms over his chest then raises a brow, watching me.

"What? I do not understand. What demands? I am an Alchemist. What could I possibly offer you as ransom?"

"For heaven's sake, John, tell the woman!" Another voice joins our conversation, but this time it is a woman. She steps into the light and my eyes widen slightly at her size. She has to be at least five foot nine or taller. Her white hair is cut short in a bob and her eyes are almost violet in color. If I did not believe in vampires, I would believe she was from another world. Her beauty definitely sets her apart from anyone else I have ever met.

I look from this woman to John, then back again. "Tell me what? What do I need to know? And please, someone untie me!"

"You will remember your place," John growls at her. "You must forgive Sophie. She gets... excited easily."

I shake my head and look between the two of them again. "Please, tell me what?"

Adam walks back into the room with a refilled glass of water. I almost gasp to taste the water again.

"If I give you this, you must promise to listen with an open mind. I will then, and only then, untie you. Understood?"

He could force me to promise to build him an army from mud. I would have agreed just to have this water. I nod a few times then lick my lips as the water comes closer. He tips the cooled water to my lips and I gulp so fast I might drown.

As soon as the water has left the glass, he sets it on the windowsill. John sighs and drops his head between his shoulders. "Where the hell do I begin?"

Sophie speaks up. "Probably at the very beginning. There's a good chance she may not know."

John nods a few times then lifts his gaze to mine. "Amelia, there is so much you need to know. I would prefer to do this outside rather than in here. First and foremost, I am not an animal."

Adam and Sophie snicker in the background. John rounds on them and growls so loud it actually scares me as well. I think I hear one of them yelp. He slowly turns back to me and his eyes glow a bright yellow, then settle back into their brown hue.

Gasping softly, my mouth is agape. "Your... your eyes."

"Yes, that is what we need to discuss. Now, if I can trust you not to scream or try to run off, I will release you. I want to warn you, though, if you do try to run, I guarantee you we are much faster and will have no issue taking you out. Do you understand?"

I swallow hard and nod a few times. "Y-Yes, I understand."

"Good." He pulls a pocketknife from his pants and opens it. Kneeling down next to me, he cuts my left leg loose, then my right.

Stretching my legs, a groan leaves my lips. He then cuts the rope binding my waist, then my hands. I bring my hands around and rub my wrists softly. The skin is red, almost raw from the rope being taut.

"Alright, Amelia, there's a lot to discuss and not a lot of time. Let us go outside for a bit. Adam," he turns to the man who has been with us, "bring out a jug of water for her. Sophie, stand guard."

The woman nods and leaves the house. I do not see where she runs to then I catch Adam glaring in my direction. He mumbles something under his breath then descends the stairs.

"In time, you'll understand why we did this today and maybe you'll forgive us." He drops his gaze for a moment. He leads me down the single flight of stairs as we make our way out the old front door.

The entryway appears to have been beaten in a few times more than it could handle. Looking up and around at it, I ask, "Are you not afraid of the top falling in?"

"It hasn't yet," John tells me. I nod and continue following him. "First and foremost, allow me to introduce myself. My name is John Hawthorne." He bows his head slightly then continues. "Are you familiar with Henry the VIII, Amelia?" He glances over at me and I nod. "I'm not sure how much you have been told about him. In the beginning of Henry the VIII's life, he wished to live a long and fruitful life. He never wanted to die and his idea of ruling meant, well, forever. Your ancestor, Zosimos, was his Alchemist. He tasked Zosimos to create a serum for longevity. He wished to be immortal.

"Zosimos was often heard to have gone mad while working on such a serum. He worked day and night until he finally made the concoction the King was seeking." John sighs and continues as we walk the grounds of the condemned home. "The King took the serum, and in a matter of days, he died. Zosimos did not understand what happened to his Master, but he was arrested and tried that same day. Zosimos was put to death.

"Henry the VIII was laid to rest for just a few days when his current wife went to visit his tomb site. She went in, but never came back out. Rumor has it she was the former King's first victim."

"First victim? I'm sorry, Mr. Hawthorne, the story is tragic, but I'm not sure I follow."

"Please, call me John. Zosimos created the first vampire in Henry the VIII." I gasp and immediately stop walking. "Zosimos did indeed kill the King, but he also created the first Undead. The former Henry the VIII went on a killing spree and took out his enemies first and anyone who did not see eye to eye with his way of the world.

"He soon realized human food no longer satisfied his palate. During a battle, while he was caught in a bloody fight, blood sprayed from his victim and some of it went into his mouth. Word has it the former King's eyes turned red as blood and he bit into his victim, draining him completely."

"Oh my goodness!" John and I both have stopped walking and the shade from a tree provides temporary relief from the sun.

Adam closes the distance to where we stand with a jug of fresh water. He sets it down by our feet then looks at John. "Anything else?"

Taking this moment to review what I have just learned, I turn my back to the two men and think of Zosimos, Henry the VIII, and the first vampire created.

Upon hearing the footsteps of what I can assume must be Adam retreating, I turn back to face John. He watches me with a curious gaze. "What is it?" I ask him.

He shakes his head. "It's nothing." He motions for me to walk as he picks up the water. "Care for a drink?"

"Yes, please."

John removes the fastened cup and opens the spout. Water fills the cup and he hands it over to me. Gulping it down as quickly as I can, I hand it back. "One more, please?"

"Of course." He refills it then hands it back over.

We continue our walk in silence for a moment before he continues.

"Henry the VIII realized by a matter of accident that he could reproduce in humans what he was. They simply needed to drink from his blood."

"Oh gosh, oh no!" Thoughts from the other night when I cut my finger on the roses fill my head.

"It's not that easy though. But now, I must ask, have you been fed blood of the Undead?"

I shake my head and lower my gaze. "No, but the gentleman actually healed my finger. I was cut and..."

John cut me off. "He didn't bite you?" I shake my head. "Michel had you that close and did not try to bite or harm you?"

"Wait," I grasp John's arm and his bicep flexes in my palm. Good god, this man is strong. I hesitantly bring my hand back and briefly forget what I am about to ask. "Sorry, I didn't mean..." I shake it off and remember he knows Michel. "Let me start over. You know who Michel is?"

"Yes, I do."

"How? I mean, have you been watching me or something?"

"Yes, we have. When word got out you had discovered the cure, we had to act quickly."

Not moving, I cross my arms over my chest. "I'm seriously confused. Why have you been watching me and Michel and what does he have anything to do with this?"

"If you'll calm down long enough for me to tell you, I will." John glares at me then looks out over the horizon. The sun is slowly beginning to set.

I sigh and lower my gaze. "Please, John, I'm completely confused here. Why have you been following us?"

John lowers his gaze then turns back to me. "Michel is not who you think he is."

"I know he's a vampire."

"It's not just that, Amelia. There was a war a few centuries back. Henry VIII fell to ash during this war. Michel was one of the first of his kind the King himself created.

"Word has it that Michel stepped into the leadership role, so to speak, to take over where his master left off. Michel knew you were working on finding a cure long before your chance meeting."

"Impossible!" I turn my back to him, not wanting to hear any of this.

"Eva has been in his pocket, Amelia. She leaked the information to him."

I shake my head no and refuse to face him. "You lie."

"No, this is the truth. Michel has been watching you for a long time. He knows your bloodline to Zosimos. He knows if an Alchemist can create the serum for immortality, an Alchemist of the same bloodline could create the anti-serum. You have successfully created this serum, Amelia."

I turn to face John and find he is standing close behind me. I almost stumble backward before he catches me. "Let me go," I demand. Shaking my arms free of him, I take a few steps back. "Well, now it has been created. They can go back to being human. What is the cliffhanger I'm obviously missing here?"

"I told you I'm not going to hurt you." He shakes his head and sighs. "He's after the serum for a different purpose. You have locked down the components to bring life back to the dead. He wishes to change it, alter it to bring death to the living. His plan is to plant it into the main water supply. Imagine if that were to happen…"

"THAT IS RIDICULOUS!" I cut him off, laughing, and shake my head. "You have no idea what you are talking about!" I am not sure if my feelings for Michel are clouding my judgment, or if all of this is just too farfetched to believe.

John growls and steps closer, getting into my face. "You need proof? I'll get you fucking proof!" He grabs my arm and pulls me forward. "Let's go!"

"Hey! Let me go! You're hurting me!"

Adam closes the distance to the carriage with a smirk. I am not sure where he took off to but it is evident now he was waiting for this moment. "Good! You need a dose of reality!" He opens the carriage door and bows as we approach.

"Get inside. I'll show you all the evidence you need!" John shoves my body up inside the carriage then climbs in after me. Adam shuts the door, closing off the late afternoon sunshine.

"Why are you doing this? What did Michel ever do to you?"

John lunges into my face and seethes, "HE WAS BORN!" I scream and try to push into the seat in hopes of getting space between us.

"John, please! I'm sorry!" My voice is a soft sob and my vision blurs from the oncoming tears.

"I told you I would not hurt you, but you're making it almost fucking impossible to keep that promise!" John sits back in his seat and breaks the eye contact. "Michel killed my family." I gasp and John's gaze snaps back to my own.

My lip trembles slightly as he crosses his arms over his chest. The carriage takes off and I dare ask a question, "Where... where are we going?"

"To get your evidence and show you there are other monsters in this world." He glares at me for a moment and my heart pounds against my chest. "Amelia, you're about to find out exactly which ones exist."

Chapter 8

The carriage slows to a halt as we reach our destination. I force myself to focus on the scenery of the countryside for minor comfort. We are on the outskirts of Savannah in a more rural area. John has practically barked in my face with hostility for challenging what he believes to be the truth. Quietness sets in amongst us and my thoughts are spinning out of control as a sense of denial sets in.

Michel is not the vicious monster John speaks of. He cannot be. The time we have spent together has been nothing but amazing. He has been sweet, romantic, and kind. Flashes of memories tease my mind as I recall the way he would look upon me. Those blue eyes of his, his lips, the way he would gently touch me. Even the night he saved me from the oncoming attack after the demise of my driver. Then, our time together at the library and the way his eyes sparkled when he handed me *120 Days of Sodom* fills my mind.

He is my knight. He saved me. No one has ever made me feel wanted and as beautiful as he has. I know I must follow what my heart tells me to be the truth. Moreover, Eva involved in all this? Absolutely ridiculous and too farfetched to wrap my mind around.

John clears his throat, snapping me back into the here and now, "We're here, Amelia," he says with no emotion, that echo of authority still in his voice.

I attempt to glance out the carriage window but it is of no use. John takes me by the arm and tugs me toward the door as Adam fully opens it. The sun pours inside, and after my eyes adjust, John pulls me in front of an old building. Sophie stands behind Adam, her arms crossed as her eyes wander around our surroundings.

The building is tall and old. Remarkably, it still stands and I am concerned if the wind were to blow, it might topple over. The windows are broken for the most part and boarded up with pieces of plywood. The front door is rusted and metal looking. The porch leading up to the building has holes and loose wooden planks.

My head and eyes lower as we step toward the mangled porch, my voice a whisper, "He saved my life..."

John turns me to face him, his eyes narrowing in anger, "For a hidden agenda. Even the devil himself was an angel, sweetheart. If you believe those sorts of tales, you're more naïve than I thought."

Pulling me toward the building's entrance, John reaches for the door handle. He pushes it open and it creeks on the hinges. We step inside and the entrance is dark, smelling of rust and mildew. Making our way down the long hall as the floor creeks under our steps, I tell myself, *there is no way to sneak in or out of this place.* We venture into a room that appears to be for interrogation purposes.

John shoves me into a chair in front of an old, wooden desk. Scratches and claw marks have mangled it in the past and I wonder briefly if they allow wild animals inside.

Folders are piled on the desk; John immediately reaches for one on top as if he had been saving it for this moment. He removes a handful of photos from it as Adam and Sophie enter, closing the heavy wooden doors behind them. They stand across the room, watching on. Their eyes meet and a smug grin forms across their features as if they are anticipating what is about to happen.

"Here is your fucking evidence," he growls out as he hands over the photos.

I watch him for a moment then slowly look down at the images copied on paper. I have witnessed news reporters for *The Times* capturing images during reports and investigations, but I have not seen anyone else have the tools to do so as well. My eyes skim the photos for something familiar. I need to prove to John that he is full of shit as he accuses the vampires... *my* vampire... of foul play.

As my eyes move over the people in the image, two of them immediately stand out. "No," I whisper. Snatching the photos, I turn them to face me and pull them closer. It is Eva, standing face to face with Michel. A woman is with them; she looks quite familiar as she stands next to my handsome blue-eyed vampire. I try to place her. My eyes widen as I remember who she is. She is the woman I noticed the night Michel and I had our date. She was there, I remember.

Flipping to the next photo, it is almost as if it moves in unison with their actions. Eva has handed over a vial of clear liquid to Michel and my heart plummets. It has to be the X280. My lower lip quivers, my heart sinking to the pit of my stomach. All the while, John, watching my reaction with intent, goes on to explain.

"You are now aware Eva is working with him. The woman with Michel, she is his progeny and his lover. They have been together through the centuries. Her name is Rene."

Adam chimes in, "Rene, what a blood sucking little whore. Sick bitch bathes in her victims' blood," he says with much disgust in his voice.

I can hear Sophie growl from her corner. "Damn right, I'd like to get a piece of that one; rip her to fucking shreds."

"They do *what?*" My eyes glance up to both Adam and Sophie. A part of me wants to wake from this nightmare. The other part wants to retch at the thought of a blood bath.

John growls at the both of them, flashing his golden eyes. "Quiet, the both of you! You will speak when it's asked of you!" He continues as he turns back to me, "Here you will see Eva handing over the serum; I tried to fucking tell you. So, here it is for your own eyes." He narrows his gaze at me.

With my worst fears confirmed, I buckle into a heap, my knees hitting the wooden floor as I fall from my chair. The photos fall from my grasp below where I kneel, my heart shattering into a million pieces. Not wanting to look upon the images any further, I push them aside as I fight the sobs that escape my throat. Eva, my boss whom I trusted with my findings, has been playing me for a fool this entire time. Oblivious to it all, t I trusted her. I had trusted Michel for saving my life the way he had. I am nothing more than a pawn in his sick game. Not to mention, he has someone else. Someone he has been loving... fucking...this entire time. It is too much. My stomach heaves and I vomit on the floor.

Wiping the back of my hand across my lips, I sit back on my bottom. My gaze is blurry as I stare across the room at the empty wall. Cracks start at the floor and work their way to the ceiling in sporadic patterns. I am staring at everything... and at nothing.

"Amelia?" John's voice has softened slightly but still maintains a harsh cruelty to it.

My voice is a shaky whisper as tears pool around my eyes falling down my cheeks, "I am nothing but a fool, a fool to him, to Eva, to you... to everyone I have ever known! I have nothing!" The words flow through gritted teeth.

John nods sternly in agreement. He squats down to my level and looks me in the eyes. "Finally Amelia, you are starting to make some sense." He rests his arms on his knees and tilts his head as he watches me.

My eyes widening in disbelief, I snap back, "Do you not understand? They have taken *everything* from me! My hopes, my dreams, my life! You feel the need to gloat about such a thing?" I turn my back to him, avoiding his gaze.

I hear his heavy sigh. He stands, moving

behind me, and I feel the warmth of the heat radiating from his body. "It was never my intent to make you feel like a fool, Amelia, but you needed to know."

"My sister was right," my head drops between my shoulders, "I should have listened to her." I miss Rachel and need her now more than ever. She would have also agreed with John on how foolish I have been acting. She is going to enjoy teasing me for eternity with this news of Michel.

"Calm down, we'll handle this, I assure you," His voice is confident as he places a single hand on my shoulder, attempting to comfort me for the first time.

I shrug his hand off my shoulder. "Please, don't," I whisper.

"Fucking sickening," Sophie mumbles from across the room.

"How about doing something useful rather than just standing there making fucking comments?" John growls at her.

I turn my head to glance at the woman as she presses her lips together. Sophie makes her way across the room, flicking a match as she lights a nearby candle to give the room light. She glances at me, then at John. Chagrined, she takes her leave. "I will check on the prisoner. I am sure he is hungry and in need of his daily dose of rat's blood. Disgusting, walking corpse," she tells us. John shakes his head, his eyes piercing her.

With his attention elsewhere, I get to my feet and push past John while pacing the darkened room. I cannot be still. Feeling utterly pathetic, I sob when a sudden spurt of anger washes over me. I grasp the chair closest to me and heave it against one of the walls with a shout. "Dammit! Everything was a fucking lie!" The sound of the wood shattering to pieces echoes through the room.

John slowly takes a step back, allowing me some distance. For a split second, sadness shows in his eyes as he witnesses my meltdown. Adam steps forward in a protective manner beside him. John simply holds a hand up, signaling he is all right. Adam steps back into his previous position, keeping watch with a serious expression.

My body begins to numb. I gaze out the musty window and stare into the open grounds. The sound of the birds singing, the familiar song of twilight, fills the air as the sun starts to set. The sky is a beautiful mixture of orange and red from where I stand. Nightfall is upon us.

John steps forward, and I can feel the heat from his body behind me. He tentatively places his hands on my shoulders then quickly removes them. "Vampires, this is what they do. I have yet to come across a human, or anyone else for that matter, whose lives are not in shambles because of them." He pauses, lowering his gaze for a split second before continuing, "They come into your life through false pretenses, when in reality their Undead heart is as black as the fucking night." He turns me to face him and looks into my eyes. A gentleness has claimed his features as he watches me intently. I am too exhausted, emotionally and physically, at this point to say much.

"This is why my kind were brought into existence," he continues. "There is so much you need to know, Amelia. We have more than one reason for being here and one of them is to fight against this cure of yours. Not only for fear of their kind getting their hands on it... which they already have...but for our own protection as well."

I shake my head, completely confused. His brown eyes stare into mine and soften with patience. "Explain? I am so confused, John. I still do not see the harm in the cure itself. The vampires getting their hands on it, maybe they *wish* to be cured," I say through furrowed brows, my heart breaking once again as Michel crosses my mind. The room feels as if it is caving in on me as my new reality sets in.

He motions toward the remaining chair, "Please, sit," he offers.

Adam steps forward, clearing his throat. For the first time, there is neither a smirk nor smug remark. Adam's expression becomes serious. "If I may explain, please?" A sense of pride radiates from Adam. John nods, giving him permission to speak, while his eyes remain on mine. I blink then glance at Adam.

Adam begins, "It started with our first ancestors. A coven of witches was called upon to bring on a force that could rid the world of vampires. As John explained briefly, early on, the Undead were beginning to take over. They moved in and gained control. That section of the world turned into a blood bath. Once the threat made its way to this coven of witches, they knew they had to get this control back before it was too late.

"They studied a magic that could create a force strong enough to kill any vampire. Once they perfected this magic, they conjured a power within the fire. An image of a man with the head of a wolf appeared. When they saw this image, they set out to find the alpha wolf and a human male. They began their hunt by conjuring a spell to lure in the perfect Alpha wolf. Legend has it he appeared in a matter of days. Their next step, they set out to find the human male. In a nearby village, they found a young, strong man and sedated him. The brought him back to their circle of magic. Tying the two together, they sacrificed them both then bound them together with magic."

My eyes widen through the story Adam tells. My lips part to ask a question and he raises a single finger, as if to tell me, *not yet.* He folds his hands behind his back and starts to pace as he continues. "The magic of the wolf was forced inside the man's body. From what I remember of the stories," he pauses with furrowed brows as if he is thinking back, "it was very painful for the human man. After the spell was completed, he was unconscious. However, when he awoke, he felt as if he had gone mad. His canine teeth descended downward and his body would contort and break. He would transform into what they referred to as 'The Wolf-Man'. He was described as a tall, thick man whose body was covered with hair. He had the body of a wolf that walked on hind legs.

"Eventually, the wolf-man began seducing the maidens in his human form, having sex with them. He would have his way with them, leaving them with child, passing on the wolf gene. So, the stories you hear of the werewolf biting the citizens? It is utter bullshit; just stories to create a scare among the people." He shrugs, less than amused by it.

I let out the heavy breath I have been holding the entire time.

John clears his throat, nodding at Adam. "I'll take it from here." Adam returns the nod then takes his place as guard back at the door.

"You see," John begins, "if you rid the world of vampires, Amelia, there would be no need for our kind. We were created to control the vampires. If they do not exist, then there is no reason for my kind to exist, either. Everything about this cure has its pros and cons.

"Ridding the world of the Undead would be the best outcome. However, there are innocent men, women, and children to consider with this as well. We would all become extinct... Understand?" He raises his brows.

I nod slowly, my face stricken between shock and disbelief. "Right, yeah. I," pausing for a moment, "I understand." I lower my eyes and consider everything I have just learned. I do understand, don't I? I sigh and offer a nod, "This is a lot to take in." Sighing, I continue, "I also understand the reason why all this went down the way it did. Had I not seen those photos with my own eyes, I don't think I would have ever believed." A single tear falls down my cheek. I quickly wipe it away with my palm.

John watches me for a moment then, satisfied that I seem to be at least partially sane, he crosses the room to Adam. They begin to plot how to get Rachel out of harm's way and our safety. I breathe an exasperated breath, realizing my life is no longer in my hands. It is now in the hands of these strangers… these werewolves.

***

After cleaning myself up in the bathroom, John provides me with a few clean towels and alternate clothing. I have never been one to wear trousers but considering our circumstances, if we need to run, my bustle is not the best choice of clothing to wear.

Pulling on the dark brown women's trousers borrowed from Sophie and the matching striped corset, I step out with a pair of brown leather boots in my hands. "Umm, Sophie?" Finding her across the room, she looks up.

John turns toward me as I step out and his eyes widen slightly. Adam's lip pulls in a smirk. Sophie closes the distance and takes my elbow, leading me back into the bathroom. "Let's get these boots on you, yes?"

"I've never worn trousers, thank you," I tell her.

She nods and has me sit on a dressings

stool. "You look... different. Better if I may say." Sophie grins as she slips the boot onto my foot then over my calf. She tucks in the material then fastens it up the side. She does the same to the other leg. "Well, let's have a look."

I stand and make my way toward the mirror. "I almost don't recognize myself. Thank you," I look at her in the mirror, "for your garments."

"You're welcome." She hands over a pair of what looks to be goggles with an elastic band connected. "Wear these at night. They'll help you see better." She shrugs with a grin. "We have our own alchemists who enjoy inventing things. Oh, these spectacles?" She points to the small eyeglass pieces screwed into the goggles. "These will aid in bringing the image you're looking at closer. Like binoculars but better."

"Oh, wow, thank you." I slip them on and they aid in holding my hair back. "I look like such a mess." I shake my head and step closer to the mirror. Turning on the water, I wash my face and hands once more. After patting my skin dry, Sophie holds out a few hairpins. Brown stones with gold feathers adorning the tops of them, they sparkle in the light. Gasping, my eyes widen. "Sophie, these are beautiful! I can't possibly..."

"Yes, you can. Take them. I have more." She

turns me toward her and helps in setting my hair. She pushes in the pins, and after a few minutes, she smiles. "Beautiful."

I turn toward the mirror again and smile. "I've never been one to really enjoy the pin curl, thank you."

I step back out this time with my boots on and hair finished.

"Alright, she's ready to go," Sophie calls.

Again, John turns to face me and he smiles. I find myself staring at him, thinking he has a nice smile. I lower my gaze and take a few steps forward, almost walking into Adam.

"Wow, you clean up... nice," Adam tells me.

"Umm..." I am at a loss for words and Sophie laughs.

"Let's go," John orders. He closes the distance to me and his eyes look me over. I almost feel as if he is undressing me. I bite my lip. "You do clean up nice," he sighs. "Are you ready for this?"

I nod and my eyes look up into his. "I'm pissed and need to shoot something."

He chuckles then leads the way outside. We make our way toward the carriage. It seems I will be seeing John quite frequently as he has put himself in charge as my bodyguard. I glance up at him as we walk alongside each other, my voice filled with confidence despite it being chipped away.

"I assure you, I'll be fine. I know how to handle myself. I am anything but a damsel in distress. My father taught me all there is to know of weaponry and how to protect myself."

"I have no doubt you've learned self-defense," he tells me, "however, carrying a vial of holy water or your... liquid sun as you call it... will not stop a vampire from attacking you."

"How do you know of this? It is not public knowledge." I wonder for a moment if my research has been leaked or if Eva shared this information as well. The liquid sun would be marketed soon, but it had not made it to patenting... at least not yet.

"One thing at a time, Amelia." Eva's words ring back to me as I stare at John.

I step into the carriage as John offers his hand to help me step into the seat. The handsome werewolf climbs in next before Adam closes the doors of the carriage in place. "You've never gone toe to toe with a vampire, have you?" he asks me with a cocky glare.

"That will be all, Adam," John informs him. He nods respectfully then disappears in front of the carriage. The reins crack as it begins to move.

John barks out a laugh. "So you know how to handle yourself just fine, huh?" His voice is thick with sarcasm, "That's just too bad, as you're stuck with me. You've gotten yourself into quite the predicament, darling'." He chuckles in disbelief at my bravery.

I roll my eyes and press my lips together. Looking away from him, I pull the window curtain to the side and gaze at the passing scenery. Eventually, the scenery of trees and open landscape is replaced with the busy streets of the city. My heart continues to sting from the news learned, knowing all my hard work, everything I have been through, has all been for naught.

"I do not need you to scold or mock me," I announce. "I've had enough for one night. Have you any decency after what I was just put through?" Releasing the curtain, I sit back against my seat and stare at John.

John shakes his head with a grin. "Woman, you are utterly amazing, you know that? You got yourself into this bind. It's what you get for trusting these damn vampires."

"Oh, sarcasm at its finest. Save it, please," I

huff as he helps me down from the carriage. I step onto the hard concrete of the sidewalk just outside my loft.

Adam, with a smirk of amusement upon his features, says, "Have a good evening, Amelia." Sophie rounds the carriage with a roll of her eyes. She politely keeps to herself.

With a crack of the reins, Adam and the carriage start down the road. John leads the way up the entrance toward my building. "If we stay the evening here, plan on me being in the room." My eyes widen at this and I am about to protest when he says, "You want me in your bed? My lady, that is too much of an advance on me!"

He chuckles as Sophie growls. "Stop fucking with her mind, John." She pushes past us toward the entrance and opens the main door.

"Please, Amelia," the way he looks at me, he makes me think I'm a child and he's been assigned as my sitter, "I would sleep on the floor. Get over yourself."

My mouth agape at the interaction we just had, I shake my head then push at his massive chest. The man does not budge. "I would really rather you didn't. As I said before, I will be fine." Pushing past him and Sophie, I lead the way toward the entrance of my loft, digging my keys out of my purse. I unlock my front door, pausing briefly.

He chuckles heartily. "And as I said before, it's too damn bad." He cocks an unamused brow at me.

With a roll of my eyes, I lead the way in. Once inside, I clear my throat as his massive form blocks the way for me to lock the front door. "Excuse me, I must lock up." My eyes turn upward toward him for a moment as he gazes down at me. His dark brown eyes have a softness to them. He simply nods, stepping toward my right as his eyes wander around the foyer with curiosity.

After securing the front door, I make my way back into the foyer. John has picked up a picture frame, looking at a picture of Rachel and me. "That was taken about a year ago," I tell him. He sets the frame down as I continue. "I have some extra blankets. The couch is quite comfortable as well." I motion around my living room, "I apologize in advance. It is a small one-bedroom place. I usually do not have visitors."

John's brown eyes fall upon me. He steps closer and leans against the wall. "I'll be fine. Bring the blankets to your bedroom."

"Oh, you were serious about sleeping in my

room?" I swallow hard and feel the blood suddenly rush to my cheeks.

He nods. "Get some rest, Amelia; I'll see you in the morning." His eyes remain on me for a moment.

I nod slowly, "Alright then. Well, goodnight." With that, I turn toward my bedroom. The exhaustion of my mind catches up with my body once I step inside my room.

Reaching behind me, I loosen the corset and exhale deeply. The garment falls to the floor as I reach for my nightgown. Lighting the lamp on my nightstand, I change my clothes, pull out a few extra blankets for John, and set them on the end of my bed. Folding Sophie's clothes from today, to ready them for tomorrow, I turn at a knock on my door.

"Umm," John clears his throat as he steps in. He keeps his eyes to the floor and steps closer. Tentatively, he looks up at me and holds my gaze for a moment.

"One might think you've never seen a lady in a night gown, John." My lips pull in a smirk.

"I've seen them in much less," he retorts with a grin.

My cheeks blush as I turn away toward my bed. I pull my comforter and sheets down. "Here's a pillow." He reaches for it and nods his thanks.

John builds a makeshift pad on the floor then unbuttons his shirt. My eyes widen for a moment and I gasp. He chuckles. "One would think you've never seen a naked man, Amelia." He glances over with a sly smirk.

I shake my head and roll my eyes. Lying back, I cover my face and turn on my side. I peek slightly through my fingers to watch him and try my best not to visibly gasp at the large, strong man undressing in my bedroom.

John's heavy steps cross the room as he bends over to blow out the light. He looks over at me just before he does, and our eyes catch one another's. Once in the darkness, he maneuvers his way back to the pad he has made. He grunts a few times as I hear him lying down, getting comfortable. He sighs, "Goodnight, Amelia."

I smile to myself, feeling safe… not that I would admit as much to him. "Goodnight." Yawning, sleep slowly takes me under.

Chapter 9

A ray of the early morning sun streams across my body, the heat of it stirring me awake. For a moment, I groan softly and pull the covers over my head. *Everything in the last few days has been a nightmare of sorts. When I emerge from bed, all will be as it was and I will never have met John. Michel will still be mine and my cure will win me the Nobel Prize.*

The terrible news of Eva and Michel begins settling in, as if my mind is casually reminding me how naïve I have been. I pull the covers down enough to glance toward my nightstand. The book *120 Days of Sodom* rests there, staring at me. A heavy sigh escapes my lips as Michel crosses my mind.

My eyes close as I envision his face. His beautiful blue eyes, his lips so luscious, the way we kissed that night. I look at the book again and anger touches my heart. "I can't believe I've been so stupid."

I sigh and look around my bedroom and adjust to the morning light. There is an unfamiliar outline of a covered man asleep on the floor. He snores as loud as the handsome beast he is.

I swallow back emotion as reality sets in all over again. "It wasn't a nightmare." I lower my gaze, staring at the dark gray fabric of my comforter and sheets as my heart plummets immediately. A single tear races toward my hairline and I shake my head. "No more tears," I whisper to myself.

Slowly peeling the covers back to sit up, I pull my legs underneath me and stare at the book for a moment. My lips curl in anger and disgust, as if the book sits there... judging me. I quickly shove it into the top drawer of my nightstand. "Out of sight, out of mind, that son of a bitch," I mutter, my voice laccd with anger.

I cover my lips realizing I have been a bit louder than anticipated, not wanting to wake the werewolf bodyguard just yet. Rising to my feet, the floor is chilly against my bare skin. Turning my head, I watch him for a moment. His chest rises and falls as he sleeps. The fearsome look he had yesterday is gone, to be replaced with a handsome, almost striking face that is at ease with rest. Thankfully, he is not able to see the slight smile on my lips as I think of the safety I feel having him here.

I have never had someone come into my life to protect me, putting his or her own life on the line. It provokes a feeling inside of me, something far deeper than Michel had ever given. I find there is something warm and comforting in the werewolf that lay asleep before me.

I whisper softly to myself, "What now?" I shake my head as I consider this. "I also felt safe with Michel before all this. I need to be careful not to fall for men so easily. Hell, I need to guard my heart. I'm such a stupid girl."

Quietly sidestepping the sleeping beast, I decide to take a long bath to ease my lingering nerves from the previous day. Gathering my clothes from the closet, I pull out a beige corset and black ribbons to tie the back, along with a lacey, black skirt to match. It is one of the newer outfits I have recently purchased and one of my favorites. After gathering my undergarments, I quietly sneak away, making a mental note to phone Rachel. I need to know she is well and safe. I need the comfort that only family can bring at a time like this. I feel as if I have walked into Hell and my life has fallen into ruins.

I carefully pull the bedroom door closed before making the short distance to the bathroom. I can hear Sophie snoring from the living room. I shake my head with a soft laugh as I push the bathroom door open. I recall times I have heard Rachel snore during her sleep, but it was because she either had caught a cold or had been drinking.

The floor creaks slightly as I reach the bathroom. Closing the door, the hinge decides to creak as well and I make a mental note to rub it down with some grease later. Reaching for the lantern, I strike a match and light it. The area illuminates from the light and casts shadows across the floor. Setting my clothes for the day on the counter, I turn and start the bath water.

After undressing myself, I lower my body into the tub and relax. "If it were easy enough to wash my worries away, I would absolutely have done so by now." I close my eyes and relax. My mind begins to drift over the events of the last few days and I can feel myself dozing in and out of consciousness.

Suddenly, my eyes open when I hear a creak on the floor.

"Amelia?" John calls for me. "Where are you?"

"Umm…" I hesitate for a moment and my heart slams against my chest. *Damn, I do not need him coming in here while I am naked!* "I am bathing."

The creaking of the floor stops and I can just imagine the look on his face while he considers whether to storm my bathroom or to leave me be. For his own sake, he had better choose the latter. The floor creaks again and the sound comes closer toward the bathroom. I shake my head and want to pull my towel in over top of me.

"So..." his voice is just on the other side of the door. "Can I help? Need me to wash your back?"

I can definitely hear humor in his voice.

"NO! Do NOT come in here, John! Do you understand me? I AM NAKED!" My voice comes out in a rush and I splash in the tub, trying to get out. Water hits the floor and my feet slip. My hands grasp the counter, and if he were to walk in right now, he would receive a full show. "Dammit!"

He chuckles on the other side of the door. "Are you okay in there? I don't mind helping." The door handle jiggles, and deep in my mind, I know he is teasing; however, I could absolutely punch him right now.

"I AM FINE! NOW LEAVE!" I scream at him.

He chuckles again and I hear the floor creak again as he takes his leave.

My racing heartbeat and red face finally begin to ease. Wrapping my bath towel around my body, I reach over and drain the tub. "Son of a bitch," I mutter under my breath. Tightening the towel around my body, I grab my clothes and make my way toward the door. I do not dare chance John coming into the bathroom while I dress.

Inhaling a deep breath, I hold it, and then slowly open the door. It, of course, creaks as loud, if not louder than earlier. I grit my teeth and finally look out. The hallway is clear and I exhale slowly. Taking small steps, I head back toward my bedroom to dress.

"You sure you don't need a hand?"

I scream and quickly turn around. John is standing at the top of the stairs and his eyes take in my body, naked underneath my bath towel.

"You will leave the upstairs right now, John Hawthorne, or so help me, I *will* hurt you!"

"Naked, I hope?" He chuckles and waves his hands at me in defeat. "I'm sorry, I'm only teasing. I'm going back down." He turns to leave then takes another look at me and whistles.

"I WILL THROW SOMETHING AT YOU!"

He quickly takes the stairs down, "As long as it's your towel!" I can hear Adam roaring with laughter downstairs.

Growling, I head toward my bedroom and

lock the door behind me. "SON OF A BITCH!" I scream out. I sit on my bed and it bounces underneath me. Shaking my head, my lips form a smile and I almost cannot help the laugh that escapes. After all that has happened, John was being playful in an effort to amuse either himself or me… maybe both. Rolling my eyes, I begin to dress myself for breakfast with my shape shifting bodyguards.

After dressing and setting my hair, I finally venture back downstairs. I glance over at John and offer a soft smile, which he returns.

"I need to see my sister. She is aware of the cure, and if I am in danger from the repercussions, she may be as well. I need to know she is okay. I would like to bring her back here with me."

John nods in agreement. "I'm fine with that plan. Does she live nearby?"

"Yes, just a few blocks away."

We take his carriage over to her home and park it on the street. I notice the area is unusually quiet. Rachel enjoys her mornings and loves to garden first thing. She may not be much into Alchemy, but the woman has a green thumb.

John helps me out of the carriage and I straighten my black skirt. We make our way to the front door and I knock. "Rachel, it's me…" I stop talking when I notice her door is not locked and pushes open. I gasp and look up at John.

He nods and pushes me behind him. Adam takes his flank and Sophie stands next to me.

"Let them go inside first. It may not be anything, but we need to make sure first," she tells me in a whisper.

I nod and watch as my guards enter my sister's home.

The area is dark and looks empty. My eyes widen and I gasp. Sophie and I step in behind the men and we look around the area. Her den has been mangled as though someone was here was looking for something. A sudden pungent smell touches my nose and I almost heave.

John and Adam look at one another then look toward the hallway that leads to Rachel's bedroom. My head shakes as I consider what they must be thinking. Without consideration of the consequences, I sprint toward Rachel's bedroom. I can hear John call after me, but I am deaf to everything right now.

I feel nothing and hear nothing. Shock may be setting in as I feel myself on autopilot. Reaching her bedroom, there is blood on the floor that leads to her bathroom. I lunge for the door and push it open. My body goes numb from my head all the way to my toes. The tub is stained and smeared with crimson, in it lays Rachel. Her body is knelt over the side of the porcelain tub, her arms hanging limp as droplets of blood continue to drip onto the tiles from a gruesome gash in her neck. Her body is pale and lifeless.

"RACHEL!" I quickly leap toward her, slipping on her blood. I land on my knees and crawl the remaining distance to her lifeless body. I grasp her face and attempt to lift it, but she does not move. "NO, NO, NO! PLEASE, SAY SOMETHING! PLEASE!" I gather her in my arms, my sister's blood smearing on the front of my clothes, my arms, and upper chest. I cradle her to me, sobbing. "This can't be happening, please God! This can't be happening!" My voice is shaking with tears in between sobs. My mind has been so clouded with heartache, loss, and guilt that I have not noticed John, Adam, and Sophie behind me. Their voices echo since everything seems so far away. I feel as if I am losing my mind from the anguish my heart is feeling.

The room spins and my stomach heaves through heavy sobs. "RACHEL! WAKE UP, PLEASE!"

John quickly kneels before me, "Amelia," his voice seems distant—miles away. He tries gently to pull me away from Rachel to no avail.

"No! John, please, I can't leave her, please!" I hold her lifeless body to me. Rachel's eyes and mouth ajar, her head rests on my shoulder as her blood seeps onto my body. My sobs build in volume as I rock with her in my arms.

Sophie comes up behind me and slips her hands underneath my arms. She begins trying to pry me from my dead sister's body. "Amelia, you need to let her go. She's gone, honey, she's gone." She pulls again but I refuse to let go. "We'll get them, Amelia, I promise you this. We'll get them."

John moves closer in front of me and runs his fingers over my hair. Looking up at him, he tilts his head. "Let her go," he tells me in a calm voice. He takes my arm with a gentle grasp and pulls. Slowly, releasing my sister, her body collapses on the floor. Not removing my eyes from her, she does not move to argue with me or tease me anymore. She is just a shell, a body.

John's arms scoop under my body to wrap around me. He cradles me to the warmth of his strong chest and I tremble in his arms. I am too far gone to stand on my own; it is almost as if he is trying to shield me from the pain, protect me from the grief. It is far too late for that.

John's gaze meets Sophie's as she watches

on, his voice strong and authoritative. "Sophie, call on the pack immediately. Tell them to get their asses down here. We need to get Amelia away from here. NOW. Afterward, get hold of Derek at the sheriff's office to handle the scene. No one is to know about this; this stays within the pack." Sophie nods firmly before she follows us out. Apparently, werewolves have ties in the police department for occasions such as this. As Sophie takes her leave, John swiftly moves us to the den. He kicks over the turned sofa and sits down. His arms tighten around me close as I continue to sob into his chest.

"John," I sob, "Rachel's gone! She is gone! Why? WHY?"

His arms tighten around me, holding me to close to him. He whispers, "I know, Amelia. I am so sorry. We're getting you out of here." I can feel the vibrations rumble through his chest as if he is holding back his emotions.

My arms tighten around his neck and I bury my face against him, crying. Tears dampen his shirt as Sophie re-enters the room. I can hear her sigh heavily before a low, guttural growl escapes her throat. "When can I sink my fucking claws into those dead sons of bitches, John? This shit has gone way too damn far."

John turns to Sophie, his eyes piercing with

anger. "You will hold back, Sophie! You are smarter than that! We need to inform the entire pack! You understand?" His voice raised, I can feel the rumble in his chest as my head rests against it.

I tuck my head underneath John's chin and cling to his shirt. It is all I can do just to stare across my sister's den. I do not flinch or even blink as his angry voice roars at Sophie's itchy trigger fingers. My body feels numb in the worst of ways.

Sophie stands down and lowers her gaze. She bows respectfully to her Alpha. "Fine." John glares hard at her and I can feel him about to yell at her again before a knock interrupts their bickering.

She looks at the door then back at John. He nods for her to answer it. She walks toward it, unlocks it, and pulls it open. Adam steps over the threshold. His eyes zero in on John holding my weary form covered in blood. He holds me close to him, as if I were a child.

"I see we have much to discuss once things settle down here," he says with a sigh before stepping aside. "The pack is coming and will be ready once we arrive."

John nods to his Beta and rises from the

couch. He carries me through the door toward the carriage. Adam follows suit just as Derek arrives.

Derek is an older gentleman, mostly bald, but like the other werewolves, his form is massive. He stands at six feet five inches and nods respectfully as he approaches the porch. He clears his throat, his eyes wandering the scene, "This is Amelia?" John nods affirmatively.

"Let me get her out of harm's way here. She's quite shaken up, Sheriff." John's voice lowered, "She made the discovery." Derek slowly nods his head thoughtfully before disappearing through the front door to speak with Sophie.

John carefully slides me into the back of the carriage. I bring my knees to my chest and stare out toward the busy street through blurred vision. He wraps a blanket around my petite form. There is no chill in the air, though the blanket brings me comfort.

John turns to Adam, "Keep watch on her for a few minutes. I need to show Derek..."

"No, please don't leave." The words leave my lips before I realize what I have said.

John looks to me for a moment and his demeanor loses the tough man persona, if just for a split second. "Amelia, I promise, I'll be right back in no time. Adam will not allow anything to happen to you." He turns away to end the conversation then gives Adam a knowing look. "Once I'm back out, we need to leave here immediately." Adam nods obediently and stands guard over the carriage.

I shift my focus to the scene just opposite of where Adam stands guard. The street is busy with a few onlookers. They gape at the commotion, mumbling speculation amongst themselves. A part of me wants to scream at them to stop staring, the other to tell them that this was a vampire attack.

People go about their business, carefree this morning. They go about their day as if they are the only thing that matters in this world— Southern Aristocrat types, some wealthy, others dressed for their day at their job. Bankers, politicians, and possibly a few 'Johns' on their way to visit the local whore house.

Some laugh amongst themselves. Women are wearing their newly bought hats, brightly colored corsets, and dresses. Men are wearing their fancy suits, some looking strapping and handsome. All that matters to them are their possessions, their lives, their businesses, and their money.

Little do they know of the true darkness in the world; I am seeing it all with my very own eyes.

A week ago, I was one of these people. I was filled with the excitement of creating my cure for vampirism. Something I was certain would win me the Noble Prize and save humanity from the oncoming plague of the Undead. Now, here I sit in my new reality. My heart and soul have been shattered. I have no one left in my family. I have lost everything—my job, my family, my sanity—all has gone to the wind. All has become as death itself.

I turn away from the world so blind and uninformed. There are far worse things to worry about than the latest fashions or big meetings and agendas that plague the normal mind. Last week I did not realize this, but now... now, everything has changed. I have had to learn this the hard way, which is my own doing. Rachel tried to warn me and I did not listen. Now, she is gone, and I feel responsible for what has happened to her.

Keep your voice down, Amelia! You never know who may be listening!

Her words come back to me like a slap in the face. I whisper to myself, "Rachel, I am so sorry. God, I am so sorry, please, just *please* help me. I have messed up... No, I fucked up." My voice cracks and I bury my face against my knees.

I did not realize at the time, but Adam has been listening through all of this. His back to me, he says nothing, but gives me the time I need to grieve. My tears continue as we wait for John and Sophie. I cry silently to myself.

***

Eventually, John and Sophie emerge from Rachel's home. Derek follows on their heels as Rachel's body is removed. Adam opens the door of the carriage and the warmth of the sun spills inside, warming my body. John climbs into the carriage, mumbling something about taking me away from the scene. He slides in next to me and his eyes look over my body as he settles in close. My eyes are filled with sadness and heartbreak along with fatigue from the ongoing chaos my life has become. As the carriage takes off toward their home, he lowers his voice to a whisper, "How are you feeling?" He studies me, awaiting an answer.

I swallow hard, my voice weakened, "I still," I pause for a moment, "I still cannot grasp the fact that she is gone. It has all been too much." I press my lips together, lowering my eyes.

John nods in understanding. "Much how I felt when I lost my family to these predators. They will suck the soul out of a person. No pun intended, but it is a fact. They feed off the life of their victim, in more ways than one." He lowers his gaze.

"I'm learning that quickly." I gaze out the window and watch the scenery pass by.

"Indeed, you are. I can assure you, though, in time, you will bounce back from this. The pain will dim in time, Amelia. Please know that."

He wraps his arm around my shoulder and I lean into him, finding comfort in his warmth. All I can do is nod.

My hand covers my mouth as I sob silently while exiting the city, a city I once enjoyed.

Flashes of Rachel's smile wash over me as I reminisce about times spent together, memories of when we were children playing on our grandparents' farm. Our nights dancing when we would get together to relax and unwind from our hectic weeks. I can still hear the echo of her laughter ringing in my head.

We eventually reach the outskirts of Savannah. I recognize it as nearly the same route we had taken the day before to the abandoned building. The carriage pulls to a stop in front of a large home. I look out the window and find it quite charming. The lawn is trimmed to perfection with a beautiful assortment of yellow, red, and purple wild flowers growing freely over the property. The building itself is red brick with dark blue shutters alongside each window. The colonial style home is beautiful with a wraparound porch and swings.

Adam opens the carriage door for John. He climbs out then turns back and reaches for me. I take his hand, stepping outside onto the gravel. With my blood soaked clothes and the blanket wrapped around my shoulders, we walk across the gravel toward the front porch.

"Your home is lovely, John." My voice is soft and weak. "It is out past town, so alone, and freeing. You could have a party out here under a full moon. I doubt anyone would notice."

He goes on looking as if he is debating on saying something further, but decides against it. His offers a soft smile and shakes his head. I wonder if I missed a joke or something.

John takes my hand into the crook of his arm, leading the way toward the front door as Adam and Sophie tend to parking the carriage. My knees remain wobbly with emotion as we step onto the porch. He reaches into his trouser pockets for his keys and unlocks the door.

I follow his lead into his home, my eyes wandering with curiosity. The air is clean; it is almost crisp. The walls are a dark shade of red with a few pictures adorning them. A brown sofa sits in the middle of a room with hardwood floors. There are recliners and armchairs in what looks like a circle situated around the sofa. The home smells of sandalwood and musk, a quite relaxing scent when I close my eyes. I try to savor it as I stand in the entrance, if only to escape my reality for a moment.

John's gaze never leaves me as he watches on. "There's a room just for you upstairs. You will have your own quarters and bathroom. No one will bother you without your permission or mine."

I nod a few times then look up at him. Fresh tears build in my eyes, "Rachel would have loved your home." A flash of my sister, drained and murdered in her tub, haunts my memory.

He steps forward slowly, and without hesitation, pulls me into an embrace. "You're safe here, I assure you."

Resting my head against his strong chest, soft sobs escape me. "I can't get the vision of her out of my head," I whisper shakily. I can feel my eyes become heavy as he continues to hold me before he picks me up, cradling me to the warmth of his body. He carries me to the room he has promised me and sets me down on the floor. His fingers begin working on my blood stained garments. "Shh, I'm only removing the top layer; you will not be naked in my presence. I have someone coming up to help you bathe."

I turn my head toward the wall as his fingers gently work the busk closure. He unfastens the skirt and pulls both off my body before he pulls the blanket up to my shoulders. Sophie steps inside the room and offers a smile. She crosses the room and opens another door that appears to lead to a bathroom.

I glance back at John as he helps me stand. "Sophie will help clean you up. Relax and try to get some sleep when you are finished bathing." He lightly touches my cheek, and then, as Sophie reenters the room, John takes his leave.

Chapter 10

A gentle breeze tousles my hair and dress against my body. My fingers pull the stray hairs back behind my ears. The sun is warm and I close my eyes, smiling up at the rays that warm my face.

"Amelia," my sister calls my name, and turning, Rachel stands in the distance on a hill. The sun behind me offers her no visibility, leaving her features in the shadows. "Come to me," she calls.

"Coming," I call back to her. Running through the field of sunflowers and daisies, my fingers run along their petals. My bare feet on the ground, it is soft and cool. I glance up at my sister and still cannot see her face.

My shadow skips along with me as we run through the field. The words of a song come to mind. It is one I am not familiar with, but I find myself singing:

Playing along the river bed,

Here comes the darkness, let's beg to be dead.

The children cry, the mothers howl,

The man will smile while taking a bow.

His teeth are long,

They shine in the light.

You better learn to put up a fight.

For he will claim thee until thy doom,

Cover yourself child, for he's in your room!

I finish singing the unfamiliar tune just as I reach my sister.

"Where on earth did you learn that wretched song, Amelia?" she asks me.

I smile and shrug. "Honestly? I have no idea."

Finally seeing her face, my eyes widen. Her cheeks are bloody and so are her eyes. There is a gash on her neck that bleeds as her heart beats. Gasping, I scream out, "RACHEL!"

A shadow of a man creeps up behind my sister. His hands touch her shoulders then move down her arms. Nails slightly long for a man, I notice dirt and debris underneath them. He brings his head around to her shoulder, licking her neck. Rachel drops her head to the side and closes her eyes.

He slowly raises his face to me. A smirk plays on his features as he licks his lips. Fear consumes me as I look into the eyes of Michel.

"NO!" Screaming, I sit up in bed, panting heavily. My heart slams against my chest and a cold sweat beads across my forehead.

My bed shifts and hands grasp my face. I can hear a voice in the distance calling my name and it is not until he finally gets into my line of vision that I see John.

"Amelia! Wake up!" He shakes me for a moment then grabs my chin with his firm hand. "Fuck's sake, woman, I will slap you awake if I need to!"

I blink and look at him. My brows furrow and I pull myself free. "You will do no such thing!" I push him away from me, "I'm fine, as you can see. It was... well, I had a bad dream." I realize then that John has no shirt on and is in his undergarments. My eyes really take him in as if for the first time. This man is huge and his chest is strong, as are his arms. Tattoos cover his biceps and a few have made their way over his chest. Scars adorn his abs and arms, and one on his neck.

He notices me staring and clears his throat. I immediately look away and feel the blush creep up my neck to my ears.

"You call this a bad dream? Look at you!" He motions to me, and as I look down, my body is shaking and my pillowcase is wet from sweating.

I lower my gaze, sigh, and cover my face. Images of the nightmare come back to me, along with the nightmare of discovering Rachel's body. I begin rocking in place as I do my damndest not to sob. I am so tired of crying that my eyes hurt.

His hand gently touches my back then he begins to move it up and down. "Do you want to talk about it?"

Glancing up, I sniff and shake my head. "I'm afraid if I do, I'll lose myself again. I don't want it to be real," I whisper.

He nods and removes his hand.

"Please, don't stop." I look away, feeling ashamed, like a little girl needing comfort from a father figure. "It was... nice." John is definitely no father figure though. He is a sexy man and I cannot help staring at his naked torso. He nods and I am thankful he cannot read my mind.

I pull my knees to my chest and wrap my arms around them. His hand moves along my back again as I rest my head on top of my knees. Inhaling deeply, I slowly release my breath and begin talking about my dream. "I know it won't happen, since she's already dead," I swallow thickly, "but it was about Rachel... and Michel. He... He..." My voice hiccups and a tear races down my cheek.

"It's okay, I get it." His voice is soft and comforting. I find myself leaning into him, the side of my head on his shoulder. I feel so weak next to him. He brings this warmth, this radiance within him that I need.

John wraps a strong, protective arm around my body and pulls me into his lap. I do not fight it and allow him to hold me, comfort me. I lean into his chest, breathing in his scent, and tuck my head under his chin. His heart beats against his chest and offers a soothing sound to the craziness that has exploded around me.

His hands move up and down my arm as he holds me close. My fingers rest against his bare chest, and for the moment, I am content.

I am not sure how much time has passed when a knock sounds at my bedroom door. It opens and John unfolds his protective arms from my body. He looks toward the door and huffs, "Yeah? What is it?"

Moving off his lap, I pull my sheet up to my shoulders and wipe my eyes. Adam sticks his head just inside the door and looks between the two of us. "I heard her yell so I came up."

"We're fine," John tells him. He rises from the bed and looks over at me. I nod once and he returns it. Reaching for his undershirt, he pulls it on. It fits tightly against him, the material almost straining against his body. "Talk to Sophie about breakfast, would you?"

Adam's brow furrows then he reluctantly nods. "Fine."

"There a problem, Adam?" John asks him.

He sighs then hesitates for a moment. "Nothing we can't discuss later."

I huff and raise my voice. "All this too much for you? Seeing a woman in tears?" I cannot help myself for being a little disparaging. "Spare me the drama, Adam. I lost my fucking sister." Rolling my eyes, I look out the window to the morning sky.

A growl comes from across the room, then a yelp. Jumping in place, I look over at the door and see Adam nursing his jaw. He glares at me then leaves the room.

"What just happened?" I ask, looking at John for answers.

"Nothing he didn't deserve," he replies. "When you are ready, come on downstairs." He watches me for a moment, "Are you alright?"

I nod a few times then lower my gaze. "I'll be down shortly."

John nods and hesitates, then closes the door behind him.

Pulling myself from the bed, I make my way toward the bathroom. The room is painted the same as the bedroom—dark red. The tub sits on what looks like paws on the ground.

Drawing the bath water in the tub, I turn to face the mirror. My eyes are dark... sunken in. I look like hell. My fingers run through my tousled hair as I sigh. "Rachel, I'm so sorry..." my voice is barely a whisper as a few tears spring into my eyes.

I turn away from the mirror and remove my clothes. I recall John removing my corset and skirt last night. Not necessarily do I want to see them as they were covered in Rachel's blood, but I am curious as to their whereabouts.

Testing the water, finding it to my liking, I turn off the faucet. I lower myself in and rest my arms on the side, my head on the back. Staring at the ceiling for a moment, my mind dances around the memories of the last few days.

Vampires are not who they project themselves to be. They are evil monsters. Every one of them. They bathe in the blood of their victims.

Werewolves are real. What other monsters in the world are out there? Fairies? Demons? Angels?

My sister is dead.

Closing my eyes at this last thought, I allow myself to sob. I deserve this; I have earned it, goddammit! I cover my face with my hands and slowly sink into the bathwater until I am fully submerged. The water moves through my hair and I can feel it touch my face and shoulders. My feet press against the tub as I push myself back up again. Pushing my hair back from my face, I shake my head.

"No more tears, dammit! My heart will always ache, but as of today, Amelia Rimos will fight back." Taking in a deep breath, I exhale and continue my pact. "I will no longer be naïve to those around me. I will no longer take shit from anyone. I will no longer be deceived. I will stand up for me and those who cannot fend for themselves. I will no longer take things lying down." I close my eyes and attempt to relax myself... failing miserably.

A short while later, I am out of the tub and dried off. I make my way back into my room and find clothes laid out for me. I am not sure when someone came in, but as John promised, no one has disturbed me. I can only imagine he delivered them.

Thoughts of yesterday—when he almost walked in while I was naked in the tub brings a soft smile to my lips. A part of me feels guilty for smiling at the memory while my sister is now dead. She would want me to enjoy myself, but I feel guilty for doing so.

I stare down at the clothes and put on a solid front. I need to be strong these coming days. I need to avenge my sister. I need to be of some support to John and his pack of werewolves.

"Shit, I still can't get my mind wrapped around the thought that shifters are real."

Shaking my head, I pull on the trousers a white blouse, and a black corset vest left for me. Pulling on my own boots and lacing them up, I tuck in the trousers. My hair is set at the nape of my neck and I secure it with pins. Pulling my goggles in place, I pull on my leather gloves.

I descend the stairs into the living room and find it empty. Voices carry from the next room, leading me toward the kitchen. Cream French doors close off the room, and as I push them open, Sophie, Adam, and John all turn to look in my direction. John's approving gaze does not go unnoticed. I do my best to hide any blush that threatens to expose my approval.

Stepping into the kitchen, the doors swing closed behind me. I clear my throat, feeling a little nervous. "I've not been one for gunnery in my time, but my father taught us how to shoot when we were children. He always wanted us prepared for anything. He left Rachel and me with weapons. They are in the safety deposit boxes at the bank. We can go there in a while and retrieve them."

"How old are these... said weapons?" Sophie asks. "Any idea what he may have left behind?"

I shrug and make my way farther inside. Finding eggs and bacon prepared, I make a plate and sit at the table. "There are guns of different sizes, and if I recall, a few bows. Like me, my father was an Alchemist. He enjoyed inventing things. My father made quite a few weapons when he was alive. People used to come to him for his inventions." I look over at John and find him watching me. My face heats for a moment as I recall him holding me... almost naked. I clear my throat as I take a bite of bacon. "Your driver? He has one of the inventions my father created. The casing on his arm helps him moments after a battle."

John nods a few times. "A few of my pack members have had limbs replaced when needed. Unfortunately, when they shift, the casing does not shift with them."

"I wouldn't expect it to," I answer as I take another bite. "They are mechanical enhancements, not magical ones." He raises a brow at this. "I didn't mean anything by that, I was only implying. That is all."

"Understood," he responds.

There is silence in the kitchen for a long moment. Sophie speaks up first, "Well, I think we need a night out before we go storming into their coven."

We all turn to her in curiosity. "Meaning?" John asks.

"Meaning, I think we need a night out. We need to hit the bars. Get drunk. Get crazy." Her eyes dazzle. "I need to find me a man that will take me to bed!"

I cough on the juice I am sipping and spit it across the table. Adam chuckles and John crosses his arms over his thick chest.

"You want a man to take you to bed?" I ask Sophie. She nods, her eyes smiling with her lips. She looks over at Adam with a wink, then back at me. "I cannot say I've ever asked to just… fornicate with someone I did not know."

"Would you with someone you *did* know?" Adam asks me and ruffles his brows. "Ow!" he yells out after John smacks him on the back of his head.

"Leave her be. She probably doesn't drink much, anyway," John announces.

I am not sure I am happy about his statement… or offended. Sitting back in my chair, I cross my legs and glare at him.

"Oh, I think you pissed her off, boss." Sophie grins and takes a few steps back.

"You don't think I know how to have a good time?" I ask him.

He chuckles. "Honestly? No. I think you are an uptight prude who has never been properly introduced to how amazing sex can be. You have probably been no further than necking in the car and I'm damn sure no one's ever tasted your pussy."

I gasp and my eyes widen along with my mouth. "Well, I never!" I quickly rise from my chair and alternate for a moment between slapping him and just leaving the room. My temper wins this one, and closing the distance between us, I raise my hand and swing.

He catches it just before my palm smacks his cheek. His firm grip holds it and he leans in with a growl. "I wouldn't do that, if I were you."

My anger toward him builds even more. "Let me GO!" I scream through gritted teeth.

"Why? So you can slap me? No thanks. Go get your things. We are out of here in ten minutes." He pushes me back and releases my wrist. Pointing at me, "Don't try that shit again." He glares then turns, walking out of the room.

What happened to the gentle giant up in my bedroom… that held on to me while I was vulnerable? What happened to the sexy, soft-eyed man-beast? I watch him as he takes his leave, just before he looks back at me over his shoulder. He smirks slightly then crosses the threshold into the next room.

Growling to myself, I stomp back up the stairs to my room and slam the door shut. I hear the other two howling and laughing downstairs. A part of me wants to walk down and kick each of them in their balls, then knock Sophie in her jaw.

The other part just wants to pack up and leave the mess I have gotten myself into.

I grab my bag and sling it over my shoulder. The heat inside of me simmers slightly, but the words still sting.

I think you are an uptight prude who has never been properly introduced to how amazing sex can be.

I close my eyes and force his words out of my mind. "I'll show him a thing or two later tonight. I have been known to drink on occasion. Why should tonight be any different?"

Closing the door behind me, I descend the stairs and find John waiting for me at the bottom. My heart skips a beat for a second then, rolling my eyes, I sidestep him. John suddenly grabs my arm and pulls me back. "Channel that anger you're feeling toward me on the enemy." He leans in just a little more. "Remember who your enemy is and know it is not anyone in this house, Amelia."

I yank my arm back from him and rub it gently. "Considering your words earlier, one would think you would rather me be dead than helpful." Looking up at him, I shake my head. "I want to avenge my sister. If it means getting drunk and fucking someone... well then, so be it." I turn on my heel and head out the door before I allow him to say anything to me. All I hear from him is a chuckle.

Turning the corner, I glance over my shoulder and catch him smiling while rubbing his neck. He chuckles to himself then shakes his head. The faintest of smiles touch my lips as I head outside toward the carriage.

***

We make our way to the bank in town and I pull my set of keys from my bag. Thumbing through the set, I press the lock box key between my index finger and thumb. I look up and catch John watching me. A part of me is still pissed at his choice of words earlier... calling me a prude. The other wants to take him up on his offer to prove I am not so sheltered. He smirks and looks out the window of the carriage once we pull to a stop.

Once inside, the bank manager escorts us back, then informs me that only one other may come back with me to the vault. I look at John and nod then take the crook of his arm. Adam and Sophie follow close behind, but remain outside the entryway.

The manger stands before us in a worn black suit; his hairline appears to be receding with age. He turns to face us as he opens the door. "Ms. Rimos, your boxes have been pulled and laid on the table for your viewing. If you need anything, simply call."

He takes his leave while John and I enter the room. Adam and Sophie wait outside as if guarding us in the room. Releasing his arm, I approach the first box. It is long, maybe four feet in length and three feet wide. I slip the key inside and turn.

The top of it pops slightly. Pulling out the key, I lift the lid and look inside. I smile as I pull out a small, brown box I hid away for dire times.

"No time is more dire than now," I tell myself.

"What's that?" John asks as he steps forward.

Setting the box down, I pull the lid off. I retrieve the old pistol inside and show it to John. "My father made this for me when I was a child. He told me it would never miss the target—simply aim and fire."

I hand it over to him then retrieve the bullets. John opens the chamber and I hand them to him. He loads it then spins the chamber as it closes.

Next to the old brown box are a couple of wooden bows, a few shotguns, and a golden pistol that looks different from the siblings it lies next to.

"What is this?" John asks as he picks up the weapon.

"This," I start as I take the gun from him, "is what my father called a weapon of the Undead. It fires wooden bullets." I smile as I open the chamber and allow one of the bullets to drop into my palm.

John picks it up from my hand and examines it. "Crafty and a great idea." He squeezes it as if testing the durability, and lays it back in my hand.

"Every bullet for this gun, the rifles, and the pistol you hold has been dipped in my liquid sun; even the tips of the arrows have the liquid on them. For good measure, everything has been covered in silver and blessed by the preacher at the church." I shrug for a moment then set the gun down. "I'm positive my concoction of UV rays in liquid form still works; however, I do not know if the blessing holds up after the preacher passes. My father was determined to make sure Rachel and I were secure with weapons if we needed them."

"I think I would have enjoyed meeting your father, Amelia." He grins down at me and pulls each weapon from the deposit box. I smile at his words and he opens his carry bag. We begin placing the weaponry inside then close the boxes.

"We have weapons as well back home. They are a little more up to date, of course, but nonetheless, these are outstanding and made to fight against the Undead. Your father was a smart man, Amelia. I believe he may have known this day would come."

"We loved our father very much. Rachel may have not been into Alchemy like me, but she knew we would need these one day. She would often talk about the vampires and how they needed to be extinct." My gaze drops to the floor. "Neither of us realized that in doing so, your population would also become extinct."

"Up until the other day, you wouldn't have known."

I nod and look up. Our gazes lock and we stand there for a moment. The intensity in his eyes almost becomes too much. I look away first and he clears his throat. John shoves one of the pistols in the back of his belt then puts the bag over his shoulder.

"You ready?" he asks.

Nodding, we leave the vault. The bank manager waves at us as we take our leave. Adam and Sophie follow close behind.

"So, antiques or something we can use?" Sophie muses.

"We got weapons and you might be surprised at the detail put into these. I think you will eat your words once we get back to the house," John tells her. He looks over at me with a wink. "Her father knew what was coming and prepared Amelia."

"Outstanding," Adam mumbles, almost sadistically, and I think I can hear him rub his hands together.

After loading the bag of weapons and ourselves into the carriage, I look at the gruesome threesome before me. They were close and had a comradery about them. It reminds me of what I have with Rachel... well, what I *had* with Rachel. The pain reminds me I am here alone.

I look at the floorboard of the carriage and cross my fingers in my lap. John climbs inside next to me. I glance over at him and consider his pack that I have yet to meet. If this pack of his is anything like these three, I might be in for a massive headache.

Chapter 11

The carriage pulls to a halt outside of John's home. The door opens and I sneak a glance over at him just before he assists me from the carriage. His hands grasp my waist as he lowers me down, our eyes locking for a moment. I slowly look in the other direction as a blush creeps up my neck.

A few of his pack mates have already arrived. I notice them sitting comfortably on the porch, talking amongst themselves. Sophie and Adam wave at them then busy themselves carrying the cases of weaponry to store inside the house so they are out of view.

The pack seems to be of all age ranges from young twenties to late forties. This is my thought, anyway. I have noticed with some women, the sun does not do well for their skin and the same could be said for this lot.

A massive, middle thirties gentleman approaches. Not an ounce of hair upon his head, he wears a sleeveless, tan military style waistcoat, which reveals a golden prosthetic arm. Gears and wiring extend from the coat and grind slightly as the arm moves. His black slacks have a large knife tucked away in a holster belt. My expression curious, he and John greet one another. John gives the gentleman a firm pat on the back.

"Tony," he nods, "this is Amelia, the Alchemist we've been watching for some time." He glances over at me with a sideways grin on his face. If it were possible, his grin could have melted me into a puddle. I have a feeling he has quite a way with women.

I flash him a polite smile. "Pleasure to meet you, Tony."

"You as well, Amelia," he responds with a curious smile before turning his attention back to John. "For what it's worth, I'm sorry for your loss." He is a polite werewolf, yet I would be a fool to anger such a large man. His eyes may be kind, but the man hovers at least six foot five with a massive bicep.

A woman approaches from the porch and makes her way to Tony's side. She looks to be in her early thirties with long hair as black as midnight. It flows to her lower back, and with the reflection of the sun, it has a blue tint to it. With her olive skin tone and beautiful hazel eyes, she is otherworldly, possibly Native American.

"Amelia," Tony begins, "this here is Catherine."

She eyes me curiously, not quite

judgmental, but the disapproving glare does not go unnoticed. "It's a pleasure, Amelia," she says, nodding before refocusing her attention to Tony, whom I assume is her mate judging by their interactions and closeness.

Tony further converses with John, "So, the Undead is stirring up shit?" Unsurprised, he acts as if this is an everyday occurrence. Maybe in their world, it is.

With my mind still playing catch up to the recent days, I lower my eyes for a moment as they speak. Thinking of Rachel, my heart plummets briefly, wishing she were here to fight against these fanged monsters alongside us. I vow to fight enough for the both of us. No more tears.

I take in what the gentlemen are saying and figure it is time to learn a thing or two from my new beastly friends.

The sounds of other carriages approaching catch my attention before I can offer any answers or details to the conversation. I have no idea who is coming or what questions will be asked, but I know I will need to prepare for a serious discussion... or maybe a series of them. A part of me wishes we could skip ahead to tonight. The prospect of booze would calm my ongoing nerves. I am becoming weary and distrusting of new experiences.

More pack members descend from the carriages. More men who are enormous, more shifters than I ever thought possible. I cannot help but shake my head. Monsters in my world are alive and I am now very much a part of their war. I wonder briefly if my father had any idea werewolves were alive.

Once the meeting has been called to order, everyone gathers around John's massive dining area. Some take seats and others stand along the wall. I immediately notice the order of how the pack takes their seats.

The ones who appear to be on some sort of 'council' sit most toward the middle alongside John. From there, they circle around the chairs in rows of three. My assumption is the longer you are in... or heaven forbid, fight your way to the top...the deeper into the circle you are.

I shudder at this, not imagining having to physically fight my sister for my father's affection. The pain of her loss, as well as that of my entire family, sits heavy on my chest.

John searches the room until his eyes settle on me. He waves me over to a seat next to him. Making my way through the pack, I lean in and whisper, "Are you sure? I don't mind..."

"Sit," he instructs.

I nod and slowly take my place next to the pack Alpha, his Beta just on the other side of him.

Sophie leans in and whispers, "You'll be fine. We do not usually have guests when the entire pack is called. Trust me; this is a great honor. Do not speak unless you're spoken to, understand?"

I nod at her, unsure of what to say, if anything.

She places a firm grip on my shoulder. "You ready for this?" Her look serious, her violet eyes have nearly changed form on the subject of battle.

Giving her a firm nod, I press my lips together for a moment as John's words from earlier this morning ring in my memory.

"Channel that anger you're feeling toward me on the enemy. Remember who your enemy is and know it is not anyone in this house, Amelia."

I look around the room and notice the women are dressed similar to Sophie in slacks and goggles. I see one woman in particular with a prosthetic arm from the same metal as Tony's. I notice a few men with gears attached to their legs and I cannot help but wonder what happened— animal attack or vampire?

Derek, the Sheriff, sits alongside Adam and

they are huddled together in some sort of discussion. Adam glances at me, flashing me a sly grin. I merely roll my eyes at this.

Turning my attention away from them, my eyes wander, thoughtful for a moment, before resting upon John. I catch him gazing at me before the meeting officially starts. I want to smile at him; hell, I would like to crawl upon his lap again… hold onto his strong body. However, I cannot, so I will not.

Sophie clears her throat with a raised brow. A smug grin crosses her features as she catches my gaze toward her Alpha.

"What? I'm just waiting," I whisper, "I've never felt more ready to kick something's ass in my life. They fucked with the wrong Alchemist. They killed my family. I want to make them pay for what they have done. I want to avenge my sister." Pausing for a short moment, I notice the others watching me. Lowering my gaze, my voice slips into a dull whisper. "I sure could use a drink or two as well, to be honest." The words tumble from my lips, catching even myself off guard.

Laughter escapes from Sophie's lips. "We'll handle the drinking tonight, doll. You are in for a treat. Once you party with the wolves, everything else will seem bleak."

Just then, John clears his throat, "Quiet! I need everyone's full attention!" he commands with a growl. The leadership in his voice is thicker than I have heard since we met. I am about to get a front row seat to what an Alpha's duties entail. I glance toward the window, the sun still shining in the late afternoon. Everyone quiets down without another word. I notice pride radiating from the pack toward their leader. For them, this is the meaning of what they are—the battles, the community, and the sense of family.

The meeting details the events of the past few days. John covers how he found me, the cure I have managed to create, and how we found my mutilated sister. My heart aches at the mention of her being drained and left as if nothing more than a convenient meal.

Then something catches me completely off my guard. John mentions Michel being in charge of the vampires.

"Wait, what?" I ask aloud and out of turn. Sophie growls at my side and I do not really care if I am speaking out of turn. This is not my pack and I do not report to them. "Go back to what you said about Michel."

John sighs and steps closer, "Can we discuss this later?"

"No. I mean, please, what did you say about him being in charge?"

"Amelia," his voice comes out in a slight growl but there is nothing menacing about it. "I believe Adam covered this with you the other day."

"I have no doubt he did, but honestly, the last few days, hell, the last week, has all been a blur." My gaze remains strong on his. I may be weak when it comes to a gentle stare but I am strong when it comes to what I need to know, especially when it could pertain to my family.

He sighs and rubs the scruff on his face. "Hell, it may not hurt to repeat it in front of my pack, anyway." He turns his back to me and begins again. "Once Henry the VIII met his true death, his progeny took over." John looks sideways at me. "His progeny is Michel."

"Oh my god," the words leave my lips in a whisper.

Satisfied I have nothing else to say, John continues with his pack meeting.

"Seriously, shut your mouth," Sophie barks at me.

I close my eyes and lower my head. There is no way my father knew all this. I cannot imagine Rachel knew, either, unless Michel compelled her to get information… then killed her. The thought has my blood pumping with heat and hatred for him… and me wanting to run out the door on a killing rampage.

As I open my eyes, hell bent on voicing my own plans for vengeance, I notice immediately the air in the room has shifted. If anything, it has become thicker.

The group of werewolves begins to growl with anticipation. Their faces are harsh and they look to be holding something back… or maybe something inside. The magic of these dual-natured creatures will take getting used to.

Coming out of my thoughts, John's voice brings me back to the present. "We're going in for an all-out blood bath with these fuckers. Going to make them deader than what they already are. Understood?"

"Let's kick their Undead fucking asses, boss!" one of the pack members howls.

Noticing their eyes are changing, I look at Sophie and see hers glowing golden. Everyone around me has stirred and I can tell the wolves are ready for battle. Tomorrow night is a full moon and I begin to wonder if they are already feeling the effects from it… or if this is pre-battle adrenaline.

I need an escape before anything happens in the den. I don't know too much about werewolves as a whole, but based on what John, Adam, and Sophie have told me, the shifting they go through is excruciating and painful. *Are they going to shift?* The thought itself scares me. Being the only human in the room with a pack of wolves... it is a death wish.

I am far from ready to see such a transformation. A loud rumble within John escapes and he growls out, "KNOCK IT THE FUCK OFF!" His voice is loud and I can feel it tremble through my bones. His nostrils flare and his lips pull into a snarl. "Fucking meeting is not over!"

Whimpers sound in the room and the pack quiets down. Glancing over at Sophie, her eyes are wide with fear of her pack master. His leadership is at its strongest; the Alpha wolf within has overtaken the gentle beast I have witnessed.

John's wolf-like eyes meet mine just then. They are oddly beautiful and I gasp softly. I know this is not something you witness on a normal basis. This is the most magnificent I have seen him... yet the most terrifying. He lifts a corner of his lips in a slight grin in my direction. I swear my heart skips a beat. Others notice and catch on quickly; all eyes are on me before the meeting continues.

The last decision is when to attack Michel and his coven. I stiffen in my seat at the thought of seeing the vampire who once made a play for my affections. The other part of me longs to stake him, ending his Undead life to avenge my sister. The feeling of fear creeps into my chest and I find myself holding my hand against my heart.

I look up at John again. He watches me for a moment, and in his eyes, I can see patience, guidance, and longing. The fear in my chest, or what I thought was fear, fades. John gives off a sense of strength to those around him. Under his protection, you never have to look over your shoulder or worry about what will come. The fear is gone and in its place are anger and rage. I am pissed and feel myself becoming just as antsy for a fight.

***

Once the pack disperses after their meeting, a few of them are kind enough to express condolences for the loss of my sister. I feel some warmth from the clan of shifters. It is true; they are quite rowdy and are stirred easily from what I witnessed at the pack meeting. A few of them seem to be kind where others come across as cold. Considering they are going on a mission against the vampires because of me, well, I would not be too warm to meet me, either.

Tony and Catherine have warmed up to me throughout the evening. Catherine seems to have melted her icy façade.

"So, you have taken a liking for our master?"

My face immediately blushes crimson. "I have no idea what you mean." I lower my face, trying to hide any evidence of a blush and fail miserably.

Tony informs me the pub we will be gracing tonight is his. "I set it up a few years back, and now, we frequent it quite often. John's drinks are always on the house, and as his guest, yours are as well."

The pack considers themselves a family bound together by the magic of the moon. I find this beautiful in some ways. I look around John's living room and most everyone is now gone. The evening is drawing to a close and the sun is beginning to set. We will be leaving soon for Tony's bar. I need to find something appropriate to wear and I have no idea what that might be.

I need to prove myself to the three wolf guards tonight. I shall drink them all under the table. Well, I will at least try.

I ascend the stairs and Sophie reaches out, yanking me into her room. I yell out and try to fight her off. She begins to laugh and shakes her head.

"Please. One swipe and you would be dead. I plan on dressing you tonight so have a seat on my bed."

"Well, don't just grab me like that!"

She laughs again then makes her way toward her closet. "Aww, here we go. Yes, very sexy." My eyes widen at what she holds in front of her. The top is a black leather corset adorned with small roses along the bust. The bottom is a black bustled skirt overlaid with red lace.

"I have never seen something like this before. I don't know if I can wear something so… wow." My eyes are wide as I take in the outfit; I am almost scared to put such a garment on.

She laughs, "I assure you, you'll look amazing in it." She gives me a wink. I blink slowly as she hands them over to me.

To avoid sounding ungrateful, I say, "Thank you, Sophie. You've been very," I pause, "kind." I press my lips into a smile.

She nods with a smirk, "I will see you downstairs."

I shake my head and move toward the door. "See you there." I step out of her bedroom and head to the room provided for my stay.

Looking over the garments once again, I sigh and lay them across the bed. I nibble my lip and consider how the others will look at me in this... how will John see me?

I do not care anymore what others think. I quickly get out of my current garments and head toward the bathroom to clean up. I wash my face and take down my hair. My golden locks billow down my back. I look through my hairpins and consider what to use.

"I wanted to give you these as well."

I almost scream as I jump at Sophie's voice. "Stop doing that!"

She laughs through her words. "I'm sorry!" She hands over beautiful, ruby encrusted hairpins. Sophie grins again and leaves my room.

"Thank you," I whisper and allow my fingers to touch the cool metal. "Perfect," I whisper with a smile.

After pulling on the skirt and leather corset, I set my hair with the pins. I apply rouge to my lips and powder my face. My eye makeup is slightly heavier around the eyes, providing me a divine evening look. Sophie is right. I look beautiful in this outfit. I smile at myself as my bust spills over top of the material. The front of the skirt just covers my panties.

"My father would have a fit if he saw me in this."

Taking a deep breath, I descend the stairs. Running my hand along the banister, I find myself looking forward to John's reaction and his approving grin.

My three werewolves are talking amongst themselves as I enter the room. I am not sure if they smell my perfume or recognize another person in the room.

A wolf whistle escapes Adam's lips. "Damn, woman, aren't you a sight." He stares and I notice John's mouth slightly agape as he stands there.

A sly grin spread across Sophie's features. "Putting me to shame, lady. You look amazing."

Placing my hands on my hips, I give John a smug grin. "Ready for this little Alchemist to out drink you big tough wolves?"

John closes the distance between us and his eyes take me in… as if for the first time. He reaches for me, maybe to touch the corset, I am not sure, then lowers his hand and smiles… big.

Turning, he offers his arm. I can see hunger in his eyes, which generously warms my womanly regions.

"I will have to see it to believe it," he teases back about the drinking.

I gaze up into those large brown eyes of his. The animalistic urge has now settled from earlier and another urge has replaced it. I do not need to be a wolf to recognize how he sees me.

I huff, "Right, you'll see, all of you."

John and I follow Sophie and Adam's lead toward the carriage. I can hear them both chuckle. They hurry ahead of us, probably to avoid John's scolding and disapproval of their teasing.

While we ride in the carriage, I notice John continues to look over at me, mostly at my cleavage. I turn my head and fight the smile that tries to form. I need tonight... hell, we all do.

We walk into the pub, and just across the room, I see Tony and Catherine in deep conversation with a few others. The room is filled with the pack as they laugh amongst themselves. The pub appears to be an older building that Tony renovated a few years ago. An old wooden texture, the walls and the bar have quite a few knots in the top. Seats have cracked leather and tables throughout the bar definitely look used. In all, the place has a welcoming feeling to it. That is, until I begin receiving gawking looks from people inside.

I receive a few stares of admiration from a few gentlemen. I also receive a few glares from the women... all of which sends Sophie into a giggle fit. Chewing briefly on my lip, I suddenly feel exposed. John must have noticed what I am feeling since he snakes his arm around my waist. This surprises me, but I will not protest. I enjoy the warmth of his arm as I fit perfectly against him.

We find an open table just along the old wooden wall as a barmaid approaches. She receives the usual whistles as she passes a table of gentlemen.

I go in for the kill, "Bring me and my friends here a glass of your finest whiskey."

"Whiskey?" John asks. "Are you sure?"

"Indeed. I plan to out drink each and every one of you tonight."

Laughter escapes his lips. "I don't think that's possible, Amelia. Our bodies handle alcohol consumption much differently than humans. If you consume the amount we can tolerate, you will be in a world of trouble." His eyes take in the surroundings, awakening my own caution.

I find myself afraid I will see Michel with his Rene... his vampire queen.

John's focus returns. The concern must be obvious on my features because he places his large hand atop of my own. His voice softens, "Hey, you're safe here. No vampire would dare step foot in a pub owned by a werewolf. It has become routine, as Alpha, to check our surroundings. You're safe here, I promise you that."

I lift my eyes to his, forcing a small smile and nod. I am feeling uptight between the exposure of my corset and realizing I will not be able to out drink them.

"Right," I sigh. "Where are the drinks? I'm absolutely parched." I had not noticed her stand, but Sophie returns with our server. The server brings four glasses and Sophie returns with two bottles of the finest whiskey.

Sophie grins. "Thought I'd help our little friend out here."

The server glares at her and a low guttural growls escapes Sophie's throat.

"Sophie, stand down. I feel like I am on a continuous repeat here. Like goddamn school children." John puts his female pack mate back in line once again.

This time I find it semi-amusing. I simply roll my eyes with a shake of my head, though. I immediately take a glass from the server, "Thank you, miss." I reach for one of the bottles within Sophie's grasp and take it from her. Unscrewing the lid, I help myself to my first drink. Finding Adam, Sophie, and John watching me, I grin and lift the shot in the air. "Let's drink up, loves. Shall we?" I plan to show them I intend to have a good time.

Adam's sly grin spreads across his features. "*Now* we're talking."

Tilting my head back, I allow the liquor to slip down my throat. It burns and I do my best to not cough or complain. John grins in amusement. A part of me wants to down the bottle to prove I am tough. The other wants to pour it over him... then lick it off. I can feel my skin flush with this thought.

"Alcohol burning you?" he asks.

"Something like that," I return.

We all continue with our night, pouring glass after glass of whiskey until the bottles are empty and clanking on the floor. I am unsure how much I have actually ingested at this point. It is a refreshing change as drunken laughter escapes from each of us.

With each drink, Adam and Sophie become closer. I notice they are whispering to one another and getting quite heated at the table. Then again, I could be imagining this through my drunken haze. I realize it is not my imagination when they begin to kiss.

I press my lips together and suddenly feel like I am watching a private show. I lower my eyes a few times, sneaking glances at John. With the effects of the alcohol, I notice the hunger in his eyes return. The heat rises exponentially between my legs as my body longs for his touch.

John leans in as he whispers, his lips grazing my ear lobe, "How you feeling, Amelia?" The warmth of his breath tickles my skin. I welcome that feeling, and for a moment, I lose myself in his closeness. My eyes focus in on Sophie and Adam, who are lost within themselves.

My voice is a whisper, nearly hoarse. "I'm… I'm fine." I try to resist the urge to nuzzle against him, then fail and my body begins to press against his. I feel him stiffen as if he is holding back his own desires before he relaxes once more into me.

"I do not feel much of anything," I giggle drunkenly, a sound that is so foreign to me after the past few days. "Truth be told, I am feeling something in my nether regions. It is quite delightful." My eyes widen at the words I have just muttered.

John chuckles as he slides an arm around me. He is playing with fire and he knows it. I give him a look full of desire. In my sober state, I would have removed his arm. Right now? I want more than anything for him to lean in and kiss me.

"Amelia," he whispers just for me. Sophie suddenly moans. I cannot help myself. The intensity is almost too much. I break the eye contact and glance over at her and Adam.

"Oh my," I mutter to myself. Adam's hands are on her breasts and he has loosened her corset. She might come out of it at any moment.

"How many bottles have we partaken of thus far, John?" I bring my gaze back to his.

He looks over at the table, "At this point, around four. I have to give you credit, Miss Rimos, you *do* handle your liquor well." He flashes me a grin that could make me melt. I feel my cheeks redden with a blush.

"Well, I have had my nights of fun, before this with," I pause, lowering my eyes as images of my sister flood my memory. "With Rachel." My eyes wander as I watch a few of his pack count to three then take a shot... "She would have enjoyed it here."

Fiddles sound in the air, a welcome distraction to the insanity that has become my life. Men take the stage as music begins to play.

Sophie climbs into Adam's lap and begins to grind against him. I close my eyes and look away. I am not sure whether to laugh or cry.

John rises from his chair, and suddenly, his absence is almost too much. He offers his hand and I stare at it for a moment before raising my eyes to his. "Dance with me, Amelia. I promise I won't bite." He waggles his eyebrows.

I cannot help the smile on my lips. "I should hope not." I tilt my head up at him. I want to tell him, *you could bite me any day of the week as long as you kiss me with those lips.* I simply give him a look as if I am debating. He grins and reaches for my hand, pulling me to my feet.

"I guess that is a yes." I grin as I wobble slightly on my feet. He slips an arm around my waist and holds me close. Holding me close, we make our way toward the dance floor.

We turn and face each other, one hand in his, and the other resting upon his shoulder. I begin to follow his lead as he swings us around to the quickened beat. The alcohol is not my friend in this moment. I feel myself leaning more into him than I would normally find comfortable.

I notice the dancing is livelier, more fun, than the dance Michel and I shared. I actually find myself laughing. I am drunk and it is blissful. This is amazing and necessary. All of our problems begin to fade. It is just us and the sounds of our laughter.

As the song ends, John holds me for a moment, looking into my eyes. My breath catches in my throat as he breaks the eye contact this time. I glance over to our table and grin. Sophie and Adam's lips look to have locked to one another.

"She was quite literal this morning when she mentioned taking a man to her bed," I mumbled. It is obvious that their tongues are stuck in each other's mouths.

John chuckles then clears his throat. "Don't worry about them. They are not quite a couple, but they will not admit one needs the other. I do not pretend to understand it."

I turn my attention away. The room is spinning, and seeing their show of affection only makes my need and hunger for John that much stronger. I look up again as Adam picks Sophie up and carries her across the pub. She wraps her legs around his waist, and he stumbles into a wall, pressing her back against it. At this moment, I wish this were John and I.

Realizing I am staring, I turn and nearly stumble. John takes hold of me in his strong arms. He leads us toward the pub entrance and helps me into the carriage. Only now do I realize just how drunk I have become.

"You alright, little lady?" he teases with his arm wrapped around me to hold me up.

Through furrowed brows, I answer, "I'm just fine, I'm better than fine. I told you, I could get just as drunk as you wolves could. Yet, I am the only one stumbling out of the pub. Now who are the prudes?"

John bursts into laughter and his voice is like magic. I love his laugh. "Trust me, Amelia. I am not drunk and I drank much more than you did tonight. The alcohol burns faster in our systems due to our higher metabolisms."

I frown at this. "Right, okay." Too drunk to think rationally at this point, I lean into strong arms as they surround me. He is my rock tonight.

The ride back to his home is quiet. I find myself snuggling into him while his arms pull me closer. Lifting my face to look into his eyes, we are inches apart. I am almost brave enough to kiss him.

I can see it in his eyes; he wants it just as much as I do. His strong hunger gives his eyes a darkened tint. He inhales a deep breath then straightens himself against his seat, providing a little distance.

I huff out frustratingly, feeling confused and rejected. Gazing out the window, I rest my back against the seat.

Once we pull in front of John's home, he nudges me. I had kept staring off, thinking of ways my life should have been. This was not supposed to happen. I was going to win the Nobel Prize. Now I am drunk, next to a man who clearly does not want me as much as I want him. I am snapped back to the present.

"Hey, we are home," he announces softly. "Let me help you out." His expression softens and my heart skips a beat. I nod slowly then slink out of the carriage where I stumble and fall into his arms. Gazing up into his eyes, for a moment, I will the man to kiss me.

He averts his gaze and helps me stand. I huff again in my drunken state. "Well, it's not really *my* home now, is it? I am unable to go to *my* home. My life is in turmoil and it is my fault. I can never go back to the way it was..." My feet trip over themselves mid-sentence, and before I know it, his strong arms wrap around me, saving me from falling.

John lifts me into his arms and holds me close. I can feel the heat radiating from his body. I find it glorious and he is making it much harder to resist my need and desire for him.

He walks us just inside the house, and suddenly, the sound of sex fills the open air. My lips part as I listen and quickly look at John.

He shakes his head. "Adam and Sophie obviously made it back before we did."

I find myself trying not to giggle. He carries me to my room and kicks the door open. Walking me to my bed, he lays me on it. "Try to sleep off the alcohol." He leans in and, just as I think he will kiss me, he kisses my cheek instead. Pulling back, his gaze remains on me.

I am not sure if I am angry now or upset that I am being rejected. "What? You did not think I had it in me to get drunk, yet here I am. And now you are afraid?" Grabbing his shirt, I pull him back to me. I tilt my head up and stare into his eyes. "I want you. I want you in my bed tonight, John. Please..." My voice shaking, my judgment blurred with intoxication, and my heart wide open for the taking, I beg him.

His body presses against mine as I refuse to let him go. His heat is a comfort to the coolness of my skin. Suddenly, his lips claim mine as he gives into temptation. Separating my lips with his tongue, he seeks dominance over mine. He kisses me fiercely with a muffled growl. Just as I think I cannot hold out anymore, he pulls away from me. He reaches for my hands and pulls them from his shirt.

I blink. "I'm giving myself to you and you turn away?" My voice laced with anger and hurt, I can feel tears sting my eyes.

"You are drunk. Like I said, sleep it off." His voice thick with desire, he rises from my bed and crosses the room. He says, glancing back over his shoulder, "Sleep well, Amelia." He stands in the doorway, almost as if he is debating with himself. Finally leaving the room, he closes the door behind him. I think I hear him lean against it.

Sophie announces to anyone who is listening how amazing Adam is in bed. The tears in my eyes spill into my hair, "I cannot believe he left me..." Unlacing my corset with drunken fingers, I grit my teeth, stumble out of my clothes, then fall onto my bed. It does not take long for sleep to claim me. All my entire mind wants to do is have intimate sex with John. The sounds of sex in the air begin to mix with the drunken sleep I am having. I know I will wake up with one hell of a hangover.

Deadly Alchemy

Chapter 12

"Well, you must be off your game," Rene tells Michel. The door to their room closes behind them with a lock of the bolt. "You seduced her to the point she was about to come out of her panties any time you were near her. Seriously, Michel, you've lost your touch," she smirks to herself as they walk further into their shared quarters.

The walls, once white, are now smeared with the blood of their victims. Splatters of red up high give the appearance someone dipped a paintbrush then scattered red paint. Down below is different. Smeared handprints, dried lines of blood, and most likely body parts, cover the bottom half.

Michel wraps a firm hand around her arm and yanks her back to him. Her body thrusts hard against his chest. He knows if she did not like it rough, his exterior might alarm her. "Are you jealous?" He keeps a firm grip on her arm while the fingers of his other hand touch her cheek. "All is not lost yet, woman. Trust me; I'll fuck her one way or the other."

"Mmm, as long as I can watch." Rene leans in and licks the tip of his nose.

"NO, PLEASE!" a woman screams in another room. She cries out once again while a rugged male voice tells her to shut up.

Michel grins sadistically. "Sounds like dinner will be served shortly."

Suddenly, their door opens and two guards stand in the entryway. Both are wearing fitted shirts, which are filthy enough they could probably stand on their own. Old crusted blood has stained the shirts beyond repair. Matching pairs of suspenders hold up their pants. One of the guards has blown the knees out in his pants where the other sports a hole near the crotch. Rene has often wondered if he did it purposely to masturbate in front of his victims.

The woman held captive between the two guards is thrust forward. She falls to her knees and her dark brown hair falls around her face. She retches on the floor, most likely from the smell of death in the room.

One of the guards, Stephen, grabs the woman's hair and yanks her head up. "Meet your maker," he smirks and meets Michel's gaze.

"Oh, let her be, Stephen," Michel tells him. "No need to be so vulgar."

"Right, because what we do is so innocent," Rene whispers to him.

"Hmm," Michel smirks then looks at Rene for a moment. "So she will soon come to realize." He licks his bottom lip and she swoons softly.

Stephen shoves the woman's head away then steps back. "Will there be anything else, sir?"

"Maybe another willing participant for Rene? I think I'll be having more fun with this one soon enough." Michel's eyes light up with desire as he approaches the woman. He leans down and touches her chin, lifting her face to meet his gaze. He tilts his head slightly as he watches her. She blinks and her bottom lip quivers.

Michel offers a smile filled with false kindness. "Child," he begins and allows his compulsion to take over. "We will not do anything to you that you do not wish to happen. If you simply wish to fuck, that is all we will do. If you will allow me to feed on you while we fuck, I shall gladly comply."

The women's eyes glaze over while she listens to his words. She slowly begins to sit up and wipes her mouth with her sleeve. "I would like that very much, sir."

"Which part exactly, love?" He leans in and whispers softly in her ear, "Do you wish for me to fuck you… or devour you?" Pulling back, he looks in her eyes.

"Whichever pleases you more, sir." She slowly blinks and stands with Michel. As she steps closer to him, Rene moves around their bodies, coming in behind her.

"Then it would please me," he begins while gently running a finger over the woman's breasts, "to fuck you *then* devour you."

"I would beg for such treatment, sir." She closes her eyes and tilts her head back, giving into submission.

Rene unties the woman's corset and loosens the strings. The woman visibly sighs as new air enters her lungs. Michel unfastens the busk closures then slowly removes it from her body.

With her breasts now exposed to the open air, her nipples harden, and a soft sigh leaves her lips. Rene begins untying the skirts around the woman's hips then allows them to fall to the floor. She is left in her panties, garter belt, and stockings.

Michel cups her breasts and sucks one of her nipples into his mouth. She inhales sharply at the sensation running through her body. Blood begins to trickle from the corner of his lips down the side of her body. Rene leans in and licks it from her skin.

Pushing her legs apart, Rene drops to her knees and turns her back to the woman, then leans back. She lifts her face between the woman's legs then runs her tongue between her folds. A loud, audible gasp echoes throughout the bedroom.

"Oh my god, I have never, no one has ever…" She becomes lost in her words as the woman gasps to Rene's ministrations.

"You have never felt, nor will ever again feel, what my Rene and I can do for you. What is your name, slave?" Michel pulls back just enough to see her flesh wound. He licks it softly and her blood coats his tongue. He looks into her eyes and watches her for a moment.

She swallows hard and reaches for his arms for support. "Rose, my name is Rose." She moans and allows her head to tilt back. "I have never had anyone between my legs as she is doing, sir."

"Hmm… well, I shall remember to give you everything you've never had, Rose." Michel captures her lips and kisses her hard. His fingers move into her hair and he tightens his grip.

Rene removes herself from between Rose's legs and stands. She licks her lips, the evidence of Rose's pussy clear on her mouth. "She tastes very innocent. She's a good find."

Michel closes off the kiss while he drags Rose, by her hair, toward the bed. "Then I suggest we taint such innocence, do you agree, Rene?" He looks at Rose and she responds with a look of desire.

Her lips part and she gasps softly. "Please, sir?"

"How do you wish to please me, Rose?" Michel shoves her on the bed.

She lies on her back and stares up at the pair of them. Slowly, Rose moves her legs apart and moves her hands down her body. Her fingers move between her folds and she touches herself.

"Well, it seems she may be ready, lover." Rene looks at Michel with a smirk. "After you."

Michel grins, and slowly, like a predator, eases himself on the bed. He pushes her legs apart then takes her hands in his. Licking her fingers, he sucks the honey away while watching her.

Rene climbs onto the bed and positions herself near Rose. She takes her hands and holds them above her head. "Allow him to taste you, and then he will fuck you. Understand?"

Rose nods a few times and she swallows hard. "Y-Yes," she tells them.

Michel looks down at her pussy. He licks his lips and grins. Gently, he pushes her lips apart and exposes her clit. "She is so wet, Rene." He leans in and swipes his tongue once, then twice.

Rose bucks her body against his mouth.

Michel presses his palms against her thighs then pushes them further apart. "Mine," he mumbles then dives in, devouring her pussy.

Rose moans as her head tilts back. Rene keeps hold of her wrists while her body writhes against Michel. Changing the grip on her wrists, Rene holds on to Rose now with one hand, while the other begins teasing her taut nipples. "He is going to fuck you soon. Be ready, slave."

"Yes!" Rose screams out as her body bucks against Michel. "Oh my god, yes!"

Michel lifts his mouth from her and licks his lips. "Your god cannot help you now, Rose." He moves up her body, and grabbing his dick, he shoves himself inside her and thrusts.

Rose yells out while Rene continues to hold on to her wrists. He thrusts hard against her and growls. Lowering his face until his nose barely touches hers, his pupils begin to dilate. Her lips part and a soft gasp sounds.

Michel kisses the corner of her lips then moves his lips to her cheek, then to her neck. He licks the vein that visibly pumps for him. It calls to him; it pumps the sweet nectar he craves.

He growls, and allowing his fangs to extend downward, he grazes them across her skin. "You are MINE!" he snarls and rips into her flesh.

Rose screams and Rene takes a firmer grip on her wrists. She thrashes against Michel as her blood pools in his mouth. "Oh fuck!" Her words come out in a scream mixed between pain and pleasure.

"Let me have some, lover," Rene tells him with a fierce gaze.

Michel rises up with a snarl on his bloody lips. His eyes completely dilated, he looks over at his lover. "She tastes like heaven!" He sinks his fangs into her skin again, this time rougher than before.

Rose's eyes close and her lips remain open as she gasps and moans from the pleasure. Her fingers wrap around Rene's hand and she squeezes. Slowly, she looks up at her captor, her eyes full of desire.

"Oh, I see the effect he has over you is working quite well." She grins and leans in. "Shall

I partake?" Rose barely nods while Michel continues to tear into her throat.

Rene lifts her arm and runs her tongue along her skin. Her fangs descend just as she snarls and bites into her flesh. Blood trickles from her lips as she suckles on the vein.

Michel withdraws himself and sits up on his heels. He pulls Rose's body up to his waist and holding on to her hips, begins to thrust hard and fast. Growling like a predator, he watches blood seeps from her throat, down her body.

Blood pools on the bed, on her body, and covers her stomach. It continues to pump with each heartbeat. Her eyes begin to close as the loss of blood has become too much for her.

Michel growls again. He quickly pulls out and adjusts Rose onto her stomach, pulling her ass into the air. He shoves himself inside of her and grips her ass, thrusting hard.

Moving down the bed, Rene lies down in the blood gathering on the bed. Leaning in, she tears into the other side of Rose's neck. She pulls on the woman's blood while her body continues to move from the thrusting against her body.

The sound of the door closing, along with the bolt, echoes behind them. The bed moves as someone new climbs on. Michel looks over at the woman who has just joined them... Eva.

She smirks down at Rose then back to Michel. "Am I next?"

"Do you wish to die like she will today?" he asks in rush of breath. He glances at Rose again and shrugs, "Or the way she has died."

"No, not at all. Just for you to fuck me the way you fuck her."

Rene lifts her gaze and snarls at Eva. "He is MINE! You will do good to recognize that!"

With a swiftness Eva never saw coming, Rene has her pinned on the bed, blood dripping from her lips onto her face. "You never interrupt a meal in progress unless you intend to become... said meal!"

Eva blinks and nods a few times. "My apologies! I am... I am sorry. I only wished to join."

"Is that so? Well..." She pulls herself off Eva then looks back at Michel. He thrusts once... twice... then leans onto Rose. He pulls her mangled body up to his and bites into her shoulder. Her body hangs lifeless in his grasp. After a moment, he removes his lips from her shoulder, and shoves her body away.

Rose lies in her own blood… dead.

Michel looks over at Eva with a sinister glare. "You wish for this fate? You wish to die today?" He moves at a speed only a vampire can and has her pinned to the bed. Rene looks on with a smirk.

"No! I only wanted to join… I did not… Oh Michel, please! Let me go!" She struggles underneath him and a tear slips into her hair.

"You should have given this more thought, human," Rene tells her. "You realize we've just had an appetizer, but have yet to have our main course!"

Michel glares down at Eva as she lies underneath him. "I think I will feed from you, but you have not earned anything in my graces! Do you realize our enemy has taken Amelia? Did you know this?"

"What? No, I did not know! I promise, Michel, please, let me go! I will reach out to her. I will get her to you! I promise! Please!"

"Please, what?" Rene asks.

She looks at the female vampire and notices the same sinister look in her gaze. Eva knew she was dealing with monsters, but it was not until this moment that she realized how deep she had allowed herself to fall. Could she actually do this to Amelia? Would she deceive her and lure her here to Michel? Could she lose her humanity if she stood up to him? Would Amelia be worth the fight? What about the human population? She knew Michel wanted this cure for his own dirty deeds. It was not until after the fact that she learned he wished to change it.

"I want to alter the ingredients, so to speak," he told Eva one night at the lab. *"I want this in the water supply of every human, everywhere. I want them to drink this... cure. I want them to change for me... rather me for them. I want to create a new breed of vampires with this!"*

"I can see you're considering something, Eva," Michel tells her, bringing her out of her thoughts. "Allow me to assist in making up your mind!" He is suddenly on her neck and tears into her flesh. Eva screams out as the sound echoes through the bedchamber.

Chapter 13

As I lie sleeping in my bed, the mattress suddenly gives way underneath the weight of someone else. Warm, large hands gently glide up my calves until they reach my thighs. Soft kisses pepper along my legs, and as I try to look down, all I can see is a figure underneath my comforter.

His hands move toward my waist and tug at the panties shielding my body. Without knowing who my visitor is, I think I should be terrified. However, in this moment, I know it is he and I have been longing for this moment.

Fingers hook into the sides of my panties and tug. Gently, he pulls the material down my legs then kisses the inside of my thigh. A growl sounds and this sends a shiver through my body causing my pussy to become wet.

He pushes my legs farther apart and the invasion of his tongue catches me off guard. My back arches and a moan escapes my lips. He pushes a single digit inside of me, pumping it slowly as he licks. I run my fingers through my hair to give my hands something to do. I want to reach down and pull him up to me, pull him so hard he would force himself inside me.

"Oh god," I breathe as he slips in another finger. He begins moving them in a 'come here' motion. My back arches again and he sucks my clit into his mouth, rolling his tongue on it. I can feel a heat begin to spiral out of control. It flutters and begins to move downward. My thighs shake and the orgasm rips through my body. He pulls my body closer as I thrash against his mouth. He sucks harder, pumps faster, until I do not think I can take it anymore.

"Please! Stop, please, I need you!" My fingers have managed to wrap around the headboard at some point, and upon releasing them, John comes out from underneath the comforter. He hovers above me and gazes into my eyes, his mouth still wet from the evidence of my orgasm.

He wipes a solid swipe across his face with his forearm, then leans in to kiss me. His tongue… that magnificent tongue…slides across my lips and opens my mouth. John claims my lips as his cock penetrates me. He thrusts and growls against my mouth.

Gasping against his lips, he pulls away and rests his forehead against mine. He thrusts again, and looking into his eyes, they glow their beautiful golden color.

My hands move up his strong biceps as I cling to him, afraid if I let go, he will leave me.

"Amelia?"

I gasp and open my eyes. Quickly looking around the room, I sit up… realizing it was just a dream. I groan and fall back onto my pillow, the evidence of an orgasmic dream underneath my body. "It was a damn dream?"

Covering my arm over my eyes, the morning sun shines into my room. My head pounds from the hangover I was anticipating.

"Amelia? You in there?" Sophie asks.

"Yes," I groan then follow up with, "go away!"

She snickers at the door. "Breakfast is ready downstairs."

I do not say anything back but listen instead. I can hear her walk along the floor as she leaves.

The floor. John. Oh, shit… is he… I sit up again so fast my head spins. I look around my room and notice he is not here. "Where did he go last night? He kissed me then left?" I fall back again and groan once more. "He kissed me."

Turning on my side away from the sun, the past evening's events come back to me.

Too much whiskey. Dancing with John. Adam and Sophie on one another as if tomorrow might not come. John kissing me. Sex noises from Sophie's room. John kissing me.

My mind reels on that thought again then I decide to speak it. Maybe saying it will put more truth to it. "John kissed me."

I sigh and shake my head then kick the covers off my body. "He kissed me then left me alone. So noble of him." My palms rub my eyes for a moment. I need a bath and I need supplies and clothes from my home. I am not in the right frame of mind for John to escort me; I am too embarrassed, and if I am being honest with myself... my feelings are hurt.

Sliding out of bed, the cold floor awakens me a little more, and I head toward the bathroom. I almost flinch when I catch a glimpse of myself in the mirror. My hair is completely tousled, my eyes are bloodshot from the hangover, and I am damn near exhausted. My mouth is dry and I almost heave when I taste the whiskey in my mouth.

I brush my teeth a few minutes too long then draw myself a bath. The warm water does nothing for my headache; I knew I would need to find some items downstairs to make a morning after concoction of sorts.

"Hair of the dog!" I recall one of my father's friends telling him once. I never really understood that meaning until I experienced my first hangover.

***

After dressing for the day in one of my own corsets and bustle skirts, I make my way quietly downstairs. Sophie is already awake… her I can deal with. At least I *think* I can. I do not want to question her about Adam nor do I want any questions from her about John… or myself claiming to be a whiskey drinker.

With my bag of dwindling supplies in hand, I make my way toward the kitchen and hear a noise. Stepping closer toward the corner that leads inside the giant room, I slowly look around the corner. Hoping not to see either Adam or John, I do not think I can face them quite yet.

His back turned to me, Derek the sheriff, stands at the sink washing his hands. His upper body is bare and he is built just like the others—strong and tall. I cannot quite see his legs and I am afraid if I enter, I will walk in on him naked.

He turns around, his full body exposed to me. I gasp and know I was correct in my assumption. I turn back to hide, a blush creeping up my face. Derek walks out of the kitchen and I quickly close my eyes, hiding my face in my hands.

He chuckles. "It's alright; I know you saw me naked. Don't worry, sweetheart, you won't be the last one to ever see me in the buff." He laughs again then leaves the room.

I shake my head and fight a smile threatening to claim my lips. "I will never, ever get used to this."

After Derek leaves and I regain my composure, I walk into the kitchen. The large, open area with an island in the middle is filled with pastries and breakfast food. Coffee sits on the counter, waiting to be poured.

Having no idea who is on kitchen duty, I decide to make a mental note to thank whoever it is... even if they did it naked. I suddenly shudder from the thought, trying not to laugh.

Opening a few cabinets, I find a mug and pour coffee into it. Lifting it to my lips, I take a sip and cringe. Whoever made this made it very strong... which today may not be a bad thing.

Munching on a piece of bacon, I begin looking through the kitchen cabinets for a few ingredients to cure a hangover. Lots of water, this

I know, but to kick start it, I need niacin, vitamin C, and some protein. I doubt I will find most of these items in the cabinets, so I pull out the bag I packed at home. I manage to locate mint leaves in an icebox. Next, I begin searching for what I may have packed.

Locating some chamomile and willow bark, I set them aside then find a few tablets of vitamin C and a vial of niacin. I cannot help but smile to myself. "The guys… and Sophie…will appreciate this once it is ready. Maybe one day they'll appreciate their liver."

Setting up my mortar and pestle, I begin grinding the ingredients together. Once the paste has been formed, I add in a little bit of water and make it a liquid. Tipping the concoction into my mug, I stir it and take a sip. The flavor has altered just slightly, but for the most part, it is the same.

Setting the cure-all for hangovers aside, I begin washing my mortar and think about how to handle the events of last night. My palms grasp the counter as I lean into it. I close my eyes as the blush creeps up my skin.

"I danced with and kissed John last night." I sigh and feel the effects of the niacin heating my skin as my hangover begins to subside.

Using a towel, I wipe my hands dry then set it on the counter. I pull my bag over my shoulder and peek into the living room. No one is in there so no one would see me leave. If something were to happen to me, no one would know, either.

"Right, not likely anything would, but for the sakes of a foul temper, I should leave a note."

Pulling out some parchment from my bag, along with a pencil, I quickly jot a note down for John… or anyone who cares to read of my whereabouts.

Use the liquid I have created in the dish. It will help with a hangover, if anyone has one. I have ventured to my home to gather more supplies and fresh clothes for myself. I will be back before sundown.

Amelia

Folding the note, I set it next to the lamp, which sits on a table by the closest window. If anyone were to light this lamp, it would most definitely be seen. Readjusting my bag on my shoulder, I head outside toward the carriage barn.

Dennis, the carriage driver I have met on occasion, is tending to the horses. His back is to me as he grooms a large, brown Draft horse. Her stall door says, "Dixie."

"Pardon me, Dennis?" I step farther into the barn as he turns to face me.

Dennis sets down the brush and runs his hands on his pants. "Yes, ma'am, how may I be of service to you today?" He looks over my shoulder, probably looking to see if John or Adam will be joining me.

"I need a ride into town, please. To my home, specifically. I need to gather a few personal effects of my own. Would you mind taking me?"

He steps forward and looks me over for a moment. His features do not show ill intent, but he does not look too pleased with my request, either. "Alone?" I simply nod and keep my eye contact with his. "I think it would be best if you…"

I interrupt him quickly before he even has a chance to suggest bringing John or Adam along. "Not today, please. It is just me. They are aware of my leaving." I figure this is truth enough, being I left a note.

"Alright," he scratches the back of his head and I can tell he is still not too sure about this idea. He opens Dixie's stall door and leads her out. "Dixie's been with me now for five years. She is an amazing animal and is used to our lot."

"Your lot?" I question him. He looks at me as if willing me to understand the punch line of a joke he just told. "Oh yes, my apologies." I muster a soft laugh. "Please, continue."

He nods and latches Dixie into the harness for the carriage. "She was just turning from a foal to a mare. She is coming into heat soon. I have considered breeding her."

"Oh, that's nice," I remark.

A moment later, Dennis is assisting me into the carriage and we take off toward town. I cannot help the feeling that settles into the pit of my stomach. I should not be doing this alone, but I really need the time away from John, from the pack... from the reality that has completely changed my entire world.

***

A sense of relief falls over me at the familiarity of the neighborhood. With it, there is also grief. I ran in the park here with my sister and I had dinner parties with my family. These events will never happen again. My heart aches for them and my loss.

The carriage pulls to a stop and Dennis assists me down. "I won't be too long. There is a watering hole just down the way. I don't mind waiting if..."

"No, ma'am, I'll wait for you here," he informs me.

I nod and lower my gaze. Turning toward my building, I walk inside and glance back at Dennis as the door closes behind me. Taking the few flights of stairs up to my loft, memories of my sister threaten to consume me.

"Amelia! Did you see how he looked at you across the bar? Oh, it was almost magical!" my sister exclaimed.

We both laughed and I shook my head, "I think he was more drunk than magical, Rachel." Our voices carried upward as we ascended the staircase.

Reaching my door, the memory quickly fades as I slip my key inside... possibly for the last time. I am not sure if John will insist I move into his home or if I may remain here. I cannot imagine being alone in his house with him. I would probably keep myself in hiding to avoid his presence.

As I walk inside, the familiar scent of my loft invades my nose and I briefly close my eyes. My perfume, the smell of cleaning products, and something new... something almost musty surrounds me.

Ignoring the foreign smell, assuming it is nothing other than stale air, I close the door behind me. Venturing toward my bedroom and stepping into my closet, I begin to gather clothes for the next few days. With a sigh, I lay them out on my bed then make my way to my dresser. After closing all my belongings into my bag, I carry it toward the living room and set it down on the couch.

Knowing I will need supplies to recreate my serum, as well as the concoction for hangovers, I walk toward my kitchen, just on the other side of my living room. Pulling supplies from the cabinets and setting them aside, with my back to the entry, I hear something… or someone… approach behind me.

My heart freezes for a moment and my first thought is Michel. Then I shove it away because it is daylight. There is no way he could possibly be out in the daytime. I know it has to be Dennis.

"I just need a few more minutes, Dennis, and then I'll be ready to go. I'm a little surprised," I pause, considering how to tell him I think it is rude to invite one's self into someone's home without permission. I turn around, and just as I am about to continue, my eyes widen at the man in front of me.

"I'm not Dennis, love, but I'm most positive Rene had a good time with him." Michel steps inside my kitchen. His long, almost floor-length, leather duster covers his body, along with his black leather gloves and oversized cowboy hat. A grey wrap covers his neck and I realize in this moment, if he were to walk outside, there is no way the sun would affect him... at least not immediately.

"How did you get in here?" I ask, backing up into my kitchen. My hands reach for anything on my counter that I can use as a weapon and locate a butcher knife. Wrapping my fingers around the hilt of it quickly, I bring it around and point it at him.

"What, are you going to stab me? Please," he mocks closing the distance. "I need you, Amelia, and truth be told, you need me as well."

My mind is reeling and I have no idea what he is talking about. How did he get into my home and what in the world makes him think I need him? "What are you talking about? I don't need you!" My head hurts at the admission of my own words. Just a few weeks ago, I had flutters in my chest at the mere mention of his name. Now, I cannot stand to be in his presence.

"If you intend to live past today, you absolutely need me." He steps a little closer and tilts his head, his eyes menacing. "How did the wolves find you? Did you know about them and played me for a fool?"

Venom laces his voice and I shake my head. "I knew nothing of them before. And speaking of fools, why did you deceive me? I thought you cared."

Right about this time, a woman walks into the kitchen. I recognize her... Rene. She is tall, slender, and almost European looking. Making her way toward Michel, she presses her body against his. She licks her red lips as she watches me.

"Wolf blood is not the best to taste, but it *is* sustainable." She grins then looks up at Michel.

I gasp and shake my head. "You killed... Dennis?"

"Oh yes, it was... good!" Her eyes widen with her words, her mouth pulling in a smirk.

The fact she refers to Dennis as an it, rather than a him, speaks a lot about her character. She is no woman... she is a monster, just like Michel. "I bet you enjoyed my sister, too."

"Oh, well for *that* little morsel, I wouldn't know." She grins up at her lover and continues, "You could always ask him, though."

He leans in and swipes his tongue along her lips. "Mmm, not too bad, but," he shifts his gaze over to me, "your sister was delicious, and from experience, Alchemists *do* taste better."

I gasp and hold my knife steady as the two vampires in my kitchen begin to stalk their prey. He killed my sister and this woman... she killed Dennis. I know I will be next and John has no idea where to find me unless he discovers my note.

What the hell have I done?

Chapter 14

With a firm grasp on the butcher knife, it remains pointed at the two monsters before me. The longer I stare into the hollowness that was once a person, the more distorted and evil their features become. The dark intentions Michel has in store are hidden behind his once beautiful blue eyes. I have no idea what he is thinking, or what Rene may be considering, aside from a slow, painful death on my part.

I pant heavily from the adrenaline coursing through my body. I am still numb at Michel's admission that he drained my sister and left her to die in her tub. Clearly, she was left for me to find...just as he wanted.

Rene's evil smirk dances across her features. "I do believe we have the little kitten tongue tied. Are we just going to stand here, Michel?" She glances over at him, "I am growing quite bored of this."

I snap from my haze and step farther back. The back counter of my kitchen stops me in my tracks. "You come near me, you devil whore, and I swear on all that is holy I *will* end you! You fucking monsters have taken EVERYTHING from me!" My voice cracks as anger rages inside of me.

I can feel my blood pumping to my face and neck. My ears are burning and my vision becomes blurred. As much as I would like to know what they plan, in the same breath, I would rather claim ignorance. All I can think of now is fighting my way out of this situation.

Michel's laughter fills the room, sending shivers of fear throughout my being. "Tongue tied no more, she is back to being the feisty little bitch." He spits with the word bitch and moves closer to me. "We shall take her back with us."

On impulse, I look toward the door and take off in a sprint. All I can think of is John and getting back to him and my safety.

Suddenly, Rene is in front of me. I slam against her body and she grabs my arms, shoving me back. She recoils as if she just touched something disgusting. "Going somewhere, sweetheart? I think not." Her tongue licks across her bottom lip then slips over her fangs. She is enjoying this sick, demented game of cat and mouse.

My sister comes to mind and the fear she must have felt startles me. I cannot imagine what she went through with Michel. The anger rises more fiercely inside my body, and with it, my hand. Without considering the consequences, I bury the knife to the hilt, deep within Rene's chest. My eyes widen and I begin to step away from her. My throat is suddenly dry as I hold in a cry that wants to escape.

Rene simply stares down at the hilt that plunges from her chest. Her blood seeps from the wound and begins to absorb into the black Victorian corset she is wearing. "Pity," she glances back to me, "this was one of my favorites." She reaches for the hilt and slowly withdraws it from her chest. Her blood oozes down to her hand, covering her wrist. "Oh, is it my turn now?" She grins with an evil glare.

I cover my mouth with a gasp and take a step back. Something blocks my path and I turn to find myself facing Michel. I turn fully to face him, and instinct kicking in for fight or flight, I kick him in the groin.

Michel buckles over and I make a run for the door. He growls and yells at me, "It's going to take so much more than that to stop me, Amelia!" Rene, with supernatural speed, runs toward me and blocks the door. Michel rises to his full height as he recovers from the shock to his balls. He slowly makes his way toward me, a hunter stalking his prey.

Struggling against her grasp, I kick against her shins and scream as loud as I can... at least until Rene's hand slaps my face and covers my mouth. There is nothing soft or gentle about these creatures anymore.

I decide fighting is my best option, even if it is two vampires to one human. I need to make a scene; I need to leave some sort of evidence for John. If he finds my note, he will come here. He will find my place completely overturned and he will then know to come looking for me.

Rene's fingers press so hard against my lips I decide biting her is my best option. She screams and I can taste her blood in my mouth. I always thought it would taste something like iron, considering the times I have bitten my own tongue eating. However, with Rene, her blood is almost... sweet.

She screams and her hand temporarily leaves my lips. Spitting every bit of her blood from my mouth, I kick at her shins again and she releases me. Falling to my hands and knees, I quickly kick at her knees in hopes of dropping her to the ground. Maybe if my heel meets her head...

Soon, the counter hits my back... hard... when Michel throws my body across the room as if I am nothing more than a rag doll. He is immediately hovering over my body and glaring down at me. His eyes flare in madness and he reaches down, grabbing my throat. He forces me to sit up and I can feel the air leaving my throat.

Rene gets to her feet and steps over with a slight limp. A part of me is satisfied I have injured her; another is pissed that I did not do more damage.

She adjusts her hair and glares at me for a moment. "Please, love, allow me to bite her. An eye for an eye, anyway." She holds her palm up for his examination.

"Merely a flesh wound. Besides," he looks back at me with a sadistic grin, "I could bite her now, and change her. Then all our troubles would be over."

My eyes widen and I quickly try to shake my head no. I can feel my face turning red from the lack of oxygen.

"Oh, being an Undead doesn't suit you, my love?" Michel asks. He leans in closer, almost touching my nose with his. "I should allow her to devour you, anyway!"

A tear races down my cheek. Michel leans in and licks it off. His grip loosens just enough to allow me to breathe and I inhale a deep, sharp breath. Rene lets out a sound that sounds like a laugh, but more of a cackle. I glance at her and find her staring at Michel. I then look at him and see he is not watching me.

Taking a chance, I swing my legs up and

kick Rene in the chest, knocking her back. Michel's eyes widen in surprise, and just as he is making a move to grab me, I slip off the counter and land on the floor.

As fast as a vampire can, he reaches down, grabs a handful of my hair, and pulls me to my feet. "You fucking bitch! You seriously think fighting us will get you out of this situation any faster?"

"If it gets me away from you then I'm all for it! Let me go!"

"Not a chance!"

Michel pulls me close and I think *he is going to do it; he is going to bite me.* Instead, he throws me across the room and my back hits the opposite wall. A few family portraits drop to the floor and shatter. Pictures of Rachel and me scatter to the wooden floor. Rene kicks the side of my coffee table and it flies toward me, pieces of it breaking onto the floor.

Michel's laughter is thick with darkness, almost with a sense of victory from my struggle. His voice is calm in an eerie sense. "Tsk, my Amelia. If I had a beating heart, it would most surely break from your lack of enthusiasm to see my home." Sarcasm thick in his voice, he bends down to where I lay on the floor. He tilts his head and watches me for a moment.

Warmth trickles down my scalp and I am afraid the smell of blood will trigger some kind of animalistic urge in him... or worse, Rene. I look between the two of them as I try to sit up.

His hands grip my arms and he pulls me up, standing me on my feet. Dizziness touches my head for a moment and my vision blurs. Michel's arms snake around my body and he pulls me close.

Rene steps forward, and as I look toward her, I think I see a tinge of jealousy. "I believe we should take this elsewhere, Michel, before her mutts realize she is missing. I am fully ready to fight; however, I would like to have my fun with this one first." She grins wickedly, showing a hint of fang. Rene reaches for my arms as Michel's tongue slowly licks along my earlobe. His fangs barely brush over my skin and the coldness of his breath fans on my neck.

"Mmm, I do believe you are right. I long to fuck her, but I believe I will fuck you first," he glances over at Rene, "in front of Miss Rimos. I'd like to give her a taste of what she is missing." He whispers in my ear, "You'll enjoy it, Amelia. After all, I could smell how wet I made you at the pub the night you were out with that tasty morsel sister of yours. Do you remember?" He grins as my mind quickly flashes back to our heated encounter at the pub the night Rachel and I celebrated my breakthrough of the cure.

It was the night I imagined Michel lifting my legs around his waist as he pressed my back against the wall. Thoughts race through my mind, and as I stare him in the eyes, it is as if he is feeding my memories to me through some memory of it himself. My fear heightens as the realization of what is happening sinks in. I start to wonder about the reality of our time at the library and my imagination grows darker.

I have studied these sorts of things in my readings at the library. However, I had always assumed the dark powers of the vampires were rumors. I thought stories of this amount of power over one's mind were only old wives' tales told through the ages.

Rene laughs in the background. "Oh, that *is* dirty, lover. Although, that is *nothing* compared to what I have in store for her." Michel's idea of a sick game is to watch me as he plants visions of us in my mind. My body numbs as I try not to consider what Rene would consider as fun.

I long for John, my protector, my wolf. Why did I not stay behind? Why must my pride be so great that it forces me to pay with my life? Coming back to the present, I am no longer able to hide my fear. "You both are sickening!" My body trembles with fear as I look between the two vampires.

Rene takes an unneeded breath as she steps closer to me. "Mmm, I am quite tired of hearing your voice. I am no longer amused, Alchemist." She balls her hand into a fist and quickly throws it toward my face. My body goes limp in Michel's arms and my world immediately turns black.

***

Images of blood and the ravenous vampires linger over my body, as their mouths sneer with wanted desire… a desire to eat my flesh. My eyes widen and I want to scream—I need to scream— but I cannot. Everything is silent except the pounding of my heart in my ears.

"May I eat her now?" My mind freezes at the sound of Rene's question. She glances over at Michel, and as I look between the two of them, his lips pull in a smirk.

"Not yet, I wish to taste her first." Michel is suddenly holding on to my body and his eyes grow dark with lust. "Lie down, Amelia. Lie down and allow me to feast on your body."

My head shakes a few times and fear explodes in my body. Adrenaline pumps through my veins and I need to run; I need to get away from this place… from this evil.

Before I realize what is happening, Michel has me on my back. My arms are pinned above my head and he stares down into my eyes. "You will give yourself to me, Amelia."

I feel as if he slips thoughts into my head, forcing me to change my mind. Like a hazy cloud, the reality of my situation begins to change. The fear begins to disappear, and in its place, lust. My lips part, and as I am about to tell him yes, his knees push my legs apart.

Rene grasps my wrists and holds me tight. Michel begins to shift down my body as his hands move down to my breasts. He squeezes them and presses them together.

Gasping, I glance down and notice my clothes have been removed. I do not recall removing my garments, I think to myself.

His tongue slips over my erect nipples and he gently nips on the buds. I gasp and my head drops back to the floor. Michel grasps my legs with his hands and pushes my thighs apart.

"I'm going to taste you now, Amelia," he tells me. I nod, finding no words leave my lips. I cannot get myself to mutter anything.

His lips move over my stomach and he licks along my skin. I inhale sharply at the sensation. Suddenly, pain rips through my side, and when I look down, Michel has bitten my waist.

"No!" I inhale and immediately choke on the dryness of my throat. My eyes open, burning at the thick haze in the air. My heart beats hard against my chest and I look for Michel and Rene, finding neither of them around. "What in the hell? Was I dreaming?" I mutter to myself.

My vision distorted, I try to make sense of exactly where I am. My face burns from the impact of Rene's fist and I am positive I have a large bruise.

I try to move my wrists and ankles, finding both are bound to the cold stone wall I am chained to. The scent of death lingers in the air. The rot of human corpses causes me to retch on the floor. It is the foulest smell I have ever experienced.

Afraid to speak, I choke out tears, trying with all my might to free myself from the chains that bind me. My voice has a shaky undertone to it and my eyes frantically wander around the dark area. I grit my teeth, "Dammit!" I was a fool to allow my emotions to overtake me and I pray John has seen my note.

The night at Tony's pub replays in my memory, like a breath of fresh air I so long for. I swallow back tears; I was safe, unafraid. I can almost feel his arms around me as we danced to the tune of the band that night. His arms fit so perfectly around my waist. Then later, his warm lips against mine. And now? I fear I shall no longer see the beautiful warmth of his dark eyes. Feel those soft, amazing lips against mine. The thought of it causes tears to pool, blurring my vision. I have nowhere to go, no way to escape from this.

Suddenly my thoughts are interrupted. "Evening, sleeping beauty," Michel's voice echoes through the darkness. The temporary sanity I had is now gone as light begins to fill the room. He approaches and his shoes echo against the stone on the floor. The light continues to grow and it provides a way for me to see this hell I am in.

"Fuck you! Let me out of here, you spineless, dead piece of shit." My words seethe with hate for the vampire I once felt something for.

"Shhh, tsk, Amelia. I never knew you spoke such language. Here I thought you were a lady." He chuckles darkly. "Turns out, you're turning into a bitch just like your mangy friends. Fucking werewolves. Smelly, hairy creatures. Wouldn't you agree, Rene?" He glances across the room.

Rene has changed her outfit from the damaged black Victorian corset dress to a royal blue corset. Her skirt is long and flowing, the train of it follows behind her as she glides across the room, lighting each candle. Just beside her sits a bathtub, its rim stained with crimson, a hook hovering above.

"Indeed, however, I only know what we've studied of her, and what you have told me of her, Michel." Her lips turn upward, forming a dark smirk as she eyes me with contempt.

Once she lights the last candle, she proceeds to a wooden phonograph, which sits beside a large bed covered with white sheets in a corner of the room. She carefully lowers the arm on the device and music fills the air. *How classy of them*, I think to myself.

Michel chuckles with a shake of his head, almost as to wave her off. "Amelia, love, that dog who *recused you* and I go way back. His family was quite tasty for what they are. I am sure Mr. Hawthorne has shared our history?"

A sickening feeling erupts in my stomach. To hear that Michel personally destroyed John's family devastates me. The thought alone makes my heart hurt for John. I nod slowly, "He informed me. Much like you murdered my sister, you murdered *his* family." My words escape me as tears of anger fall.

"Ahhh, Werewolves are not as innocent as they seem. Trust me." A dark grin crosses his lips. "Foul, savage beasts that stick to their own kind, more so than the vampires. At least we have the option of turning you. They tend to stick within their pack." He begins to pace. "So, you see, you and he can never be possible, Amelia. His pack, as well as himself, see you as beneath them. They are merely watching over you for their personal interests."

"I don't believe you," I spit back.

"Aww, come now, Michel. You'll break the poor dear's heart." She laughs as she steps out of her darkened corner, approaching me. The flicker of the candle light partially illuminates her skin. I freeze with fear, chills running up and down my spine as she leans in to sniff me. She runs the tip of her cold tongue along my cheek. The area where she hit me still throbs and I am sure it is swollen. She allows her tongue to touch my bruise then sends it down my neck.

What if Michel is right? Maybe I am simply a decoy in a bigger plan. I lead them to Michel and his coven of monsters and they attack. Nothing seems to matter since he will be too late if they do come for me. I will either be on the other side of this battle, turned into the werewolves' enemy, or Michel and Renee will completely do away with me, drain me, and leave me for dead just like my sister. I only long to flee this place, to feel safe and secure again in my own home.

"Mmm, even her skin tastes sweet, lover." She pulls back just enough to grab my face and force me to look at her. "Just a taste? I promise not to drain her." She looks over her shoulder at Michel.

He shakes his head, "No, my lover, not yet. There are still a few things we need from her. However, I shall allow you to play with her, fuck with her mind some more." His eyes darken as he gazes upon me. "She's been far too headstrong and it's time to change that. We need to weaken that mind of hers." His attention returns to Rene. "Just do not taste. I fear you'll lose control and drain her without getting the information about her cure."

My body visibly shakes as they discuss their plans of torture. My wrists are raw from where I struggled against my shackles earlier.

Rene's eyes widen, a hint of defiance in her tone, "I suppose that will suffice." A sigh escapes her lips as if she has been scolded and wants to argue his command. "Shall we bring in our current play thing? Let's show her what she has to look forward to should she not cooperate."

Michel nods and his lips turn upward into an approving grin, "That I will allow, as I do believe our little friend has some life left in her. We may as well finish her off in front of our... guest."

A smirk creeps across Rene's features just before she turns on her heel. She approaches the tub, anticipating her sire's command of the guard.

Michel simply calls out, his voice calm yet authoritative, "Stephen, bring us the woman." My focus turns toward the guard named Stephen as he emerges from outside the heavy wooden doors. One would question how often he bathes, as his shirt is stained with dried blood.

He nods, catching my gaze, and gives me a sideways smirk. "Right away, Your Majesty." He bows, his eyes never leaving mine, before turning to capture the woman they spoke of.

Rene runs her fingers along the edge of the tub with anticipation. Michel paces, anxiously awaiting their prisoner's arrival. All I have left to do is watch the two monsters before me.

Stephen returns with the woman, and she is screaming. "PLEASE, NO MORE, LET ME GO!" She struggles against his grasp as tears fall from her cheeks.

I gasp and whisper, "Oh, no. Eva." I swallow hard, choking against the dryness.

Eva's beautiful features have been torn apart. I notice the tear along her neck, much like Rachel's, and her normally dark features are now pale from the amount of blood drained from her. Her face is stained with tears, and dirt clings to her skin. She looks to be Undead herself.

"Oh my god, what have they done to you?" My voice is barely a whisper.

Eva's nearly dead eyes glance in my direction. It is as if she does not recognize me, or she hasn't the strength to say so.

Rene throws her head back as wicked laughter escapes her lips. "Your god can't help you now, Amelia." Her is tone mocking. Michel slowly makes his way toward her; all the while Stephen continues to grip a distressed, broken Eva. Her screams turn into a whimper that she can no longer hold back.

Michel unties Rene's corset from behind with a wicked grin. It loosens and drops to the floor as he chimes in. "Your god will not, and cannot save you from the power of the beast. Not tonight, my dear."

Michel begins running his hands along Rene's thin biceps, kissing along her neck as his hands slide toward her breasts. He grasps them, fondling her before pinching and playing with her nipples.

She lifts her legs out of her skirt and kicks it away. She grabs Eva roughly by her arm, which causes her to whimper. "P-please, I beg of you. I will not say anything. I promise you that..."

Rene glares at her, "You are most pathetic when you beg and plead." Her fangs descend and she glances toward Michel, "Shall we drink some more, then hang her like the piggy she is, my King?" Their form of affection causes my stomach to churn as they prepare to torture and butcher Eva further. I wish I could turn away, though I am afraid to.

Rene's lips peel back over her fangs, exposing them even more. She jerks Eva's head to the side as she ravenously sinks them into her neck. Eva is so weakened she does not cry or try to fight them off. Rene violently pulls away, removing a large section of her neck. Eva's body goes limp. I have no idea if she is alive or dead.

"Simply beautiful, my love. This is why I chose you, my progeny, my mate." Michel steps forward and runs his finger along the gash in Eva's neck. His fingertips follow the river of crimson flowing down Eva's body toward her breast. His fingertip circles around her nipple before he places it to his lips, licking the crimson from his fingertips with a smirk.

Through tears, I cry out, "Please! Don't do this... you monsters!" I pull at the chains and pain ignites where they dig into my wrists and ankles.

Stephen, the vampire servant, stands at the entrance, gazing at the scene through darkened eyes. He licks his fangs as if he is turned on by the show his superiors provide him.

"Stephen, prepare my bath," Rene commands.

His grin widens as he steps forward, following orders. He grabs Eva's weakened body from her grasp. Kneeling down, he takes her by her feet then lifts her up as if she weighs nothing. The blood from her neck drips into the contents of the tub. He reaches, grabbing the hook above the tub, and lowers it. Forcefully he shoves the hook through the bones of her ankles. I can hear the skin tear before Stephen steps away, leaving Eva dangling.

I cannot hold back my screams of the terror I feel as I witness a world so dark, so evil, "Oh my god! OH MY GOD! Somebody help me! PLEASE!"

The words escape me and as loud as I scream, I have no idea if anyone, anywhere can help me... or hear me.

Rene steps forward as Michel reveals a knife tucked away in the holster of his belt. He removes it and watches me intently, his lips stained with Eva's blood.

Rene takes the knife from his grasp and places the blade to Eva's throat. With one even cut, her blood pours out as if a butcher were slaughtering an animal.

My eyes and mouth widen with fear. Never will I forget what I am witnessing tonight. This nightmare will forever haunt me. With the little life that courses through her, Eva gurgles from the massive blood loss.

Michel takes the blade from Rene, licking it dry. He closes his eyes, savoring the taste. "Not the best, but she shall suffice for tonight."

Rene removes the remainder of her clothes. "I suppose she shall; at least she has ceased shrieking like a bloody banshee. Now, I shall fully enjoy my evening as our special girl watches." She glances over at me with a sadistic grin. Rene steps into the tub, lowering herself. "Scream all you want, but know that if you continue to scream, I will cut out your tongue. Screaming will do you no good." The crimson liquid covers her body before she fully submerges herself. She disappears inside the tub as Eva continues to dangle over her, intensifying the horrific scene.

The remainder of who I am, any innocence I had left is ripped from me. There are some things not meant for one's eyes, this is one of them.

Michel slowly makes his way across the room toward me just as Rene rises from the bloody bath. Her hair, her face, and her body are fully covered in the crimson liquid. Michel grabs me by the chin as I lower my eyes. I have seen far too much; I cannot bear to watch anymore.

He hisses through his fangs, "You will watch. Humans are here to serve and to feed us, my dear. Do you understand?"

My lip quivers as I nod slowly, too afraid to look away from him.

"You will give me the ingredients, whatever remains of your notes to the cure. Do you understand? Your boss did not cooperate the way she had promised." He forcefully positions my face toward where Eva hangs. "Look at what has become of her." His lips are inches from my face, his breath reeking of death, and I find myself wondering how and why I had not noticed the stench of it before this.

Rene slowly ascends from the tub. She steps to the floor as her body drips with the remnants of blood. "Michel, please join me? Let's give little Amelia the show she so deserves." Her voice nearly pleading, she saunters toward him.

Michel traces his fingertips along the bruise on my cheekbone before backing away. His gaze locked on me, he stands then turns to face Rene as he disrobes.

He is built just as I envisioned. His skin pale, but built to make any woman fall to her knees. His biceps are large and pulsing as he readies himself to join Rene. He flashes me a fanged grin as Rene drapes a bloodied arm around his waist.

They make their way toward the tub and her gaze fixates upon my features. They step inside it and he lowers himself first as she straddles his body.

His hands move up her thighs and he guides her down. She finally breaks our eye contact as she looks at her lover. Rene's head tilts back as she gasps. Michel begins to thrust against her and her moans echo throughout the room.

I become nauseous, holding back the vomit as blood smears against each of their bodies. It is not an act of love, but lust and pure evil; low guttural growls echo throughout the room.

Has this become my reality? Will this become my reality for eternity? Michel has a way with words, a way of convincing me I am less than what I am. I have never felt as though I were a victim, until tonight.

Chapter 15

Grumbling in his sleep, John's eyes begin to open and he takes in his surroundings. He reaches up and rubs his eyes with his palms for a moment then lets out a loud, heavy growl as he stretches. His arms pull above his head and his legs extend while his feet hang off the end of his bed.

"Fuck... what a night." He moves a hand over his face as his scruff scratches against his palm. Thoughts of kissing Amelia make him groan again, but differently from before. "It'll be damn awkward. Outstanding."

He moves from his bed and makes his way toward the bathroom. "Damn that woman," John mumbles to himself. He draws hot water into the tub and sits on the edge of it. Waking with an erection from the festivities of the night before, he gingerly wraps a hand around his cock. He strokes his erection a few times and groans softly to himself. Picturing Amelia while they kissed last night, he imagines her body naked, what she would look like... feel like...against him. Thinking of how her pussy would taste against his tongue and the way her walls would clamp around his cock, he mumbles to himself, "Fuck, she would be so tight."

His cock twitches and his balls tighten more than before as he finally comes. He runs a finger down the vein and empties the last of his seed. The relief is welcoming, but he is far from satisfied.

Finally lowering himself into the hot water of the tub, he reaches for the soap and begins running it over his body just as he hears Adam's voice.

"John, are you in here?"

"In here, yeah," John answers. "What's up?"

"Would, umm," he hesitates for a moment, "Amelia be in there? With you?"

John can hear the hesitation in his voice. He raises a brow. "Hell no, she's not in here with me!" he lowers his voice and continues just to himself, "Not that I would mind her being in here with me."

"I'm sorry. Just..." Adam hesitates again.

"What is it, Adam? Where is she?" Adrenaline spikes briefly in John and he tries to calm it. She is probably out in the barn or maybe walking the property.

"She's not in her room and Dennis is not outside. I thought maybe she would have asked him for a ride, but I cannot find him, either. Derek talked to her this morning, but hasn't seen her since."

His heart drops for a moment then he shakes his head. "Alright, I'm sure she's fine. Now where the hell is Dennis?" John rinses the soap off his body then turns off the water. He reaches for a towel and wraps it around himself. Water droplets hit the floor as he walks into his bedroom. "Talk," he tells Adam.

His Beta looks at him for a moment, then nods. The alarm on his face does not go unnoticed. "I think Dennis took her to town. She is nowhere around. The carriage is also gone."

"Shit," John mumbles under his breath. "Alright. Get word out. I will take a few to her place. Maybe she got a bright idea to venture there for who the hell knows what." He runs a hand through his wet hair. "Who the fuck knows what runs through that woman's mind?" he mumbles to himself.

"Right," Adam starts as he turns toward the door. "See you downstairs." He closes the bedroom door behind him.

John drops the towel and makes his way to his dresser. He pulls out a pair of underwear and slips them on. He then pulls on an old, fitted t-shirt. The material pulls against his chest and his biceps.

"That shit makes you look… different," Sophie told him one day.

"What the hell is that supposed to mean?" he asked her.

"Nothing." She turned her back to him and he watched her blush.

He recalls this conversation with Sophie. Shortly after, another female in his pack mentioned how it made him look… pleasing to the eye. He considers removing it, then decides to keep it on. John is more focused on finding Amelia than what he wears.

Pulling on a pair of jeans, John tucks in the shirt then pulls on his shoulder strapped gun holsters. He buckles a belt into place and pulls on a brown leather vest, buttoning the three buttons. The vest covers the guns as a sort of disguise.

Picking up a brown top hat fitted with a few gears attached to it, as well as night goggles, he puts it on. The gears attached are actually weapons he can throw. If needed, he can bend the metal to be long enough to decapitate a vampire.

He has done it before and would definitely do it again.

John makes his way downstairs, intending to load up on a few weapons. He enjoyed the bows Amelia's father left her, as well as a few of the guns. Smelling the breakfast, he grabs a few pieces of the sausage and stuffs them into his mouth.

"Headed to a fight?" Sophie asks across the room.

"Don't know yet," he answers her. "Going by her place first."

"We'll come along," Adam responds and makes his way toward Sophie.

"No," John tells him as he turns to face his Beta. "You can come, but she," he looks to Sophie, "you're now a liability since you're involved. I need his head in the game."

"John!" Adam challenges.

John growls at him then closes the distance between them. "You challenge my ruling? My authority?"

Adam shakes his head a few times and backs off.

"Sophie," John calls to her in a growl.

She walks across the room and stands next to the Alpha and her Beta. "Yes?"

"Check the barn then report immediately."

"Yes, sir." Sophie lowers her gaze then leaves the room.

Shifting his eyes back to Adam, "You do that shit again, you're out," John threatens. "Understood?"

Adam lowers his gaze then nods, demonstrating submission to his master.

"You offered your neck to me as your Alpha. You go against me, you fight me for it."

"I was not challenging your authority. It's just," he glances up at his Alpha. "There's a lot riding on the line with Amelia."

"And?" John leans in as his eyes glare into Adam's.

"Nothing, it's nothing."

The screen door in the other room bangs and Sophie comes running into the kitchen, almost breathless. A look of fear covers her features and she reaches for John.

"The horse... Dixie is back! There's blood on the carriage and Dennis is not on it!"

"Shit!" John glares at Adam once more then runs through the living room.

"Wait," Adam calls to him as he crosses the room. He stops in front of a lamp on one of the nearby tables and picks up a piece of parchment. He quickly skims it then looks over at John.

"What is it?" John reaches the front door and stands there for a moment. "Speak up!"

"There's a note... from her." Adam closes the distance to John and hands the note over with a thrust.

"What the hell is your problem?" John growls.

"This! All of this is my problem! I sleep with Sophie and now she cannot help us because *I* might be off my game. Fuck, John! You've not bedded the woman but *you're* running out of here all guns a blazing and hell-bent on finding her without a goddamned plan!"

John growls and thrusts Adam against the wall, his fingers gripping his shirt. He leans in and his words spit as he talks. "You want to try that again?" The note has wrinkled in his grasp.

"Stop it! Both of you!" Sophie calls.

"Read the damn note, John!" Adam tells him. "Your fight isn't with me."

He growls then slowly lets his Beta go. "This isn't over."

Rather than speaking his mind, Adam decides to keep his mouth closed. He straightens out his shirt then looks over at Sophie. He reaches for her and she moves to his side. "You okay?" he asks.

She nods and leans into his embrace. "What did it say?" she whispers.

"Just wait for it," he tells her.

She looks him over then sighs. Sophie turns her attention back to John as a few other pack members enter the room.

"We heard a ruckus," announces one of their males. His tall, thin build is a sharp contrast to the thickness of John and Adam.

Adam shakes his head no to the pack member then turns his attention back to his pack master.

John opens the note and reads it over once, then twice. He growls and his eyes glow golden. His blood rushes to his face and he lets a growl erupt from his chest so vicious, Sophie jumps back a few feet in fear.

"WE. LEAVE. NOW!" John growls each word and walks out the front door. His voice comes out in a command. Adam and Sophie both feel the pull and follow him outside. His entire pack makes their way to the front and fall into formation. "We ride on horseback. Anyone without a horse will join us as shifters. Understood?"

The pack acknowledges their master. Deuce, John's draft horse, waits for him around front. The Friesian male is tall and his coloring is dark brown, almost black. Deuce is large for his breed, standing close to eighteen hands tall. John approaches his mount and climbs into the saddle. He takes the reins and looks to his pack.

"Looks like Dennis has been murdered. Amelia left this morning. According to her note, she went home to gather more supplies and has not returned. The sun will be setting soon and tonight is our full moon. We will have no choice but to shift." John's eyes light almost in excitement to his announcement. "If the vampire coven has Amelia," he growls, "there is a chance we could be too late, but that is not a chance I'm willing to take... nor accept."

"All the better to destroy the dead fuckers," Tony calls from the side.

John looks at him as Catherine clings to his side. He offers his friend a slight nod.

"A few will need to remain here. Amelia could show back up," John looks at Sophie, "and if she does, word needs to be sent to me immediately." He looks at his pack again. "If we have any wounded return, they will need to be tended to. Sophie," he looks at her again with a nod, "you will put out the word for any available Alchemists to assist us. There are a few in our favor."

"On it," she tells him then mounts her horse. The thoroughbred takes off down the driveway, leaving a dust cloud in her wake.

"Now, we ride," he tells his pack. A few yell out in excitement of the oncoming battle, others simply mount their horses.

The shifters without horses grin and look at one another, knowing their change is coming. The pain of shifting is never pleasant, but the end result is always worthwhile. The moment after being in true form is the most euphoric state to the werewolf.

***

Arriving in town, the pack reach Amelia's building. A few of the men dismount with John and they begin to look around the area. He gives orders to a few to look around town and ask if anyone has seen her recently.

John steps onto the front porch and skims the side of the building until he lands on Amelia's window.

"John," Tony calls to him, "there's blood."

John looks to his pack mate then looks down to where he is pointing.

Tony squats down and touches the blood, then rubs his fingers together. "Pretty fresh, I would gather, but it has been here since at least this morning." He looks up at John.

He nods. "Let's get inside."

Opening the door, John steps inside the building first. A few of his pack, including Tony, ascend the stairs with him. As they reach Amelia's landing, John immediately notices her door is slightly ajar.

He holds up a hand to stop his pack then glances back at them. They shuffle in the hallway as quietly as they can manage, the floor creaking underneath their weight. John holds a single digit to his lips and they nod in return.

Approaching the door slowly, he barely touches it as he gently pushes it open. The room comes into view and the first thing he notices is the room is in complete disarray.

Adrenaline kicks in and a growl begins to form. The heat from wanting... needing to shift... burns through his body. Suddenly, there is a hand on his shoulder. John snarls and snaps at Tony.

Tony shakes his head and squeezes his shoulder, as if willing his friend and Pack Master to calm down.

John looks him over then shoves his hand away. Giving Tony a nod, he moves his eyes back to the open room. He pushes the door open a little farther and it creaks on the hinges. The entire living room comes into view and is a mess. Evidence everywhere indicates a fight has taken place. The couch has been turned over and ripped. He glances toward the kitchen and the area is a disaster.

"Fuck," he snarls in a whisper and enters the loft. He sniffs the air and his nose curls. "The Undead have been here." He ventures farther inside and glances toward the kitchen again, then in the other direction toward her bedroom. "I pick up her scent as being here," he announces. "Look around for anything that will help us."

Two men head off in the direction of the bedroom while Tony joins John in the kitchen. He sniffs the air and glances toward his Pack Master. "Are they aware she was staying with us?"

"I have no idea. She's not been around here for a few days so I suppose anything is possible," John answers.

"When you took her to her bank, did anyone see you? Did you see anyone familiar?"

John shakes his head no. He presses his palms on the counter and leans into it. "Her note said she was coming back here for supplies." He glances up at Tony. "If they have her, they could force her to make the cure again… or hell, even alter it."

"What's the likelihood of them keeping her alive?" Tony's head suddenly slings back. He yells out from the pain of John's fist against his jaw. "What the hell, John?" He rubs his jawline and moves his mouth around.

"Don't say shit like that, Tony. They need her alive." He opens the icebox and looks inside. "Hell, we need her alive." He wants to tell Tony *he* wants her alive, but thinks it better to leave it be for now. John shakes his head and closes the icebox. "I wish she would have told me she was coming here."

"From what I remember last night," Adam announces coming back into the room, "she may have been too embarrassed."

John watches his Beta across the room then raises a brow. "What do you mean, too embarrassed?"

"She seemed pretty into you last night."

"Like you remember with Sophie in your lap?" Tony asks him.

"As much as Sophie was on me last night, I never stop watching my pack. If anything were to happen to John…" His words trail off for a moment and he clears his throat. "All I'm saying is I think she may have been too preoccupied with what occurred last night to consider coming to you this morning."

John nods a few times and considers this. "I kissed her then left her room."

"How drunk was she?" Tony asks.

He looks at his friend then sighs, "She was pretty inebriated."

"Then you left her to pass out?" Adam asks him. John nods in return. "Well, if you needed to talk with her first thing in the morning, would you have sought an audience?"

"Probably not," John answers and averts his gaze. "Now listen," he inhales and his chest puffs out as he gathers himself. "This isn't about me. We need to figure out what happened and get her back." He looks between Adam and Tony. "What are the last whereabouts of Michel?"

Chapter 16

Stretching, my body pulls, and pain erupts from my wrists. I gasp and my eyes open to the darkness surrounding me. Sleep has crusted in my eyes and there is a dryness in my throat that almost causes me to choke. I need food and water. I need to be able to see. I need...

My mind pauses as the events begin to return to my mind. Panic rises inside of my chest.

Michel and Rene.

"Oh god, no, Eva..." My breath catches in my throat as memories of yesterday surface. Eva's body hanging limp and upside down over the tub. Her body draining into the basin as Michel and Rene fuck underneath her.

The thought alone is enough to make me retch on the floor. I cough and try to inhale, but the stench of death is too strong. Tears well in my eyes and burn, from the pain I am feeling, and from the fear of not making it out of here alive.

"John," I whisper in the darkness, "I wish I could tell you where I am. I wish I had not cared for my pride. I wish... I hope you find me."

Suddenly, hands grab my leg and I scream. Whomever it is tugs and pulls at my body.

"Stop it!" I scream. Nails dig into my flesh and it is all I can do to scream at the pain. It radiates up my thigh and they twist me, causing me to turn away from them.

Something moist moves up my leg, and for a moment, I swear something licked me. It happens again and I try to look to the side, but see nothing but darkness. The tongue moves across my calf again and I try to jerk my leg away.

"Hold still if you wish to live."

I gasp and my eyes widen. "Michel?" My heartbeat quickens and I shake my head. "Please, stop this. Let me go." A sob escapes and my voice echoes in the dungeon.

"Only when I'm good and ready." He licks my calf again, and this time, I can feel his fangs. "Mmm, you taste," he licks my legs again, "so good."

"Please stop this," I plead with a squeak. "It's madness!"

"You know NOTHING of madness!" he yells and his voice surrounds me as it bounces off the dungeon walls.

"Then tell me." I know I am grasping at straws in getting him to talk, but I have to do something if I intend to live through this. "Tell me what it is you want... what you need."

"Oh, my Amelia. Are you trying to get inside my head?" I can feel him move against my leg. His hands move to either side of my hips, and suddenly, death is breathing into my face. "What do you know of madness?"

I whimper softly and shake my head.

He leans in and licks my lips.

I shudder and turn my face away from his.

His tongue licks across my neck and I cannot help the cry that follows.

"If I truly wished for your death it would have happened already," he tells me. "But don't worry, love," he licks my neck again then kisses my ear. "You'll be dead soon enough." He grips my face and forces me to face him. "Just as soon as you give me what I need."

"Oh god," my voice is between a whisper and a cry. "What could I possibly give you that you don't already have?"

"Oh, you silly, silly girl." His nose moves alongside mine as he inhales deeply. "I need to know how you created this cure of yours," he chuckles darkly and continues, "Then have you alter it into… something more."

"S-something more?" I ask. "What if I don't comply?"

"Well, let's see… How about this?" He pulls away from me; at least I think he does. I no longer feel his breath or smell his personal stench. "I'll give you two options."

I am not sure I want to hear what this is, but whatever he has to say will prolong the inevitable.

He is back in my face again and his fingers gently glide down my cheeks. The monster from earlier seems to be at bay while he plays gently. Well, his version of gentle that is. I am not sure which scares me more: the evil vampire he is or the gentle monster in front of me.

"Are you ready, my love?"

I swallow and almost choke. "I need water first, please."

Touches of water dribble on my lips and I gasp. I lick my lips and taste what could be my salvation. Then it stops.

"More, please Michel, more!"

"Not until you've heard what I have to say."

My eyes close and I focus on the water that just touched my lips. I think of food, think of what would make me salivate. John's lips suddenly come to mind. *God, I wish he were here right now.*

"What are your plans for me, Michel?" I ask, hoping like hell I survive whatever it is he has planned.

Michel tilts my face upward and his nose runs the length of my neck. He inhales deeply then releases me. Blindness in the room makes whatever he is about to divulge that more sinister.

"Option one," his voice is still close but there is a bit of distance now. I can hear his shoes on the ground and it sounds like he may be pacing. "You will willingly create what it is I need." He pauses for a moment then clears his throat. "Well? Ask me what it is I need, Amelia."

I shake my head, afraid of what he will say. My voice squeaks when I try to speak and my heart slams against my chest. Sweat beads on my forehead and I can feel it race down my back. "W-what is it you n-need?"

He chuckles sinisterly. My skin crawls and I feel my body shudder. "I need you to make me a formula similar to your cure."

Attempting to swallow, I choke and cough hard. "Water, please," I beg gruffly.

Michel grabs my hair and forces my head back. He pours water over my face and into my mouth in such a rush that I fear I will drown. Adrenaline spikes in a fight or flight mode. He finally pulls the water away and I cough again, spitting water up.

"Now if you're done with the dramatics," he begins, "go on and ask me about this... new cure."

I cough a few more times and clear my throat. Inhaling deeply as I try, with what strength I have left to ask, "Why don't you just tell me what it is you want me to do?" I cannot believe these words just came out of my mouth, but there it is.

"Oh, I like it when you're feisty." He is suddenly back in my face and he inhales my scent again. He makes me feel like I am a steak dinner and he is starving for a bite. "I might have fun with you yet, Amelia." He licks my lips and I quickly jerk away.

"I want you to make a different type of cure, as you call it. I want a creation made in liquid form that would change humans into vampires... without a flesh wound."

I shake my head a few times. John's and Adam's conversation come back to me the night they filled me in. "No! I couldn't possibly..."

He cuts me off and grabs my throat. Michel squeezes it and his nails dig into my skin. He cuts my air supply off and he is in my face again. "You WILL do it or I will *force* the deed upon you. This is your other option! You see, Amelia, I will simply change you into one of my vampires and take the will away from you." His voice is calm as he talks while continuing to squeeze.

"I think I would enjoy having you on my arm," he continues. "You are a bit of candy I could have on occasions while Rene is… shall we say… feeding her need for blood baths. She is quite mad and the only thing that seems to keep that bitch calm is her blood bathing. You do this for me and I shall give you immortality. That or just kill you."

I choke and the chains rattle as I try to reach for his arms. The links restrain me and I can feel myself fading into a darkness that lies outside of the dungeon. I beg for this release, just to be away from this hell Michel has brought me into.

"Oh, Amelia, I almost forgot I had you in a strangle hold. My apologies," he tells me. He addresses it as if I simply tripped and he has helped me back to my feet.

Gasping for air, my vision begins to right itself. "You are a MONSTER!" I scream out. "I will

NEVER help you!" I begin to sob and try to back against the wall, away from him.

"Oh Amelia, I'm not the monster. It is *you*, my love, who is the monster." Michel chuckles his sinister laugh and continues, "It was not my kind who created themselves."

I gasp and shake my head. "I am not responsible for any of this! How dare you even consider it?"

"How dare I?" He laughs. "Do you have any idea what it is LIKE to live for an eternity just to see everyone around you DIE?" His voice darkens in anger and I immediately regret my words. "Do you have any idea what it is like to chase something, right in front of you, just to lose it every single fucking time?"

"Michel, please, I'm sorry! Please, stop!"

"You have no idea what it is like to live this life. You have no idea what it is like to be hunted, to be targeted, to be called blasphemous! You have no idea what it is like, Amelia!"

"Michel, no I don't understand, and honestly how could I? You have chained me up, forced me to watch the mutilation of Eva, and all the while, you fuck your whore in a tub filled with Eva's blood! How can I feel sorry for you? How can you honestly ask me for anything after that?"

A growl fills the air and it suddenly turns cold… very cold. I know I am about to either die or be changed into one of his kind. I pray it is not the latter. His hands grasp my face and he yanks me forward. The chains on my wrists force my arms back and my chest bows forward.

"YOU WILL DO AS I COMMAND OF YOU!" His voice is full of rage and torment. His grip becomes tighter and I cry out from the pain.

"Lover, if you rip her head off, you'll never get what you need." Rene's voice sounds across the room and for the first time since being here, I actually feel grateful for her presence.

Michel loosens his grip and eventually releases me. I fall slack against the wall behind me. My back is raw from the cement rubbing against it and the sweat running down my body causes a fierce sting.

"Why are you down here?" he asks her. "I did not call for you."

"No? Well, upon hearing you threaten to put me away for this tasty tart, I figured it was time to make myself known."

Michel growls and a breeze shifts over my body. Rene screams on the other side of the room and a thud sounds against the wall.

"Michel! Let me go, dammit!"

I wish I could see what is happening since I think he has pinned her.

She suddenly screams and I quickly hold my breath.

"That will shut her up for a while," Michel mutters.

"Wh-what did you do?" I stammer out.

"I ripped her throat out. Don't worry, she'll heal and be fine in a few hours."

"Oh my god!" I try to look toward where I hear Rene's voice. "Why? Why did you do that?"

"She would have killed you before I had a chance to get what I needed. Trust me, the bitch is pure evil."

I have no idea what to say to that. Michel is threatening to change me... or kill me... yet he mutilates his mate to allow me to survive a moment longer.

"Michel, I cannot do this. Please, do not make me. I do not wish to be part of this plan."

"Then I shall change you and be done with it. Once you have made the transition, you will have no choice but to do my bidding."

"Wait, no! Don't do this!" I try to think of a way to get him to keep talking but come up with nothing. "Please, you showed me kindness the night Henry died!"

"Oh that, yeah well, I killed Henry," he announces.

"You? I do not... I don't understand?" Confusion plagues my mind as I move over the events of that evening.

Henry screams.

Michel runs in past me.

There are sounds of a fight.

Michel looks out to find me. I think he has saved me from an attack.

Realization sinks in. My eyes widen and my lips part.

"Ahh, I see you understand now," Michel states.

"You... you staged that?"

"That I did. I have known about you for a long while now, Amelia. Eva has been great at monitoring you. Oh, well, she *was* great. Now that I have you, I am no longer in need of her services, as you know."

"You... monster," I whisper.

"No, love, remember *you're* the monster here, not me."

"No, I'm not! I did not stage a murder! I did not kidnap me and force me to watch that... that... murder!"

Suddenly Michel is on me and grabs my face with his hands. "Yes, it IS you!" He spits the words out. "It was your kind who created us and it will be YOU who destroys the entire human population, starting with you tonight!"

He forces my neck to the side and sinks his fangs into my neck. The dungeon fills with my screams. The shock is too much. I can feel my body begin to shut down as the blackness of my mind takes over.

Chapter 17

The sun has fully descended, and with it, the internal fire begins to burn through his body. John, Adam, and Tony dismount their horses and tie them to a tree just outside of Michel's homestead.

John growls and he looks at his pack mates. "We go in. We kill. We get her. We leave. No fucking around!"

Adam nods a few times and his neck twists to the side. "Fuck… it's time."

"Being out of earshot gives us the advantage on the attack. Be ready for anything," John orders.

"What if," Tony growls as he grits his teeth, "we are too late? What if they already got the cure, or worse, changed her?"

"It's not a fucking option!" John yells out.

Adam and Tony yelp as they back away. John shakes his head and turns away from his men. Suddenly, a loud enormous growl escapes his lips. It echoes through the forest and the birds in the trees cry out as they fly away.

The pack begins dropping to their knees and then fall to their palms. John yells out as his body, with a loud crack, begins to break. He groans and cries out from the pain. His legs break at the knees while his back begins to bend and shift. The glow of his yellow eyes strain for a moment, just before he squeezes them shut. A scream sounds from a few of the pack members as hair begins to grow across their bodies.

John reaches for his face and holds it for a moment as it cracks. His face distorts and begins to shift into a canine appearance. He groans and cries out while his ears change... taking on a canine point, and his body continues to shift. He falls back a few feet and grabs at his shirt, ripping it across his chest. The rags fall to the ground and the chest of a wolf pushes into view.

Falling forward, he catches himself. Human hands and feet have disappeared underneath the pads and claws of the wolf beast.

As most of the pain has receded, John pants heavily and looks around at his pack. A few are still in transition while others work on catching their breath.

Getting to his feet, John stands tall. Taking on the body of a wolf within the body of man, he steps forward and stares toward Michel's homestead. His voice comes out in a heavy, dark growl. "We will kill any Undead who cross our paths. We will rip their heads off and tear their bodies apart."

Adam is next to his left flank, Tony on his right. The two men growl in agreement.

"What of Amelia?" Adam asks.

John turns to look over his shoulder at his Beta. "Leave her to me."

"And if she's changed?" Adam growls out.

"I said, leave her to me!" John bites toward Adam and his Beta jumps back.

"For Dennis," Tony announces.

John growls once more and faces forward. "For Rachel and Amelia."

Howls erupt around them and John snarls while his lips curl. "Now!"

They depart the forest and make their way toward Michel's property. The pack begins to split apart and surround the area. John and Tony make their way toward the front porch while Adam and a few other wolves move around back. A few move to either side of the foundation.

Giving a nod, John looks at Tony and growls. "You ready for this?"

"I am," he tells his Pack Master. "Are you?"

"What's that supposed to mean?" John asks.

"Your head in this?" he asks him.

"You're kidding me, right?" John glares at his friend then begins making his way toward the front door.

"I'm dead serious," Tony states. John glares at him once again and shakes his head. Tony grins at his use of words, then the two stand on either side of the front door.

John reaches for the door and gives it a push. "It's open," he states. Tony nods and John pushes the door open enough to peer inside.

The room is dark except for a faint light from another room. His vision adjusts to the darkness and he continues to look around, taking note of what obstacles are in the way.

He pulls away and leans against the outer wall. "Three vampires, a few chairs, and two doors. There's a hallway and a light that appears to be coming from what looks like the kitchen area.”

Tony nods and turns to one of the pack members on the ground. “Go, tell the others.” The wolf-man nods and runs off. “You ready?”

John nods and turns back toward the door. “They have no idea we’re here. If they do, they’re putting on a good show.”

Nodding, Tony readies himself for an attack. John opens the door again and looks inside. He begins to push it open a little more then lowers himself to the ground.

He and Tony crawl across the floor and make their way inside the house. Voices sound as the vampires talk to one another, carrying small talk of the happenings in the dungeon.

“Rene is one fucked up bitch,” says a vampire closest to John. “She gutted that woman then bathed in her blood, right in front of the Alchemist.”

“Too bad it wasn’t me. I would have fucked her in the blood rather than making her watch.”

This is all John needs to attack. He growls and Tony shakes his head, nudging him.

"What the hell was that?" the first vampire asks.

"Sounded like a damn dog," the other one replies.

John glares at Tony then back to the vampires. "Now," he growls under his voice.

The two wolf beasts slowly begin to stand as they watch the vampires. In return, the vampires' eyes widen and they ready their weapons.

"How did you get in here?" the first one yells.

Without offering an answer, John lunges at the vampire and knocks him to the ground. His scream is immediately muffled. The other vampire attempts to run from the room but Adam stops him. He runs into the Beta's chest and Adam snarls. He jumps on the vampire and begins ripping at his throat.

Tony walks the room, checking the corners and sends a few of their men into the connecting rooms.

"Clear," comes one of them.

"Clear," announces another.

Everyone returns to the den as John gets to his feet. His snout covered in vampire blood, he uses his arm as he wipes his face clean. "Where are the others and where is the dungeon?"

"Behind you," yells a woman's voice. The pack quickly turns as one of their own is attacked. He yelps in pain as the vampire sinks his fangs into his shoulder.

A loud explosion sounds from the den and the vampire's eyes widen. He releases the wolf-man and pushes his body away. He turns to find Catherine behind him with a shotgun.

She gives him a grin and cocks the weapon again. Tony growls in approval. The vampire attempts to inhale as his mouth widens. His eyes begin to glow and a golden light radiates from his mouth, his nose, then his eyes and ears.

"Get cover!" Catherine yells.

The wolves turn away from the Undead as a loud scream sounds from his lips. He suddenly combusts in fire and burns, falling first to his knees, then to his face.

John turns to look at him and nods. "The UV bullets are..." he is at a loss for words. He considers the reasons why Amelia would have created such an instrument, then kicks at the dead carcass of the vampire.

"Fucking brilliant!" Adam finishes for him.

Chaos then breaks out as other Undead venture down the stairs and enter the den. They look around at the pack of wolf-men in their home, then to the dead body on the floor.

"You want war? You've got war!" John snarls at them.

The vampires jump into action and lunge toward the closest werewolf. Snarls, screams, and growls fill the air as the fighting begins.

***

"What the fuck is going on up there?" Michel crosses the room vigorously and grabs Stephen. "What has happened?"

I look between him and Stephen and can hear what sounds like... dogs? Wolves? *John*, I think to myself. *He has found me!*

Stephen shakes his head a few times and his eyes widen. "I don't know, Master!"

"Then I suggest you go find out!" Michel thrusts him away. He follows Stephen to the large, wooden doors then closes them behind his servant. He locks the bolts and tosses the keys off to his right.

I make a mental note of where I see the keys tossed. Suddenly, Michel in front of me and grabs my arms.

"You are coming with me. I'm far from done with you!" He presses a few notches on my shackles and they unlock from my wrists. My arms ache as they drop to my sides. I cannot lift them or attempt to examine the sores on my skin.

Michel does the same to my ankles. I pull my knees to my chest and watch him carefully.

"Get up, now!" he orders.

"I can't, I won't be able to!"

"Fucking weak human!" He grabs my arms and pulls me up. I scream from the pain radiating through my body.

"Allow me to take her, love," Rene tells him as she makes her way over. Michel was right about Rene mending her wounds. She could not stop staring at the vampire. Her throat had been removed, yet here she was. "I'll take care of her."

"No," he tells her. I think I hear her growl, but I am not sure. "You will guard this area and kill any mutts that get through. Do you understand?"

"What do you intend to do with her?" she asks. I can see the defiance on her face. She looks between Michel and me and I think I see a bit of jealousy.

"You question me again and I'll kill you myself! This time there will be NO return!" Michel grabs my body and tosses me over his shoulder as if I were nothing more than a pillow. He turns to face her. "Guard the fucking door!"

Rene growls then I hear her shoes striking the ground as she walks away from us.

"As for you, my delicious Alchemist, you have a choice." He begins to walk out of the dungeon and closes a solid, thick door behind him. He locks it then continues to walk.

"Where are you taking me?" I ask in a hushed breath. I look at the walls and see they are grey stone. The hallway is set up with lamps and Michel grabs one. He quickly lights it then makes his way down to the hallway; the only light we have is the one from the lamp he carries.

There is a loud thud against the door behind us and I scream. Either the wolves got through and killed Rene, or they are fighting, trying to get through. Another thud sounds and I can feel my hopes begin to spring to life.

"Where I plan to take you is to safety. You will change that cure of yours into what I need, or at least leave instructions on how to do it. You'll be kept alive until we've successfully created it."

"And if I refuse?" I ask, feeling a little bold.

"Then I'll change you and force you to do it. The choice is yours, Amelia."

Michel walks into another room and locks the door behind us. He crosses the room and sets me on something soft. Maybe a bed, but I cannot be sure. He leaves my side and, taking the light of the lamp with him, the room grows dark.

In the corner, a light begins to burn. The lamp moves across the floor as another one is lit, then another and another. Before long, the room is bathed in the glow of the lamplight and I finally am able to take in my surroundings.

Daggers, swords, knives, and scythes line the room and I gasp. A few tools created by former Alchemists line the wall—a shotgun, a modified bow and arrow, and a few guns that looked similar to the pistol my father made.

"Welcome to my weapon room, Amelia. Look around. Each of these has been used on the wolves... as well as Alchemists...in the past. Each one has a story. Each one has been retired, but trust me, each one still works." He picks up a dagger and allows the sharp edge to run across his inner fingers. Blood trickles to the floor as he watches me. "We can do this the easy way, and you tell me what I need to do to make my elixir for the humans." Michel squeezes his hand as he makes his way toward me. He allows the blood to trickle onto my lap as he smirks. "Or I can simply change you and force the will upon you. Your choice, love."

"I would rather you kill me, if that is even an option on the table. Any human out there would rather die than become a monster like you!"

He suddenly grabs my neck and pulls me to my feet. His blood covers my neck as he brings me close. "Oh, Amelia, we are about to have so much fun together." Michel grins as he thrusts me back onto the bed. He licks his fangs and makes his way toward me.

I scream and try to move back on the bed, willing my arms to work. I kick at him as he grins, inching closer. "John!"

"Your wolf-man can't help you, love. He will need to get through my guard to find you."

"Did you know he's willing to sacrifice himself and his pack in order to end your kind? Did you know he's willing to rid the world of the Undead?"

"He is a weak-minded creature, Amelia. Take my hand and be mine for eternity. Allow me to be your maker." He holds his hand out for me and I am at a loss for words.

I look from his hand, to his eyes, then back at his hand. "You cannot be serious!"

"I am very much serious," he grins and climbs onto the bed.

I try to scoot away from him unsuccessfully. "What about Rene?"

"She's a liability. Come now; trust me when I say you'll enjoy this life with me." He grins and suddenly pins me on my back. "Give me what I want or I'll take it. The choice is yours."

I shake my head. "Fuck you!"

"As you wish." He grins and pulls my hands above my head, gripping my sore, battered wrists with one hand. I cry out from the pain as he lingers in my face. "Welcome to the world of the Undead, Amelia."

I scream as his fangs sink into my neck. Tears slip into my hairline and pain radiates from my bite wound, my wrists, and my head. I can feel his essence begin to pump into my system slowly, like warm water bathing my skin.

My eyes begin to flutter shut as the lights in the room dim to a dull blackness.

Chapter 18

"Are there any left standing?" John pants as he takes a few strides across the den. The ashes of vampires lie in piles as evidence of their demise; blood stains the ceiling, walls, and wooden floors. Aside from the creaking of the floors as they step, the only sounds in the room are from the wolves growling as they sniff the air.

"Not in here," Adam offers, "but they're not all dead yet. I can smell their stench."

"Yeah," John answers, "I can smell them as well." He crosses the room toward a door. "Adam, take a team with you through the door over there." John points across the room. Adam nods and waves a few of the wolves to his side. "Check it out and call out for help if you need it. Tony, me, you, and the rest of us, we're going down this way." He motions to the door in front of him. "Each team has a runner." John looks at a young wolf in his pack with blond hair covering his body, his golden eyes glow for a moment as he nods. "When the area is clear, we'll send the runner with the update. No one needs to be a hero today. In and out!"

"In and out!" the rest of the pack calls back to him.

Adam nods at John and grabs his door handle. "Three, two, one…" He slowly opens the door and candlelight provides enough light for him to see into the room. "Got it, let's go!" One by one, they venture into the room and the sounds of steps begin to fade into the distance.

John turns toward his door and grabs the handle. "Right, ready?" Tony nods behind him.

Catherine pumps her shotgun. "I'll stand guard."

John nods at her and Tony stares at his wife for a moment. He growls, "I love you, woman."

"Hurry the hell back or I'm coming after you!" She grins at her husband and takes watch between the doors.

John turns the handle on the wooden door and it does not move. "Dammit, it's locked. Stand back," he orders and backs up. He inhales, and with a growl so loud the walls begin to shake lightly, he makes a run for the door and slams his shoulder into it, causing it to splinter. He pulls a fist back and slams it into the splintering area, forcing a hole through it.

"There's a light inside," he tells his pack. "And the smell of death." He steps back and kicks in the door enough to make a visible entrance. Kicking it once more, he forces his way through the opening. Immediately taking in his surroundings, John finds blood on the walls and a tub in the far corner and he freezes in place… not moving. "There's a fucking body hanging over the goddamned tub!"

Stepping farther inside the room, he finds devices of torture—ice picks, tooth pliers, and daggers of many kinds. He shakes his head and the sound of metal scraping the ground catches his attention.

"Oh hell, look at this!" Tony picks up a set of rusted chains lying on the floor. "There's fresh blood on them, John." He looks back at his Pack Master and holds the chains up in the air. "These are some sick pieces of shit."

"You think you know our kind?" Rene's voice echoes through the room. The pack turns toward her and a snarl erupts from each wolf. "You think you know *anything* about us?" She cackles and steps out of the shadows. Her hair pulled up on top of her head in a bun held with hairpins, she stalks forward with a sword in her hands. The hilt is ivory in color with silver on the ends.

John looks the sword over and his eyes widen slightly. "A silver sword? You really think that will stop us?"

"If I sever your head it will, mutt!"

He growls at the woman and makes his way toward her. "You are brave to take us on alone, Undead whore. Where is your maker? Where has he taken Amelia?"

She grins and licks her bottom lip. "What makes you think I'm alone, mutt? My maker is not here, obviously. As for Amelia, I'm positive he's either killed her, made her a vampire, or fucked her by now." She shrugs, "Possibly all three." She grins and stalks forward a few more steps.

"Ahh, hell, you shouldn't have said that, Undead whore," Tony tells her. "You see," he takes the flank on John's right, "Amelia means a great deal to us, more so than your lot. We need her back, and you'll give her to us willingly, or we'll just have to kill your Undead ass." He grins and bends his knees in a fighting stance, growling. "Your choice."

"I don't think I'm giving her a choice," John tells him. "I think I might just rip her head off right now." He steps forward and continues to watch Rene.

She looks between both werewolves then at the others standing behind John. "Well, Hawthorne, I didn't think I'd get the pleasure of killing you, taking out your family, *and* tasting Rachel and Amelia both. Hmm, call me lucky!" At the end of her words, she is across the room and raises her sword in the air, intent on killing John.

Suddenly, Tony dives toward her and wraps his arms around her waist. They tumble to the ground and he forces himself on top of her, sitting on her chest. He grabs her wrists and slams her hand into the floor until she drops her sword. She hisses up at the wolf holding her.

"What in the hell did you just say?" John is suddenly down on his knee and has a hand around her throat. "You took out all of my family, aided in killing Rachel... and did you say, *tasted* Amelia?" He squeezes harder when she does not talk.

"TALK, YOU WHORE!" He slams her head down on the ground and Rene yells out in pain.

"Fuck you, mutt!"

A howl erupts when a wolf is tossed into the wooden door on the other side of the room. John looks up, startled, and growls as more vampires enter the room. He mentally counts the numbers as they arrive. Adrenaline skyrockets through his veins and the growl begins to vibrate through his chest. "Go warn the others!" John orders the runner. "We need their help! GO!"

"Fuck, yes, you need help, mangy dog!" Rene kicks her legs and lands one against Tony, throwing him off her. John tightens his grip around Rene's neck as Tony grabs her legs, holding her down.

"You got her, John? Hell, they're closing in!"

"Go!" he orders. John looks down at Rene once more and moves a little closer. He positions himself, straddling her chest, and pins her arms with his knees. "You kick me; I'll break your damn legs!" He grabs her chin and forces her to look up at him. "Where the hell is she?"

"Why the hell should I tell you?"

"You tell me, I'll make your death quick." John snaps in her face with his snout. Rene visibly flinches and he grins to himself. "If you don't, then I'll make sure to draw out your torture until you're begging me for death." He leans in closer, almost touching her nose. "Even then, I'll prolong it."

A loud boom sounds and Rene quickly looks to her right. Tony lands next to John with a vampire on top of him. The vampire hisses and his fangs drip with saliva.

"KILL HIM!" Rene screams. The vampire leans in a little more. John looks between the two of them while pinning Rene to the floor.

Adam suddenly rushes into the room with the rest of the pack members. The vampires are now outnumbered easily, two to one.

Tony quickly grabs a dagger from his belt and plunges it into the side of the vampire. The distraction buys him just enough time to throw the Undead man off his body. "Not today!" he answers Rene. He quickly gets to his feet and turns on the vampire. "Sneaking up with a sucker punch is not the way to fight." He pulls out a vial of liquid sun Amelia had given him and grins. "This is the way to sucker punch someone!"

The vampire looks at Tony's hand, unaware of what he is holding until it is too late. Tony throws the solution at the Undead; his skin begins to burn and he screams in pain. The vampire visibly melts, where he stands, into a pile of ash, the dagger dropping to the floor with a clank.

"Now," John turns back to Rene, "where the HELL is she?"

Rene looks at the wooden door across the room then back at John. He grins then grabs hold of her head.

"You said you would make it quick!" she pleads with him.

"Oh, give up that easy, do you?" he taunts.

"Look around you! My clan is dead!" She makes an effort to weep. "Michel is my mate and my Master. If he comes back to this, he'll kill me himself!"

"Seriously?" Tony asks her. "That's barbaric as hell." He shakes his head and makes his way toward the wooden door.

"Good, you deserve nothing less," John tells her. He stands and lifts her body by her neck. Her feet barely graze the floor and her hands grip at John's. She scratches and flails in his grasp. "Say your goodbyes, Undead whore." Her eyes widen in panic as he makes his way across the room toward the weapons hanging on the wall. He slams her body into the daggers and Rene gasps and closes her eyes for a moment, then she presses her palms against the wall in an attempt to free herself.

John shakes his head and grips hers, then in one quick motion, breaks her neck. She falls lifeless underneath him.

"You're not killing her?" one of his pack members asks.

"Nope, you heard her," John turns to face his pack as Adam comes to his side. "Michel will do it for us."

"You alright?" Adam asks him.

John nods and dusts himself off. He points across the room to the shackles. "I guarantee you Amelia was in these."

"Fresh blood on'em," Tony offers.

"Any idea who's hanging over the tub there?" Adam motions to the hanging corpse.

"No idea," John offers, then turns to his runner again. "Work on getting whoever that is down. They deserve a proper burial." His runner nods and makes his way over to the tub.

A gunshot sounds upstairs along with a growl of laughter, breaking the eerie silence. "I love that woman," Tony offers.

"Right, well we need to get through the wooden door." John crosses the room to it and the claws at the end of his fingers roughly scratch down the door. "It's thicker than the other one. I doubt I can break it down with my body."

"Nothing this ax can't get through." Adam bounces the hilt of an ax in his palms.

"Excellent." John backs out of the way, as Adam takes a swing at the door.

***

"You really made this all too easy for me, Amelia," Michel begins. "It was so easy to come into your life, show you interest, and seduce you. Honestly, I could not have planned it better myself. Add Eva into the mix, she made it even that much faster for me to gain my prize. She wanted me, and in return for her help," he leans into my ear and whispers, "I fucked her while my Rene watched."

Michel chuckles to himself and withdraws from the bed. I can feel the mattress shift as his weight is removed. My eyes barely open as I watch him unbutton his shirt and pull it from his body. His hands move into his hair and push it back. He stares at himself in a mirror in the room, running his tongue over his teeth. I am positive he tastes the remnants of my blood on his teeth.

He lifts his wrist to his mouth and bites it. *Oh my god, he is going to feed me his blood.* I can't... I won't. My heart stammers in my chest and I am positive he can hear my pulse quicken.

Suddenly, a loud boom sounds from the other side of the door. I quickly look at it and watch as it shakes. Something hits it again and the door shakes once more.

"Dammit," Michel mutters to himself. He is back on the bed at such a speed I did not realize he had even moved until he is in my face.

Gasping quickly, I flinch backward. "No!"

"Aww," he grins down at me, "you're awake. Soon you'll be mine for eternity, Amelia." Michel forces his wrist against my mouth. "DRINK IT!"

I try to scream against his cold flesh but it comes out muffled. My eyes widen and I shake my head no. His blood begins to smear across my face. Michel grabs my nose and holds it in an effort to force my mouth open for a breath.

"Unfortunately, humans need to breathe air; the Undead do not." He smirks as he watches me.

I can feel my head becoming dizzy. I need to breathe but I cannot open my mouth for the chance of ingesting his blood. I blink slowly as he leans in closer... his lips just a breath's distance from my face. "Drink it, Amelia, and it will soon be over."

The door finally opens and these... what in the world are those? My eyes widen in a renewed fear at what is before us. Tall men with the head of a wolf, hands that appear like claws and bodies covered in hair...

Michel removes his arm and I quickly inhale oxygen. I sit up and wipe my arms across my face to remove his blood from my lips.

"Did you feed her your blood?" the closest man-beast growls. Michel looks at me then back at the man-beast. "Even with a small drop, she will turn." He smirks and backs up to the other side of the room. His hands move behind his back, as he appears to be searching for something, which he finds. A door opens from the wall and Michel quickly ducks out, speeding away.

"After him," the same man-beast calls. Three different beasts follow in step to find Michel.

Panic sets in as the beasts in the room turn their attention to me. The one speaking makes a few steps forward and I shake my head no. "Please! Don't hurt me!"

"Amelia," he growls.

"Who… who are you?" I try scooting as close as I can to the wall, hoping I will find an escape like Michel did.

"Amelia, it's me, John," the creature growls.

I gasp and stare at him for a moment. "John?" His golden eyes stare into mine and he slowly inches closer. "John?" My voice comes out as a whisper. He nods and steps even closer. He told me he was a werewolf. He told me there were other monsters in this world. Now he is here… in wolf form… for me.

"I'm not going to hurt you," he growls. "I promise; it is me. Need me to prove it?"

"Umm," I have no idea what to say. I glance at the others in the room, then land back on John. His body seems to move with his breaths. Blood is on his snout and hands. Suddenly, tears race down my cheeks and a sob fills the room. I do not realize it is me that is crying until I gasp for air.

"It is over, Amelia. We found you," this beast tells me.

"It really is you?" I ask.

He nods and steps closer until he's flush with the bed. He lowers himself to the mattress and slowly takes a seat. "We found your note, foolish woman."

Letting go, I can feel the adrenaline suddenly rush out of my body.

"Oh, I think she may pass out," one of the man-beasts in the room calls.

John is immediately in front of me. He scoops me into his arms as the room becomes darkness... just darkness.

***

"Make sure she's cleaned up," the familiar voice growls.

"Right away," a female returns.

I try to open my eyes. The room is a little dark, barely lit with candlelight. I glance toward the voice and see the man-beast that earlier claimed to be John.

The door to the room closes with a click of the handle. Small, tentative hands begin working on my clothes. I think she feels me flinch.

"Don't worry, Miss Rimos. I am an Alchemist, just like you. I am simply going to give you a bathing. You have been through quite a terror. Please try to relax. No one here will hurt you."

Her voice is soft and gentle. She reminds me of my mother with her tone. I look toward her and find she has dark hair, almost black. Her eyes are a sea of endless green and her skin is porcelain.

Someone scoops me in their arms and my body is carried toward the bathroom. I glance down at the tub and images of Eva come to mind.

"NO!" I scream, my body flinching. "You will not drain me!" My hands slap at the man holding me and someone grabs my arms.

"Miss Rimos," the Alchemist begins, "I promise, no harm will come to you. Please allow us to clean you."

Panic rises in my chest and I look between the man holding me and the woman consoling me. He is tall like John but bald with dark brown eyes. He scowls when I slap at him to let me go.

"Please, look down. There's only water with a touch of lavender to relax you, nothing more."

Tears slip down my cheeks as I shake my head. "They drained Eva over a tub... then did things in it! Horrible... horrific things!"

The woman's eyes widen in shock and she shakes her head. She closes her eyes and tries to contain her own emotions then she looks back at me. "I promise you are safe here with me. Please trust me, Amelia."

I close my eyes and swallow the lump in my throat. "Please, set me down," I ask the man.

"I do not wish for you to fall, Miss Rimos," he tells me.

"I will catch her," the woman tells him. "Set her down." He nods and slowly lowers me. My feet touch the cold floor and I work on keeping my balance. The woman reaches for me and I grasp her arms.

"I'm okay, leave us," I tell the man. "And thank you."

He nods and takes his leave, closing the door behind him.

"Help me in the tub," I ask the woman, "but please, do not leave me."

"I promise," she insists, "I will be right here. Sophie is just outside the door if you would like a familiar face with you." I nod a few times. "Sophie, please come inside," the woman calls.

"What should I call you?" I ask the woman as Sophie steps inside.

"Sarah, my name is Sarah."

"You're a sight for sore eyes," Sophie tells me. I want to smile, but I cannot. I want to tell her to be quiet, but nothing comes out. I simply stare at her and begin to cry again. She crosses the room and pulls me into a hug. "I have you, Amelia. I promise no one will hurt you. No one can get to you. You are safe here."

Chapter 19

Slowly, I come to my senses the next evening. I am resting against the soft comfort of a bed as my heavy eyes gaze upon the ceiling before they begin to wander the confines of the room. At first, I am unable to decipher where I am. Fear strikes me momentarily; the pain and fear I have experienced has altered my mind. It has altered my perception of reality. I fear I have hallucinated my rescue from the clutches of Michel and Rene's dungeon of torture.

"I can't be here; it isn't possible," I tell myself, my voice a hoarse whisper. The soreness from my nights of screaming returns. I turn my head to the side to study my surroundings.

The room appears to be the one I stayed in at John's home. The bed appears to be the same; even the smell of the fabric is familiar. The window allows in the sun of the setting evening and I can feel the heat of it against my skin. The warmth of the sun is something I briefly thought I would never feel again.

I close my eyes as I consider this for a moment. The torture replays over and over in my mind. Eva's screams, the blood-filled tub, being chained to the wall, Michel biting me and finally, being surrounded and saved by men and women that looked like large beasts all fight for top billing in my mind.

Swallowing a large lump in my throat, I half expect the fanged monsters to enter and further torture my broken mind and body. Eva sold me out to the vampires for her own, personal gain, and that resulted in her death. A part of me feels sorry for the way she died. The other part, the damaged part that seems to have lost reason thinks well, maybe she deserved what she got. I sigh and slowly shake my head.

"No, no one deserves a death like that."

I slowly pull my arms in front of me to look upon my wrists... my bruised and bloodied wrists. Wiping the tears from my eyes, I fear everything around me will melt away to reveal that I am still in the vampire's lair. My wrists are stiff and sore from the shackles. Pulling the covers off my body and slowly sitting up, my body is sore, but I am not as broken as I feared I would be. Glancing down at my ankles, I see similar bruising has appeared.

It takes a little bit for my new reality to settle in; I am truly here, in the protection and comfort of John's home. I am safe amongst those I call friends, my werewolf companions.

My eyes widen as visions of John's wolf form ricochet in my mind. I replay the images of him as he carried me away from Michel's clutches. He felt different; he looked different. He was… different. He was a beast… a wolf-like beast. His arms were stronger than when he was a human. When he held me close, his warmth engulfed me. John's strong chest was covered with hair and his hands were different… distorted into the claws of a beast as he carried me away. His eyes were a beautiful golden color, like that of a wolf.

I straighten myself from where I sit. Everything I have known has changed. We are no longer alone in the world with vampires. There are werewolves as well. Not that I did not believe John before, but actually witnessing it for myself makes everything more real.

For the first time since bathing, I realize I am no longer naked, nor am I stained with blood. I gasp and reach for my neck. The scars from Michel's bite have all but healed. The Alchemist, Sarah, having washed me clean the night before, must have treated the bite. The bite. *Oh no, did I ingest his blood? Did they force the cure down my throat? I bit Rene but I am positive I spat it from my lips.*

Panic rises briefly. If I ingested the cure

then I am fine, I will live, which is the goal for right now. Long-term effects... well, I will have to record what happens, I suppose.

Recalling bits and pieces with Sophie, I begged her to stay with me, having been too afraid and needing her familiar face. Sophie, above all others, and I am still amused inwardly by this. She has treated me as an equal, unlike the story Michel told me. The inferiority of human beings to vampires and werewolves does not seem to be true with her. Is it with John?

"One worry at a time, Amelia," I tell myself. I need to see John and the others. As I stand from the bed, I remove the night clothes, then glance through the clothes I have handy.

Deciding on a white, button down blouse, tan corset and brown skirt, I dress myself and pull on my boots. Setting my hair in a neat bun on the top of my head, I pin a small brown hat just in front of it.

Reaching for the door, I pause for a moment as my hand turns the knob. I am not quite sure what to expect on the other side. Praying to myself that I am not dreaming... and that Michel is not on the other side, I slowly inhale and exhale. I turn the knob and quickly swing it open. A hiss escapes through gritted teeth as moving so quickly twists the freshly scabbed wounds on my wrists.

Stepping out of the room I stand in the hallway, almost feeling lost. The stairs are just in front of me and I stare down at them, daring them to move. I have most likely lost my mind… completely. Taking in another deep breath, I take a few small steps toward the stairs, slowly descending toward the voices I hear talking. I hear their voices as the kitchen area comes into view. No one has seen me yet, for which I am grateful. I take a moment to listen before making my presence known.

Adam's voice, full of excitement, echoes through the kitchen. "Fucking vampires didn't see us coming. We got them real good. You should have seen John, too. Man had that dead bitch of a whore, Rene, pinned, squirming, and begging him to kill her Undead ass! She was afraid of her fanged bastard maker." Sophie's laughter echoes afterward, followed by several others. I'm not sure who Adam is retelling his story to, but I do not like hearing this retold again.

"Damn, I hate that I missed it. Did you bring me a souvenir of some kind?" someone's voice teases, "You know what? Never mind, the fact that y'all dusted a heaping number of them is more than enough for me." The male's voice laughs again and it is all I can do not to retch on the floor.

I look at the wolf pack gathered in the kitchen: John, Sophie, Adam, and Tony discussing last night's fight with so much passion, almost as if they were high from the aftermath of it all. I take in a deep breath and descend one more step and the floor creaks.

I quickly look at the others and Sophie stands, clearing her throat. "Amelia! My goodness, you're up early," is all she can manage to say. Her features shift from humor to concern, the first I have seen since we met.

Adam, Tony, and John immediately turn and face me, echoing the same concern. I am unable to decipher if it is for my wellbeing, or if it because of the trouble and torment I have caused their pack over the vampires.

John immediately rises to his feet and rushes to the stairs. His eyes capture mine and they are no longer that of a beast, but of his humanity. My eyes feel heavy with the tears threatening to spill. I had not expected to return to their headquarters, had not expected to be amongst my werewolf allies.

Inwardly, I begin to think if I can still call them my allies. Michel's mockery and hateful words of mingling with their own takes residence in my mind as I stand before the man who has saved my life... the man who I know, regardless of any possibilities, I am falling for.

John's gaze turns tormented, almost as if he feels pain... maybe for the torture I experienced or maybe, possibly, he also feels something for me.

The lump returns to my throat once more, emotions take hold, and my knees threaten to buckle. The tears I have been holding back spill from my eyes. "I can't... I can't... Please, I, I, I am so sorry. I am..." John takes me in his arms. He pulls me close and his arms surround me. His temperature is warm and I feel safe in his embrace.

"Shh, it's okay, Amelia. You're okay," he tells me. His cheek rests upon my head as I sob into his chest.

If it was not for him, I fear I would be in the fetal position, clutching what I have left of my life to my chest. He holds me close, whispering encouragement that I will get through this. His pack mates watch, witnessing my breakdown.

I lean into him and he turns to the side to guide me. We make our way to the back door and venture outside. The warmth of the Georgia evening and the fresh air does wonders for me. He leads me farther out back.

We walk upon the softness of the grass. The setting sun warms my back and I snuggle against John a little tighter. My world has been spinning out of control. He turns me to face him and his strong, warm hands lightly grip my upper arms. Looking into my eyes, he watches me for a moment. My lips tremble as I try to hold a brave face, and I know I will fail very soon.

His voice a whisper, "Amelia, it is okay. It is over now; you are safe. We will not let anything happen to you." His hands grip my upper arms a little tighter then he releases me. He moves his hands to my shoulders then gently cups my face. "I promise, I'm here and I won't leave you."

My lips tremble and I begin to falter. I grasp his hands and remove them from my face. I need a little space; I need to step away to break the comforts of his contact. "John, they, they killed her; they killed Eva. It was as if she was nothing but a piece of meat! She did not deserve that!"

My voice begins to rise. "Rene ripped out her throat and drained most of her blood. This was just before their servant hung her upside down by her feet, as a butcher would do to a cow. She hung over the tub, John! I can still hear her screaming in my head." I sob again, my words running together as I go on to describe the details of that monstrous night.

As I gaze across his property, I try to collect my thoughts and calm myself. I try to focus on something other than the past, but all the emotion I have held inside comes flooding out. "Before you saved me, Michel, he... he threatened to turn me into one of his, one of the Undead. He wanted to take me as his lover, his new progeny. He wanted to do away with Rene." I swallow hard. "He bit me just before you arrived. He was forcing his blood on my face and... and...” As I recount all of this, I feel nausea rise within the pit of my stomach.

John watches me intently, giving me the space I need. He remains quiet up until this point of the story. Turning me to face him again, "Amelia... did he make you drink from him?" he says as softly as he can, but his voice is a low growl. If he is holding back his anger throughout my melt down, he is doing a damn fine job.

I shake my head and take a few steps closer toward him, collecting myself. I need to take hold of my emotions, so I don't lose my mind to it all.

"No, I don't think so. Did Sarah mention anything to you?" He shook his head no. “She didn't mention giving me the cure?”

“No, she didn't. Should she have?”

"Only if she gave it to me, I suppose. I did bite Rene's fingers to free myself from her, but I spat anything out that may have resulted in doing so." My head leans to the side as I pull my coller away from my neck. Showing him the location Michel had bitten me on the left side of my neck, I tell him, "It's still stiff and hurts like hell. So do my wrists and ankles. They had me chained for the majority of the time." John leans in and his fingers gently move over the marks on my neck. His touch is soothing and I close my eyes. For a moment, I tell myself we are in a different situation and John is wooing me, rather than checking my bite marks.

I am jolted back to the present when he speaks. "He didn't go through with the transition then, and it looks like you'll heal in no time. You're lucky, very lucky."

My own relief a mirror image of his own, he clears his throat. I place my coller back over the bite mark and nod a few times. "I fought him hard." My eyes focus on his. "He tried to force his blood, but I wouldn't have it... I'd rather die and join my sister and my family, than be his fuck toy for eternity."

John's features distort with anger for a moment and his eyes flash golden before returning to normal. "Anyone would be better off dead than to be one of the filthy Undead."

I nod slowly in agreement, searching his eyes for some sort of answer to all this, maybe some sort of affection. *Oh, now's not the time*, I scold myself inwardly as my thoughts return to the subject at hand. Maybe I am still in shock even to consider this thought. I am definitely going mad.

"Dennis..." I whisper, recalling the day I left. "I caused his death. I asked him to take me back to my home to gather more belongings. He wanted to wait and run it past you, wait for you to escort us. I told him it was fine, that we should go, and I'd left a note." Lowering my gaze, a single tear slips down my cheek. I quickly wipe it away.

"I was inside packing. Michel and Rene, they were there waiting for me. They knew I would be there. Michel's lips... they were stained with blood, Dennis' blood. He was gloating about how they killed him." I cannot bear to look John in the eyes as I tell him what happened. "He was drained and died because of me."

My voice trails off, "I allowed my pride to get the best of me, after what had happened the night before I left. Rather than think logically, and wait for you, I took off. Had I not done so, none of this would have happened... and he'd still be alive."

John reaches for me then pulls away abruptly. I swallow hard, holding back the tears threatening to escape. I have come undone enough and I refuse to let my emotions overtake me again.

Michel was right; he does not want me. When this is all done and over with, he will send me away.

I feel guilty for thinking such a thing with the topic at hand. I am pathetic in the worst way.

With a serious undertone to his voice, John says, "No need to feel any such way, what's done is done. He made the decision to go; he could have said no, Amelia. He had no idea you would both be ambushed. There was no way of knowing any of this would happen." I look up at him and watch as his eyes scan the property. All I can manage is a slow nod. John turns back to me and catches my gaze. He seems to relax, and just as I think he's about to step closer toward me, Adam emerges from inside.

Clearing his throat, he says, "Sorry to interrupt, I have news." Adam becomes nervous as John look toward him, a low growl emitting from his chest. I tilt my head slightly as I watch him, curious what he was about to do, then finally look over at Adam.

"Alright, what the news, then? Don't just stand there." John narrows his gaze, impatience radiating from him. I know that the closer to nightfall, the more he will feel the pull of the moon. Is it aggression he feels toward his Beta or is it something more? I watch the two closely, listening with intent to the news Adam has to bring.

Adam nods submissively as he stands tall in a button-down shirt, the sleeves rolled up to his elbows, dark beige slacks, and the holsters, which hold his guns. "The Alchemists with the Undead are still working on the cure." His eyes rest upon me before returning to his pack leader. "So far, they've been unsuccessful. Each experiment has resulted in death."

John nods with a low growl. "Good, let's hope the sons of bitches keep coming up short." John turns his attention back to me.

I consider the attempts on the formula and my expression shifts from somber to alert. I look from John to Adam. "They won't be successful. I am the only one who knows how to mix the ingredients. It's," I pause for a moment, "tricky. I have my notes, but if they're working with Eva's copies they have the wrong ones." I inch closer to John, my voice rising in warning. "Making this cure and following the notes alone won't work." I lower my eyes, "He wants to turn the entire city into the Undead.

"He was just as you warned, even crazier than I ever would have imagined. I know this now, far too well." I recall his threats of killing me savagely, or worse… turning me into his progeny, his lover, and his slave. My expression contorts in discomfort as I remember Michel's words.

John immediately steps forward, his arms surrounding my petite frame. I am not quite sure what to make of this gesture. Regardless of whatever it is, I submit to his embrace.

Adam rolls his eyes, obviously disapproving of such affection as the seriousness of the situation arises. "Right, that's my cue. I'll," he mumbles, "just step back inside and get back to work." John flashes Adam a disapproving look, growling lowly. I can feel the vibrations from his chest and it brings a soft smile to my lips. Adam retreats into the house.

I melt into John's embrace, releasing a deep breath I feel I have been holding forever. His arms hold me close and I rest my hands upon his chest. He feels strong and comfort washes over me as I lay my head against him.

His voice is a comforting whisper, "You'll be staying here for the meantime. You'll be safe, and that son of a bitch won't lay a single fang on you ever again." He gently touches my chin and lifts my face up. His eyes narrow in seriously and he gazes down at me. Concern and affection touch his features, something he has fought showing before now. "This I promise you, Amelia."

I simply nod slowly, my gaze never faltering on his. We hold each other's gaze for a long moment. "I, I promise not to leave. Not after everything I caused, John." My eyes lower for a moment; "I'm still so sorry for causing all this."

He tilts my face up once again. John watches me for a moment then leans in and kisses me on my cheek, close to my lips. My heart begins to pound hard and I hope he is not able to hear it. "No more I'm sorry, Amelia," he whispers against my skin. His breath is light against my cheek. "Let's get you inside and get you dressed. I mean, I am all for the nightgown look. It is sexy. But for the rest of my pack, you need clothes." For the first time since this nightmare, a soft laugh leaves my lips. I nod in agreement.

"Alright, that sounds good." I continue to look into his eyes as the sun sets in the distance. I can almost see the shadow of the moon in his eyes, his wolf within, as the next night of the full moon draws closer.

I start to think he may lean in again as he

looks from my eyes to my lips, then back to my eyes again. Instead, he rests his forehead against my own. "Let's get inside."

***

On the outskirts of the forest, as his army of Undead clansmen begin surrounding John's home, Michel stands watching... waiting. A devious smirk plays upon his lips as he witnesses the affectionate embrace. "I see now, to get what I need, the bargaining chip is the woman. *My* woman." He slithers back into the forest again, mumbling to himself. "I'll taste her. She will be mine!"

Chapter 20

John closes the bedroom door behind him and stands there, staring at it. I take a seat on the bed, and for a moment, I am afraid to ask him what is wrong. I open my mouth to speak as he turns to face me.

"I thought I'd lost you." He takes a seat next to me and stares into my eyes. Reaching for my hand, his fingers gently move over the scars on my wrists.

"John," I begin softly, "I'm so sorry. I didn't mean…"

"Stop, please." He lowers his chin and it touches his chest. He inhales deeply then slowly exhales. "I thought you were lost, Amelia. I thought Michel would have changed you, or worse, killed you." John glances to the sidewall, now almost refusing to make eye contact.

"John," I try again and shift myself closer to him on the bed. "Like I said earlier, with everything that happened, I was confused. There is no excuse for my actions other than me being stubborn and allowing my pride to drive my emotions." I pull my hand free from his and adjust myself on the bed.

Pulling my legs up, I hug my knees to my chest. Laying my cheek on top, I look over at his still form. He is so strong, but at this moment, he appears completely vulnerable. I pray I am not misreading the signs in front of me.

Foul, savage beasts who stick to their own kind. They tend to stick within their pack. You and he can never be possible, Amelia. His pack, as well as himself, see you as beneath them. Michel's words return to the forefront of my mind and I lower my gaze to the comforter on the bed.

"You put us all in danger with that pride of yours, Amelia." John slowly lifts his gaze to mine. He sits a little taller on the bed and runs a hand down his face.

"I apologize, John. If I could take it all back, I would have never created this... cure. I hate what it has done to my life. I hate everything about it."

He tilts his head slightly and raises a single brow. "You hate everything that you've experienced since creating it?"

I nod and watch his expression for a moment. "Well, maybe not everything." I shrug and turn my head to rest my chin on my knees. "Sophie seems kind." I glance sideways at him with a grin.

"Just Sophie?" he shakes his head with a small smile.

"I'm glad I met you, John." I can feel a blush touch my cheeks, and to hide it, I look at the opposite wall. I close my eyes and can feel my heart almost break in my chest.

He will never want me. I do not know if I can ever sleep alone again without nightmares of Eva, Michel, and Rene. A tear slips from my eyes and lands on my knee. I sniff softly to myself.

"Amelia?" John asks, and gently touches my back.

"Yes?"

"Are you okay?" His voice is soft and comforting, very different from his wolf form not too long ago.

Lifting my head, I look over at him and shake it no. "No, I do not think I will be okay for a long time. But for now, I have to be." I shrug slightly and lift a brow. "I think a part of me is scared to fall asleep. I don't want to face my nightmares."

"Nothing will get you here, you know that."

I nod and shift on the bed to face him. "Yes, I do know that but I'm going to be honest: it is not enough. I need someone who will be there for me, John. I have no one left. My parents are both dead. My sister is gone. I'm alone." I look away to keep myself from losing it and crying. I sound so pathetic. My eyes burn from the tears that want to escape but squeezing my lids seems to keep them at bay. I wish he would hold me, tell me it will all be okay, and sleep next to me in my bed… or even on my floor… just something.

"Amelia," he says my name and it is almost a whisper. He touches my cheek and turns my face back to his. "Look at me."

Taking in a deep breath, I slowly exhale and meet his gaze.

"There's something you need to know, something I think you need to hear from me. I hope you understand…"

I cut him off. "I think I know what this something is. Michel told me you do not mate outside your pack so please; you do not need to give me the speech. I just need you to be patient with me while…"

This time he cuts me off. "He did what?" His eyes change from patient and kind to anger filled sadness. "What did he say, exactly?" he growls out.

I swallow and look in his eyes. "He had me pinned against the wall when he said this, so bear with me. The memories are a bit fuzzy." I am lying. I know it. He knows it. I remember everything about what happened. A part of me just wants to forget.

He nods. "Go ahead."

I lower my gaze and shrug slightly, raising a single brow. "I don't even know why this is important now, but he said your kind… you do not mate with anyone who is not a werewolf. He said your kind felt everyone else was beneath them."

"Do you believe that?" he asks.

"I'm not sure what to believe. We have never really talked about it. Plus," I look into his eyes and see he looks almost hurt, "I never considered us going any further than where we are now. I think you made that pretty clear the other night after the pub."

"You were drunk, Amelia."

"And you kissed me. You wanted me as much as I wanted you and you left." I shake my head and stand up. Crossing the room to the window, I look outside. The trees blow gently with the breeze and my eyes are burning again from unshed tears. *Damn these eyes of mine.*

Warmth touches my back and strong hands move up my arms to my shoulders. He steps closer and his chest brushes against my back. "I kissed you because I wanted to. I wanted to do more, but I would never take advantage of you that way." He leans in and his lips are close to my ear. His breath fans across my skin and it takes everything inside me not to shudder. "I want to kiss you again."

My breath catches in my throat and I close my eyes. I pray I am not dreaming. I pray this is happening. I reach up behind me and touch his cheek. The growth of facial hair touches my palm and I visibly sigh. "I want you to kiss me." All the torture, the death... everything I have been through, I need this distraction; I need John.

John slips a hand around my waist and pulls me closer to him. His fingers splay across my stomach and I lay my head back on his shoulder. His other hand gently takes my chin and tilts my head to the side. He kisses a soft line along my neck and the scruff of his facial hair tickles my skin. My breath exhales in a rush.

"You've awoken a side of me that has been dormant for a long time, Amelia. I want you." He nibbles gently on my ear. "I want you, no one else."

"John," I whisper his name and he turns me to face him. His fingers gently move down both sides of my cheeks and he tilts my head up. Looking into his eyes, longing and need stare back at me. He closes the distance and gently captures my lips. We hold this for a second then he presses his forehead to mine.

My lips part and I cannot take this any longer. I wrap a hand quickly around the back of his neck and pull him down to me. Our lips crash into one another's in a hungry kiss filled with need.

He pushes me against the wall and leans into my body. His hands move to my back then slip down over my derriere. He lifts one of my legs around his waist and presses into me. I gasp and my arms tighten around his neck. "I need you," I whisper to him.

He lifts me and my other leg wraps around his body. John carries me back toward the bed and lays us down on our sides, facing each other. He cups my face and continues to kiss me. "There's another full moon tonight," he mumbles against my lips. "I can't do this, not now."

"What?" I pull back and look in his eyes. "Are you afraid of losing yourself to me?" My voice comes out slightly concerned.

His eyes stare into mine and they are very serious. "Yes, I am."

"Oh," is all I can whisper. "I had no idea..."

He shakes his head. "I just need you to understand what you would be getting into with me, Amelia. Life with a werewolf is not easy."

I blink and I am almost speechless... almost except for the obvious question I need to ask. "Do you accept... umm... lovers outside of your pack?" I know my skin is blushing, but right now, I do not care.

"Typically, no, unless there's a damn good reason."

His fingers gently glide over my temples and he pulls my hair behind my ears. "What would be the exception?"

"We can't help who we fall in love with." He grins and softly kisses my lips. My heart flutters at the words he has spoken. "As Pack Master, it is usually me who makes these decisions. However, here it may be up to Adam."

My heart suddenly drops and I shake my head. "I don't think Adam cares much for me."

"Adam will accept you. If he didn't, he would not have gone in willingly to find you."

"But you're like his boss, right?" He nods. "If you give an order, he must obey."

"That's correct."

"So did you force him into this situation?"

He shakes his head. "No, I did not."

"Are you sure about that?" I sit up and look down at John. "I don't want any animosity among your pack."

"Don't worry about that." He reaches up and pulls me back down to him. His hand moves over my waist, and gripping my side gently, he pushes me on my back and moves on top of me. My hands move up his biceps, biceps as wide as my palms. My breath comes out in a rush and my stomach flutters. He kisses me and his tongue slips across my lips, opening them. His tongue wrestles for dominance with mine and I allow him to win. I am like putty in his hands. I would conform to any mold, any shape he needs.

John moves his hand down my hips to my leg then pulls it up around his waist. He presses into me and I gasp, feeling his erection rub against me. His lips kiss along my jawline then to my ear. "I need you," he gruffly whispers.

I whimper softly and my fingers pull at the shirt on his back. Wanting to rip it off his body, I need to feel his skin against mine. I need him.

"JOHN!"

Suddenly, Adam's voice sounds from the staircase. Steps sound as they climb the stairs in a rush.

He pulls himself away from me, but not before whispering, "This is not over." He grins and kisses me again, then rises from the bed. He adjusts his crotch and I cannot help the smile I am wearing.

The door opens and hits the wall behind it with an abrupt force. Adam's face is full of fear and rage. He is seething as he looks between John and me. For a moment, I am scared he is pissed, knowing John has been kissing me, picking me as his mate. Then I second-guess myself, knowing there is no way Adam would actually be this visibly upset with his Pack Master. Why would this even matter to him?

"What the hell, Adam? What's wrong?" John glares at his Beta then furrows his brows. "What is it? I can sense your fear. What's happened?"

"They're here, John! They are fucking here! They're here for *her*!" Adam points to me and keeps his eyes on John. "They've surrounded the house. Michel is leading them and they plan to attack."

"Then let them bring it!" John roars his words and his body shakes slightly as do the walls in the room.

"John? What can I do?" I want to kill Michel. I want to end his Undead life. I want vengeance for my sister.

"Nothing," he says to me. "You'll stay here. I cannot chance you being caught, Michel getting his hands on you, or worse, dying. Understand?"

"But I can help!"

"NO!" he roars at me and I cower slightly. He lowers his gaze and shakes his head. "I'm sorry, I need you here." He walks over to the bed and takes a seat. Taking my hand in his, he lifts it to his lips, and kisses it. "I need you safe," he whispers.

I nod and keep my eyes on his. "Okay."

He nods and begins to stand. Adam clears his throat, watching us.

"Take the liquid sun with you." Getting up from the bed, I cross the room for my bag. I pull out a few vials and hand them over to John. "The guns I provided, do they still have the UV bullets?"

Adam nods and steps further into the room. "They were great when we swarmed Michel's coven. Catherine enjoyed them the most."

I nod and lower my gaze. Just the mention of Michel's name causes me to shake. "Right. Leave me the bow. I can shoot one pretty well."

"Let's hope you won't need it," John tells me. He makes his way toward Adam and claps his shoulder a few times. "Let's do this."

Adam nods and keeps his eyes on me. "Stay hidden. Just in case." I nod a few times. Adam turns to leave, then hesitates at the door. "We'll talk soon about whatever is going on between you and John." I do not say anything. Adam closes the door behind him and it is quiet.

I grab my bag and head back to the bed and empty the contents—one vial of liquid sun, a dagger, and one vial of the cure. I want to snarl looking at it. I want to smash it on the ground. I want more than anything to turn the clock back and meet John under different circumstances.

Instead, I sigh and look out the window. The sky is just past nightfall and a growl fills the air, then another, and another. A few howls sound in the house along with a yelp that sounds like a dog scream.

"Holy shit, what is that?" I want to rush to my door but I am afraid to look at what may be on the other side.

Then it begins. Screams sound outside as snarls erupt in unison. I rush to the window and look out. Man-beasts are in the yard fighting what look to be humans... but they are not. They are the Undead.

I cannot help but look for Michel and Rene. There are so many out there. The numbers are not good in John's favor; it seems they are fighting two to one. Suddenly, an explosion occurs. Five vampires turn into dust and a beast howls into the air.

Amelia... My name is whispered. It is Michel's voice. I hear him, but cannot see him. *Amelia...* Scanning the grounds, I want to find him; I want to know where he is, knowing he cannot get to me. I cannot handle him again, not right now. *See me...* My gaze hazes over for a moment and I see him.

Dressed in a black long-sleeve shirt and pants, Michel is wearing a top hat and carrying a cane. Coming to a fight dressed up makes him look like a damned fool and very arrogant. He reaches up and pulls something from the side of the hat and it looks like a round saw blade. Breaking eye contact with me, he throws the blade. It lands in the side of a wolf, causing him to howl in pain. The beast drops to his knees and begins pulling at the weapon. Another vampire takes advantage of the downed beast and tackles him.

I am coming for you, he whispers in my mind. *You will be mine.*

I gasp when he suddenly disappears.

Suddenly, my door is thrown open, and turning around, I scream.

"Michel! Oh God, please, no! Leave me alone!"

"You will be mine, Amelia! All you need is a drop." He closes the door behind him and stalks toward me. "Willingly or forcefully, you *will* be mine. You will do what I need. You will help me in this venture!"

I scream as loud as I can. "JOHN!"

My back hits the wall when Michel's hand surrounds my throat. He presses hard against me and his breath fills my nose. The stench of death floats around my head and I want to vomit.

"Where is it, Amelia? Where is your cure? You have it still, don't you?" He leans in closer and his tongue touches my cheek. "Help me change it. Make it what I need so we can populate the world together."

"Get off of me!" I try to push against him but he is too strong. His body is like a wall and I cannot penetrate it. "I will never help you!"

"Oh, love, you should never say never." He gives a sadistic grin. "You will once I change you. You will do exactly as I need. Mmm," his nose rubs against my neck then he licks against the vein in my throat. "I can almost taste you on my tongue, and I don't mean your blood."

Fear escalates inside my body and a sob escapes. "Please, Michel, don't make me do this!"

"Oh, love, I find it only fitting it was your kind who created us. How poetic it would be to have our kind rid the world of humans. Of course, that would be the downfall of the wolves as well."

"You cannot destroy the wolves of the world. They are here because your kind is here. They will always be in existence." I push against his body again. Michel slams me back against the wall. "Please," I beg of him.

"If you leave me no choice, it will be your own doing, Amelia. This decision is yours."

"GET THE FUCK OFF HER!" John's voice growls into the bedroom, and suddenly, he snatches Michel off me. He slams the vampire into the wall then snarls at him. Michel's eyes widen in fear and he turns away from the sharp fangs in his face.

I quickly jump across the bed and the contents fall to the floor. Michel quickly finds the cure as it rolls to a stop. He grins and makes eye contact with John. "Do you wish to die, mutt?"

"You will not kill me, you blood leach!"

Michel lands a blow that causes John to bend over, gasping for his breath. Michel quickly speeds across the room and grabs the cure. I scream when his hands grab at my body, pulling me to him. He yanks my head to the side and snarls. "I'll kill her if you don't back off, Hawthorne!"

John stands tall and watches us for a moment. His eyes glow their golden color as he steps closer. "Go ahead."

"What?" I whisper. *Did I hear him right? Did he just tell Michel to end my life?*

"Don't act like you don't care, Hawthorne. You reek of her!" Michel pulls my hair again and I whimper from the pain.

"I don't care if you kill the girl. Do it." He crosses his arms across his chest and raises a brow. "Without her, you can't take over the human population. You need her for it."

Michel snarls and suddenly there is pain in my throat. Michel has bit me… again.

"NO!" John screams out.

The next few moments happen so fast, it is almost a blur. John knocks me out of Michel's arms. His arms wrap around Michel's waist and he takes him to the floor. My side hits hard and I knock my head against the wall. Black dots blur my vision as I watch the vampire and werewolf fight.

Michel drops the cure and it rolls across the floor to a stop a few feet from me. Rolling to my stomach, I stare at it for a moment. Warm liquid touches my hands when I look down; I realize it is my neck, bleeding from Michel's bite.

The two men snarl and fight one another. Punches land, snarls erupt, and a few hisses fill the air. I begin to crawl across the floor toward the vial. The needle inside it is ready; all I need to do is push it into Michel's flesh and empty the solution into his body.

"John," I whisper in a hoarse voice, "pin him down."

"I'm trying," he growls. A loud crack sounds and Michel yells out in pain. John shakes his hand out and I realize he must have punched Michel... hard. He grabs the vampire's throat and squeezes. "I've wanted to end you for a very long time. Now I get to do that."

"Hardly," Michel huffs. "You think you can beat me? You think you can best me? Without my kind you wouldn't be in existence!"

"That may be true," John begins and he brings Michel closer, "but we have nothing to lose if you're gone from this world; dead *or* human."

Quickly, I jab the needle into Michel's leg and empty the entire syringe. He screams and kicks at my side, sending me across the room. Pain erupts in my chest from the blow and my back stings at landing against the wall. With the fresh wound on my neck, I feel myself falling into blackness once again. The last words I hear are John's, "Shit! Amelia! Stay with me!"

Chapter 21

Inhaling deeply, I look myself over in the mirror. Six months have passed since Michel bit me. Six months have passed since the fight took place between vampire and werewolf. Six months have passed and we have not heard any rumblings from the vampires. A part of me wonders if it is because they lost their King, and the other part is curious if they are torn as what to do: move forward with his plan for domination or take it easy for a while and enjoy their immortality. My hope is definitely the latter.

As with anything, only time will tell. I glance up at my clock to check the time. "Seven PM. John should be here soon." I grin to myself, feeling the flutter of butterflies in my stomach. Thoughts of Adam accepting me in their pack tease my mind briefly.

"I want her, Adam," John told him. His words made me smile.

"But she is not a wolf by nature," Adam replied. "How can she be your mate? She may not carry on the gene if you have children together."

"Jesus, we're talking about taking on a mate, right? Not children!"

My eyes widened at these words. Children are not a subject I was ready to talk about quiet yet. I casually looked over at John and I caught him glancing at me. I can see he did not consider this, either.

"How often have the pack mated outside of the pack?" I bravely asked.

"Not often," Adam growled in a low response.

John snarled at him as I continued. "But it has happened, correct?"

Adam nodded, "Yes."

"They were able to bear children, too. Not that it is of importance to us right now," John offered.

Adam shook his head. Sophie casually strolled over to her Beta and slipped her hands on his shoulders. She whispered something in his ear and he turned to look at her. He nodded and she smiled. Adam turned back to John and me.

"She's more than proven herself worthy of our pack," Adam began and I felt myself gasp, holding my breath. "There are a few things you need to consider, though. Once you are pack, you are pack for life. There is no breaking up because it did not work out. This is a life changing decision you need to consider, Amelia. Not one to take lightly."

I nodded and glanced at John. "I understand what I would be getting into." John pulled me close to him and kissed my cheek. "He's worth it."

Adam cleared his throat. "Right. I don't necessarily agree with it and it's nothing personal against you, Amelia; however, if you truly feel you two are meant to be, then I approve."

John chuckled. "I appreciate it, brother." Adam nodded then left us, taking Sophie and the other pack members with him. "So you're mine, now," John said as he stared into my eyes.

My body temperature flew up a few degrees and I felt my face become hot, my heartbeat pick up, and my stomach flutter all at the same time. I swallowed hard and nodded.

He took my hand in his and led me from the den, up toward his bedroom. Once he closed the door behind him, he raised his brows. "Are you sure about this?"

"Y-yes," I offered. "This is so formal, so… I don't know."

He chuckled. "You'll become accustomed to it soon enough. There is one more piece in becoming part of this pack, Amelia. It's something that will not be pleasant."

I knew there was something to rain down on my excitement. I sighed and nodded a few times. "Okay, whatever it is I can handle it."

He raised a single brow and smirked. "I have to mark you as my own."

My mind began mewling over thoughts of how a wolf, or man, would mark a human. Would he rub his face or body against my own? Oh hell, I can handle that. This thought made me grin. Then I recalled memories of when my father would tell me about dogs marking their territory. Horror ran through my mind at the thought of him actually peeing on me.

Then in some tribes around the world, tattoos are inked on skin. I think I can handle a tattoo… hell, I healed from a vampire bite; I can definitely heal from a tattoo.

"You just went from a sexy look to something horrid. What gives?" he asked me.

My gaze dropped to the floor and I chewed on my lip for a moment. "How do you, umm, go about marking me?" I slowly raised my eyes to his.

He brushed the hair from my face then cupped my cheeks. John kissed me for a moment and the gentleness of his lips took away any fear I had before. "I would bite you. My essence would embed itself into your skin and you would carry my mark."

"You... you bite me?" I asked, almost breathless. He nodded. My lips opened to say something but only a squeak came out.

He chuckled. "Don't worry, I won't tell you when it'll happen. I'll... surprise you so you won't expect it." He leaned in and pulled me close, nuzzling in my hair. His lips kissed against my neck, over the scar left from Michel. "Any wolf in our pack or any other would pick up my scent on you. They would know you're spoken for."

"What..." I gasped softly at his lips on my neck, the way he made me feel was almost like a current running through my body. "What about you? Will others know you're spoken for?"

He chuckled and nibbled on my ear. "Yes, without a doubt."

I swallowed hard again when I considered my next question. His hands moved down my back, over my derriere. My fingers dug into his strong biceps for support. My goodness was he big. "This is a forever kind of notion, right?" He nodded and tilted my head further back as he kissed down my shoulder to my cleavage. "Oh god," I whispered.

He chuckled and briefly buried his face between my breasts. My fingers moved to his hair in an effort to pull him even closer. "What is it you wish to ask, Amelia?"

The man sees right through me. I could not help the grin I wore. "Is this like a marriage of sorts?"

John pulled away and stood straight. Oh no, I asked the wrong question. His face was serious and he wore almost like a frown. "Do you wish to get married?"

I blinked, not sure what to say to this. "Maybe not right now." I looked at the ground and felt shame cover my face. "I mean, I just thought…"

"Amelia?" he asked. I sighed and looked up to see him smile. "Yes, it is like marriage."

My eyes widened and I gasped. "Were you teasing me?" He chuckled and I slapped his arm. "Not nice, John!" He laughed harder then pulled me close again.

"You and me, Amelia, no one else. I have fallen in love with you. I need you by my side. No one else has affected me the way you have."

I think my eyes watered because my vision became a little blurry. I sniffed then nodded. "I have fallen for you as well. You have been there for me and I cannot think of another man who would do the things you have done for me. I mean, aside from the shifting, of course."

He grinned at this. "Of course." He winked then pulled me closer toward him. His fingers gently glided down my cheek then he cupped my face. "You're beautiful in so many ways." My heart melted and he kissed me.

We had not had sex prior to that point and the mere thought of it made my nether regions quite damp. I was ready for him and it seemed he was ready for me, if the erection in his pants was any indication.

John turned me around and began loosening my corset. Inhaling sharply once it was released, his hands moved around my body and he grasped my breasts. He pulled me to him and pressed my back against his solid chest. His lips kissed along my neck, almost as if he were devouring me.

I gasped as he moved a hand to my chin. He pulled my neck up and over as he exposed more of my skin. He growled softly in my ear, "Mine!" John turned me to face him and his fingers began working on my skirt. It fell to the floor in a heap and I was left standing in my garter and stockings.

He looked down at my body and growled again. "Damn, you are sexy as hell."

I smiled at this and allowed my hands to move over my breasts, down my stomach. "You like what you see?" I backed up to the bed until I felt it against my legs. I sat down and scooted back. I raised a single brow then pulled my legs apart, setting my feet up on the bed.

"What the hell are you doing to me, woman?" John asked fiercely. He grabbed his shirt and began pulling at it, not caring if the fabric ripped. My god it was hot. He pulled the sleeves off his arms and tossed the material to the ground. Kicking off his shoes, he removed his pants and underwear. John stood in front of me like a God… perfectly sculpted from his shoulders to his calves. The man was like nothing I had ever seen.

My eyes widened at the size of his cock. My brows rose and I looked up at him to see humor had taken over his features. "Don't worry, I promise I won't hurt you."

"I certainly hope not," I told him.

John grabbed my legs and pulled me to the edge of the bed. I gasped and quickly grabbed his arms. His muscles contracted at my touch. "Lie back," he ordered.

I propped myself up on my elbows and bit my lower lip in anticipation. His eyes roamed down my body, and when he stopped between my legs, he licked his lips. A shudder ran through my body at what was to come.

He lowered himself to his knees, his hands grasped under my thighs, and he pulled me even closer to the edge. I could feel his breath against my inner thighs, his hair barely tickling the insides of them. He leaned in closer until his nose touched my pussy. He inhaled and moved upward, the touch sent a shiver throughout my body.

"Damn, you smell good," he told me. Fingers lightly touched me as they massaged against my skin. He pushed my folds together, causing a friction against my clit. I gasped quickly and his eyes shot up to mine. "Did I hurt you?"

Did he hurt me? Oh, dear lord, no. "Not at all. I wasn't expecting the sensation…" He did it again and I gasped then closed my eyes.

A single digit slid inside me and he curled it, teasing it against my walls. I lay down completely, submitting to the pleasure he intended to give me. He motioned his finger in a 'come here' fashion, which caused a moan to escape my lips.

"You like that?" he whispered in a gruff voice.

"Yes," I answered.

He pulled his finger free, then using both hands; he pushed my lips apart, exposing everything to him. He sighed and his breath was warm against the wetness that seeped from my core.

Suddenly, his face was against my body and he sucked my clit into his mouth. My back arched and a moan filled the room.

"Amelia, you ready?" John's voice calls from downstairs, bringing me from my daydream fantasy. My stomach flips a few times in delight at this memory. After running my hands down my dark violet skirt, I catch a glimpse of myself in the mirror. My violet corset is in place with my shoulder jacket and hair set with a few hairpins. Placing a little bit of rouge on my lips, I sigh, looking at myself, and smile.

"Coming," I call back.

Swiftly making my way down the stairs, John is at the bottom, his back facing me. Taking him in, I see his black suit and top hat look divine on his body. I want him to turn and face me so I can get a good look at him and allow him to see me in my new garments. I am hoping he does not shred these to pieces later.

As if hearing my thoughts, John turns and glances up the stairs. His white button-down shirt and black tie make him look damn good tonight. He is a stunning man, even more so naked. Damn, I cannot wait to come back home.

He takes a few steps up and meets me halfway from the bottom. "You look amazing tonight, Amelia." He leans in and inhales, his eyes dropping to my bust line. He growls softly then looks back at my eyes with a smirk. "I want to bury myself inside you."

I inhale sharply at his words and I smile. "Then let's hurry up and go so we can get back that much faster."

Inside the carriage, John cannot not keep his hands off me. I have no complaints. We come to a stop in front of the theater, and upon looking out the window, I smile when I see what is playing.

"*The Countess and Her Sheep*. I'm looking forward to this." I turn back to face John and lean into him. "Thank you for tonight. I've not been able to frequent the theater as often as I would like."

"You're welcome." He kisses me softly, and as our carriage door opens, he holds me for a moment. "I would rather take you home," he chuckles against my lips.

"Soon enough. Just keep that thought on hold for a little while longer." I wink at him then allow the driver to assist me to the ground.

We take our seats, and halfway through the play, his fingers begin to play with my ear lobes.

"What are you doing?" I whisper to him.

"Making you remember what you're in for when we get home."

I playfully glare at him and he winks.

When the play finally ends, John is the first to applaud and rise to his feet. I laugh softly to myself and stand next to him, offering a few claps of my own.

As we take our leave, there is a slight chill in the air. Fall has arrived and soon winter will be here, the holidays, and Christmas. Sadness plagues me for a moment as I think about Rachel. She will not be here with me to celebrate; I will be alone for the first time in my life.

"What's wrong?" John asks solemnly. "Are you okay?"

I smile and offer a nod. "I'm fine. I was thinking of my sister and the holidays. I will be alone for the first time." Lowering my gaze, hoping I do not sound pitiful to the man I love.

"You're not alone, nor will you be ever again." He lightly touches my chin to lift my head. He gazes into my eyes and smiles. "I promise."

I nod and close my eyes, willing the tears away. I want to cry for Rachel because I never got to say goodbye. I also want to cry for happiness with the love I have found with John. Instead, I let go of a long sigh. "I know, thank you."

"Are you ready to go home?" he asks. His hands move to my arms as he moves them up and down, his attempt at keeping me warm, I think.

"Yes, I'm ready." Stepping closer into his embrace, my cheek presses against his chest. I can hear his heart beating against my ear. I slip my arms underneath the warmth of his coat and his arms wrap around my body. I am at home here, at peace. I love the feeling John brings me when I start feeling anxiety take hold.

We have both been through so much, and in the end, we found each other because of it. John became my knight in shining armor through this ordeal. I cannot imagine spending a single moment without him.

***

Closing the door to our bedroom, I begin pulling the pins from my hair. Large drop curls hang down my back and I run my fingers through them, enjoying the freedom of having my hair down.

"John?"

"Yes," he answers from our bathroom.

"Will I grow old with you? Do you age as a werewolf? How does this work?"

"Well? Once you become my mate, you will change, somewhat. Not a lot, I mean, you will not shift into any kind of form, but you'll take on our life expectancy."

"Which is?" I ask.

"As long as I'm alive, you'll remain alive by my side."

"Oh, wow, okay. Will we age together through the years? Do we remain youthful? I'm sorry, I know these questions are silly, but honestly, I'm curious." I remove my corset and set it on the dresser then step out of my skirts. Unclasping my garter, I slide my stockings down my legs. Walking toward the bed, the cool air sends goose bumps over my naked body. Sliding into our bed, the sheets are cold against my skin.

"It's okay to ask." John finally ventures from the bathroom and I sit up to take in the sight of him. He is so tall; I believe close to six foot five is what he told me. His eyes are dark and lustful. His facial hair has grown a little since this morning; it is absolutely sexy. His broad chest and strong arms flex slightly. The rivets along his stomach invite my tongue to explore.

When I finally meet his eyes again, there is an amused expression on his face. I clear my throat and I know my cheeks are pink. "Like what you see?" he asks.

"Obviously," I retort. "Come to bed. I miss you."

He growls and suddenly jumps on the bed. I laugh and squeal when he makes a dive for my neck, kissing along my skin. He pulls back and smiles at me, then leans in, capturing my lips.

John pushes the covers away and I realize I am no longer cold. This man makes me warm in the right places. He pushes a knee between my legs and adjusts his body weight so to not crush me. His cock rubs longingly against me, causing me to whimper, and then nibble on his bottom lip.

"We will age together, but at a slower progression. When others your age turn sixty you may still appear to be twenty." John moves his lips to my jawline, then to my neck. "Our lifespan works differently. We're not immortal since we do age."

"As long as I am able to spend my life with you that is all I need."

He suddenly pushes inside me and I gasp, tilting my head back. He kisses up my neck and pulls back enough to thrust forward, completely filling me.

"Oh my god," I whisper. My arms wrap underneath his and I hold on to him. I match his rhythm as he continues to thrust against my body. My head tilts back again and my back arches. "Harder," I tell him.

He growls and sits up on his knees. Grabbing my hips, he pulls my body up to his waist. Driving himself inside of me hard and fast, I reach up and grab the headboard for support; my moaning begins shifting into a yell.

John grins down at my body. "Fuck, you feel good, woman!" He growls once more then begins to slow down. Releasing my body, he lays me back. I pant for a moment to catch my breath.

I feel him pull out of me and I look at him, confused. "Are you okay?"

He nods with a smirk. "You bet I am. Now relax, I'm going to make you come quite a few times tonight before I'm done."

"Oh shit," is all I can manage to say. He chuckles then kisses me. Quickly moving to my breasts, he sucks a taut nipple between his teeth. I gasp when he nibbles, his hand squeezing the other breast. He switches sides and does the same to the other nipple.

My hands move through his hair and I give it a tug. He glances up at me and I whimper softly, "I need you."

"Be patient, woman," he tells me with a playful glare. He bites my nipple again while watching me. This is the most erotic thing I have ever witnessed.

John moves from my breasts and kisses along my abdomen. His tongue licks the line down my stomach that leads to my navel. My body shudders at this sensation and my pussy grows that much more wet.

He reaches between my legs and his fingers begin massaging my clit. My body bucks suddenly at the pleasant sensation. "Oh shit, John... oh god!" My body suddenly explodes as the orgasm rips through my body.

"Mmm... first of many, I hope." He moves down my body while his fingers continue their assault.

Grasping the sheets, I fist them in my hands. I am afraid I will rip them here in a moment. Suddenly, his mouth replaces his fingers. He sucks my clit between his lips and rolls his tongue across it, thrashing it.

"Oh my GOD!" My hips buck hard and my fingers dive into his hair. I pull him harder against me, not wanting to let him go. "Fuck, John!"

I can feel the buildup of another orgasm as he continues to lick me. My body begins to tremble as I come again. "John! Please, stop for a... oh god! Please!"

He growls against my lips and it is all I can do not to rip his hair out. My hips begin grinding against his face. Growling louder as I continue to ride out my orgasm, he removes his mouth from my body as the aftershocks of my orgasm continue to pulsate through my body.

John growls louder, and suddenly, a pain rips through my right leg. I scream, and when I look down, he has bitten my thigh. He releases it, and when he looks at me, his eyes are glowing their golden color. Blood seeps from the wound and the pain is just a gentle throb.

Moving up my body, John growls as he brings his face closer to mine. There is nothing scary or menacing about him at this moment; the man is absolutely beautiful. "You are MINE!" he growls again as he shoves his cock inside me with a hard thrust.

I gasp and my lips part. He thrusts hard, much harder than before, and I grasp the headboard for support. "You marked me?" I ask in a shuddered breath.

"Yes," he tells me in a lower octave. With each word he speaks, he thrusts hard. "You. Are. Mine! Mine, Amelia!" He growls and it sounds like a snarl. If I did not know this side of him, this sound would scare the hell out of me. At this moment, though, right now, I feel protected and safe.

His face moves to my neck and he kisses my throat. "I love you," he tells me in a gruff voice.

"I love you, too."

Epilogue

Adam returns from a hunt with a few deer in the back of the carriage. Sophie and I make our way outside to help with the cleaning of the carcasses. The kitchen help beats us to it and the chef shoos us away.

Since some of us do not shift to kill our meat, it has become necessary to bring food back to the home for preparation. We also find we enjoy cooking together as a family: John, Adam, Sophie, and me.

Sophie and I have become close friends, almost like sisters. She knows she could never replace Rachel, but she has come close.

Christmas is a few weeks away. She has been teasing me that John will ask me to marry him.

"Well, I'm his and I'm marked. It's not like I'm going anywhere," I tease her.

"I know, but it would be so romantic to have a wedding here at the plantation." Sophie appears a little dreamy-eyed. I glance over at Adam and he shakes his head with a chuckle.

As time moves forward, Adam has softened some around me. He seems kinder… in a tough, asshole kind of way. He treats me more like a little sister rather than an equal. I suppose that in his eyes I will never be an equal since I am not a wolf.

From behind, John's arms wrap around my waist and he kisses my neck. "You hungry?"

"For you," I whisper back. He growls in my neck and I grin. "Adam just returned from a hunt. We can clean the deer and…"

He cuts me off. "No, we have the kitchen help to do that. I want you to come join me in the basement for a bit." He turns me to face him. "Are you up for this?"

I inhale and slowly let it go. I knew I would need to do this at some point. "Might as well get on with it," I tell him.

He nods and we make our way back into the house. He closes the back door then turns to me. "If you're not ready for this, I can go it alone."

"No, I'll be fine. I need to do this for research purposes, anyway."

"You're positive?"

I nod in return with a smile.

We make our way downstairs and the descent is dark, save for the candlelight. John begins lighting other candles in the room then hands me one of them. The light illuminates the area and across the room, I can hear him. His seething, his breaths, sound labored with congestion.

"Come to torture me some more, Hawthorne?" He smells the air and he cackles. "I see you brought me some dessert."

"You will never taste her again, Michel."

Michel. I have not seen him since I injected him with the cure. John brings the candlelight closer to his face and I gasp.

Michel looks to have aged at least forty years in a matter of months. "What's happened to him?" I ask. His hair is all but white, his skin appears a bit wrinkled, and his eyes... his eyes are dark... almost black.

"He seems to be aging, almost like he's catching up to the years he missed while frozen as an Undead." John sets the candle on a table by Michel.

I step closer and bend over to get a closer look.

"He cannot reach you, Amelia," John tells me. "Get as close as you need to."

"Okay." Tentatively, with a shaky hand, I reach out to touch his scalp. He hisses at me and I flinch back. "Stop it!" He laughs then coughs. Phlegm covers his lips and he spits. I shake my head and reach for him again. My fingers run across his scalp and I feel for his texture. His skin feels almost like thin leather that has been worn through. His hair is rough and it falls out from his scalp at my touch.

"Get me a syringe?" I ask John.

"What are you going to do?" Michel asks. "Test my blood? See how old I should be in the next day or so? I am your science experiment. Why not cut me open?"

"Because I would not give you the satisfaction of death after what you put me through," I hiss.

A hand touches my shoulder and I look back at John. He offers a smile then hands over the syringe. I turn back to Michel and take hold of his left arm. It is withered and his skin is very thin. I am afraid if I push up on his skin, like pushing a sleeve, it would peel away. I need to be careful with drawing blood or it could lead to a bigger mess.

As I shove the needle into his arm, he hisses at me and tries to snap at my face.

"I hope your teeth fall out," I tell him under my breath. His stench is strong, and being this close, I want to gag. Once I have enough in the syringe, I withdraw the needle.

"Are you just going to let me bleed?" he asks.

"I don't see why not. It would do you good to bleed some. Lord knows you made enough people bleed for you in your reign..., which, by the way, is over. Your coven assumes you're dead, and by the looks of it, you will be soon enough."

"NO!" he screams. "RELEASE ME!"

"No," John interjects, "you will live out the rest of your days down here; out of sight from the rest of the world. You are one less monster the world does not need."

"You cannot play God with me, Hawthorne!"

"Let's go," John tells me. We head back up the stairs and Michel's screams begin to muffle as we reach the top. We close the door behind us and the screams become non-existent.

***

"I have the results." I take a seat next to John at our dining room table. Sophie and Adam look in from the den as they take a break from opening each other's Christmas gifts.

Sliding the folder over to him, he opens it and scans the information.

"I have no idea what this says," he tells me with a chuckle.

I smile and walk around the table to sit in his lap. He wraps his arms around my waist.

"Look here," I point to one image. "This is blood from a vampire. You see how the red blood cells here are mutated?"

"Umm, yeah, sure."

I roll my eyes and continue. "Here," pointing to the other image "is Michel's blood. His red blood cells are completely normal; however, his white blood cells are attacking them. They can sense the disease he once had, combine that with the X280, and he begins to age rapidly. His body make up is trying to condition all the years he missed while he was Undead. Most likely," I stop and turn in John's lap to face him, "he will be dead in a few weeks, and long shot will be a month."

"I see," John starts. I can see thoughts are churning in his head.

"What's your question?" I ask.

"Well," he reaches up and scratches his head for a moment. "What happens if, for instance, a vampire would bite him in the state he is in?"

"There is no way he would survive. The vampire who bit him would drink his blood and Michel would most likely perish right then."

"Right, I figured that much, but what about the vampire who ingested his blood? Michel has this... X2whatever inside him."

"X280."

"Yeah that," John nods. "What happens if a vampire ingests Michel's blood? Would he become cured as well?"

"That's a good question and one I cannot answer right now." I shrug and look back at the documents. "Unfortunately, that is something I never got to test." His hand moves over my back and he pulls me close.

"Then we'll just have to be sure no one sneaks in and bites him."

"I doubt that would ever happen." I grin and kiss him.

"Exactly." He considers his next words for a moment. "Seeing him the other day, are you…"

I nod before he finishes. "I'm fine. I have been for a while. I feel safe with you."

"As you should." He motions for me to step off his lap and I stand. I smile over at Sophie as she gnaws on a fingernail. She has this grin that appears to be mischievous. I want to ask her what she has done, but I am distracted when John takes my hand.

Not realizing he is down on one knee, I gasp and cover my mouth with my other hand. *Oh my god, he is going to ask me to marry him… on Christmas Eve.*

"Amelia," he begins, "my life changed so much when you came into it. The darkness surrounding me began to lift the moment your light touched me. When you walk into a room, people cannot help to notice you and your beauty.

Any man would be lucky to have you on his arm; I am fortunate you chose me. I hope to spend the rest of my days proving to you how much you mean to me, how much I love you, and how much you have affected my life. Amelia Rimos, will you marry me?"

Sophie gasps and Adam chuckles next to her. I feel a little light headed and quickly take in a breath when I realize I have been holding it.

John opens a small, black box and inside it is a diamond. It is round in shape and set in a gold band. It easily looks to be one carat. My fingers lightly touch the diamond. "John…"

I meet his gaze and he looks more scared right now than he did when fighting against Michel that day he attacked me. "I love you. Of course, I'll marry you!"

His expression begins to soften and he lets out a long breath he had been holding. He pulls the ring out and slips it onto my finger. As he stands, he wraps his arms around my hips and lifts me in the air. We laugh at the same time and I hold onto him tightly.

"I love you so much, woman."

"I love you, too!"

Sophie squeals in delight and rushes over to us. "Let me see!" John sets me down and she takes my hand, giving it a close look. "You might need a wheel barrel to carry your hand in, honey. Adam, come look!"

I smile and shake my head. I meet John's gaze and he smiles, then leans in and kisses me. "How would you like to celebrate?" he asks.

"Let's have a party here." I pull him closer to me to whisper in his ear. "I plan on celebrating as much as I can with you in our room."

He growls softly then pulls me close. "You two, out now." He points to Adam and Sophie. "I have some celebrating to do!"

I laugh as John picks me up over his shoulder and rushes toward the staircase. "Bye!" I wave at Sophie. She laughs and shakes her head as she slips her arm through Adam's.

The End

I hope you enjoyed the story of Amelia, Michel and John. It took me almost four years to understand their story, then another year to write it. I have ideas in the works for a sequel to this story so keep the love of the characters close to your heart.

Keep on the look out for more books coming soon. Follow my newsletters here:
www.juliemorganbooks.com/newsletter.html

About the Author

Hailing from Burleson, Texas, and growing up in the country with big tractors and bonfire parties, I would daydream about far off lands, hoping to get inside their worlds one day. I can remember daydreaming about flying; not in a plane, but like an angel or a bird. I would occasionally write these thoughts in my journal, but never did much with them beyond that. I've worked in IT my entire career and have always had a fascination with electronics. I like to take things apart and see how they are put back together, preferably with nothing left over.

I've always had a love of books in the contemporary and paranormal genres. After encouragement from my family, I finally made the leap from writing in a spiral notebook to writing in a laptop.

Now residing in sunny Florida, I spend my free time with my daughter. She's my light in this dark world. You'll find us putting together puzzles, playing games, or reading stories about animals or princesses.

As a family, we volunteer our time with the local Autism Research center here in Polk County, in hopes of finding a cure one day. Once you learn to see the world through the eyes of an autistic person (child or adult), the world never looks the same again.

For more information on Autism or how to volunteer, go to www.autismspeaks.org

Where to find me:

Amazon: www.amazon.com/author/juliemorgan

Facebook:
https://www.facebook.com/juliemorganbook

Twitter: @juliemorganbook

Web site and blog: www.juliemorganbooks.com

Good Reads:
https://www.goodreads.com/juliemorganbooks

Instagram: <u>JulieMorganBooks</u>

Deadly Alchemy

Made in the USA
Charleston, SC
11 December 2014